1 MONTH OF
FREE
READING

at
www.ForgottenBooks.com

By purchasing this book you are eligible for one month membership to ForgottenBooks.com, giving you unlimited access to our entire collection of over 1,000,000 titles via our web site and mobile apps.

To claim your free month visit:

www.forgottenbooks.com/free151234

ISBN 978-0-428-97854-9
PIBN 10151234

SELF-MADE;

OR,

LIVING FOR THOSE WE LOVE.

BY

MRS. E. A. WELTY.

"An honest tale speeds best being plainly told."

NEW YORK:
SHELDON AND COMPANY,
498 AND 500 BROADWAY.
BOSTON: GOULD AND LINCOLN.
1868.

Stereotyped at the Boston Stereotype Foundry,
No. 4 Spring Lane.

TO

MY NUMEROUS AND BELOVED

NAMESAKES

These Pages

ARE AFFECTIONATELY DEDICATED.

CONTENTS.

6 CONTENTS.

SELF-MADE.

CHAPTER I.

THE WIDOW AND HER SON.

"I need not say how, one by one,
  Love's flowers have dropped from off love's chain:
Enough to say that they are gone,
  And that they cannot bloom again."
                              MISS LANDON.

"Home is the sphere of harmony and peace,
  The spot where angels find a resting-place."
                              MRS. HALE.

T was midwinter, and all day long had the stiff drops pattered against the pane. All day long had the widow Miller sat at the one low window in her dark little cottage, occasionally raising her tear-stained eyes, and sending their dim light out over the dreary waste of snow, which began to fall in thick, heavy masses, shrouding the tallest trees with a mantle as pure and white as an angel wears, and bending to the earth the tiniest sprays with the weight of their soft, fleecy burden.

While she counted the beads in memory's rosary, her tears flowed fast, and her fingers moved with less alacrity over the coarse garment she was making. Now and then, as the

silent depths of memory were stirred within, a great sob
escaping, that seemed, to keep it down in her heart longer,
would be to break it.   It was her fortieth birthday — the
day, too, when, five years ago, a path was made, in the deep
snow, from her doorstep to the graveyard over the hill.
Care and trouble had forestalled age in furrowing her once
beautiful features, and silvering her once glossy hair.   The
mild light of those eyes that once shone with the placid
expression of a Madonna's had been dimmed by tears more
than by the alternations of time.   Hers had been a life of
sorrow and suffering ; no train of obedient pleasures waited
around her.   From her very girlhood she had been the kind
and patient companion of an invalid and decrepit father,
breathing an atmosphere of want, and grief, and fear, and
the paths to the graves of her loved ones were well beaten,
and strewed with few flowers.

One by one were the dark pictures, which the death-angel
had hung in the " twilight gallery of memory," turned to
the light, dusted of all that dimmed their olden brightness ;
and then was summoned to her presence the semblance of
those fair beings who filled her heart with the holy sentiment
of love, or moved it with the fiercer storm of grief.

Darker and darker hang the clouds above the cottage ; the
wind moaned piteously, and the snow beat drearily against
the panes ; and far down in the depths of that heart, unknown to any but herself, lies the remembrance of her early
love.   How simply, and yet how earnestly, he had loved her,
the chosen of her youth, the father of her children !   How
steadily he seems to look at her, with those mild eyes, as in
years agone, ere they faded under the film of death !   And
then another form rises out of the shadows, and gazes upon
her so tenderly.   How beautiful she is ! — the very type of
innocent and lovely childhood.   Heaven's own blue is not
purer than those liquid eyes, as she looks up from that little
chair yonder, which she has consecrated by her touch.   Her

golden hair seems like the radiance which floats around the
infant Immanuel's head ; and as the dim outlines fade into
space, the mother's thought pursues that loved form along
its angel track, until from her heart to the innermost sanc-
tuary above there seems a. pathway paved with the visible
glory of God.

The storm has lulled for a moment, the elements are
calmed, and the cloud rolls heavily away from the widow's
heart, and faith, that keeps watch with her through the mental
storm, sheds a halo of light over the brow of her dead, and
the voice that never murmurs beneath the allotments of God
is raised in a humble prayer of thankfulness, that one great
blessing is still left.

She wonders why Mark does not come : it is getting late ;
the snow is towering high above the wood-pile, and old
Brindle has stood shivering in the sleet since morning, often
sending forth a pitiful mo-o-o-o, as though she cannot understand the reason of the pitiless storm. Poor " Bossy l "
There are many heads as white with the snows of time as
yours is with the snows of to-day, which have been sorely
taxed with a similar problem. It is not given to us to know
the deep mysteries of the kingdom of heaven, or God's deal-
ings with us. In his own appointed time the Christian spirit
will meet with its reward, and over her night of sorrows
stars shall arise, and she will walk by their heavenly light.

The lifting of the gate-latch, and Mark's cheerful voice, as
he jocosely talked to Brindle about the snow-storm, caused a
sudden glow to overspread the widow's features, and again
the old calm brooded over them as before. Yes, the world
had one bright spot left, and the sky an expanse of blue ;
amid the darkness and the dews that fell so thick around
her, one star shed its serene lustre over the horizon of her
heart.

" You are late to-night, Mark," said his mother, as she
handed him the bright tin milk-pail from the dresser, at the

same time relieving his shoulder of a bag of corn, and depositing it in the doorway. "I thought you would have been home sooner, as the night was coming on so cold."

"Yes, I know; but I wanted to finish my job, as it is Saturday. You know I commence thrashing for Mr. Sloper on Monday, and though I've had to work pretty hard this week, I've got something to show for it, and that's more than I always have."

So saying, he took the pail and went out, whistling a merry tune, while the widow prepared their frugal evening meal.

After the tea things were cleared away, and the cheerful fire beamed brightly throughout the little cottage, the fitful flashes of the burning wood danced over the walls, making Mark's plump cheeks shine with a ruddy glow, as if health and contentment had taken a life-long lease of his manly frame.

"O, it will be capital sleighing by Monday, and I hear the boys are talking of a grand sleigh-ride out to the 'Corners.' You'll get my new coat done for me to wear — won't you, mother?"

"O, yes, my son, the coat shall be finished if I have to sit up all night; you haven't seen it since I put the buttons on." And stepping to the chest in the corner, which answered for bureau and wardrobe, she brought forth the half-finished coat, of brown domestic cloth, the product of her own spindle and loom, and displayed to Mark's admiring gaze the double rows of shining brass buttons, and, trying on the sleeves to see if they were too long or too short, asked, "Do you think it will suit?"

"Suit? Why, it fits like a 'T.' How nice you have made the button-holes! and this stitching is as fine as a tailor could do it. Why, mother, that coat will be nice enough to wear to a wedding."

And so it appeared in the eyes of Mark, who was not

accustomed, as you may suppose, to many of the refined elegances of life. A new coat, although it was coarse and homespun, cut, and fitted, and made by no artist's hand, was to him a matter of as much moment as the purple robes of kings and popes. His was no connoisseur's eye, to detect the flaws, if any there had been, in either the quality of the cloth or the making up; indeed he, thought this a very superior garment, " most too good to wear every day."

And so the mother and son sat by the bright fire, — which was made of large logs, and needed no replenishing, — and chatted pleasantly of the coat, their week's labor, the coming holidays, and Lizzy Brown's Christmas party; and then Mark looked in his mother's face, which had assumed an unwonted cheerfulness, saying, —

" Mother, this is your birthday : had you forgotten it?"

" No, my son, but I was beginning to think you had."

" Did you, indeed? You shall see ! "

And tripping lightly to the bag of corn, still remaining by the entry door, he untied the string, and taking out a small bundle from the " sack's mouth," he held up to his mother's view a nice, warm shawl ; and before she could express her surprise, or venture a word of disapprobation, he had laid it over her shoulders, and then, perking saucily around, gave her cheek a smacking kiss, that told a whole story of love and devotion.

" There, you see I was not the undutiful son you thought me."

" Why, Mark! Surely it was not in this way I hoped, or wished, to be remembered."

" I could not very well reconcile myself to the thought of wearing a new suit of *broadcloth*, while you were obliged to stay away from church for the want of a respectable shawl. It was only four dollars. Mr. Rawson threw off half a dollar, and that, together with this half pound of tea, just made up the sum that was coming to me."

" But where are your new Arithmetic, and Grammar, and writing paper to come from? You know you cannot commence going to school without the books."

" True; but I have agreed to cut some cord-wood for Mr. Jones, and Hugh Weeks is to give me half a dollar for my skates, and the two fat turkeys at Christmas will bring more than enough for these."

" I hope there will be no necessity for parting with your skates, Mark; it will be fine skating when the snow drifts off the pond. I love to see you take the lead among the boys while enjoying this healthful sport. There is the money Mrs. Maynard owes me for weaving, which will probably be paid soon, though I am ashamed to ask for it again, as. it is a debt of such long standing."

" Yes, and she had the impertinence to ask you to spin her flax and warp that piece of linen before she paid you for the weaving of last year. I am glad you refused: some people have no souls, and I think Mrs. Maynard one of that class. . By the way, her son 'hopeful' and his sister Helen arrived to-day from Albany. I suppose they are home to spend the holiday vacation. I happened to be standing at the store corner when they passed, and raised my cap; but they were so bundled up in their furs, I suppose they did not see me; at least, they did not recognize their old friend. I think they have brought company with them, for there were two ladies in the sleigh."

" She is probably some schoolmate come to pass the holidays with them."

" She is pretty, at all events; for I saw her sparkling black eyes, full of mirth and intelligence, and her rosy cheeks and lips, and long dark curls, fluttering in the wind, as they drove slowly past. *She* nodded gracefully to my salutation, stranger as I was. I am sure she has a good heart, whoever she is. Though it is queer Sam didn't know me. I wonder if he is not putting on airs."

" O, no, I think not. You were always good friends before he went away, especially after you risked your life rescuing him from his perilous situation in the pond when his boat upset, and you came near being drowned yourself."

" Yes, I had hard work to keep his head and my own above water until help came. He wouldn't let go of me and give me a chance to swim, but clung to me like a drowning girl. The boys always laughed at him because he was too great a coward to learn to swim. And, mother, do you remember the skating frolic we had three years ago, when, in trying to trip up one of his competitors in the race, he fell, and nearly broke his skull? I've heard it whispered that his head was never the soundest, but after that accident it seemed there was a soft spot somewhere." A right merry peal of laughter now rang through the room, interrupted by a gentle reproof from his mother.

Then followed a long silence in the quiet little cottage, broken only by the tick of the old-fashioned clock, which was nailed against the wall, and the sonorous breathing of Jowler, who lay stretched at his ease on the ample hearth. The pleasant fire-light flashed upon the bright tin pans on the dresser, and the white dimity curtains around the bed, and the small mirror hanging over the spare table. That glass was in a frame as bright as paint and varnish could make it: years agone it had reflected the infantine features of Mrs. Miller, as well as those of her brothers and sisters, and was a part of her wedding portion. On the table was a spread of snowy whiteness, with long netted fringe depending midway to the floor. The old family Bible, and a few quaint-looking volumes, which comprised the library, and a pair of shining brass candlesticks, not used for common, were the ornamental part of the household furniture.

A yawn from Mark and the hour of ten struck simultaneously on the widow's ear. Then the Bible was taken carefully from its resting-place under the mirror, and a psalm was read, and they bowed down in prayer together. Did not angels hover over the family altar to waft to the heavenly Father the tender words of gratitude, and trust, and hope, which fell from the poor widow's lips?

"Are you asleep?" said my aunt Bessie, as she gave me a slight nudge, to know if I had been an attentive listener.

"Wide awake, and very much interested with your 'narrative.' Go on, please."

"No; it is getting late, and the fire is almost out; so give me your good-night kiss, darling."

"But you did not commence at the beginning. I want to know all about Sorrel Hill, and its inhabitants."

"Well, to-morrow evening we will begin the story anew."

"And I will remember where you left off this evening. So good night, dear aunt Bessie."

"Good night, my dear, and God bless you."

CHAPTER II.

THE GRAVEYARD ON THE HILL.

" Our vales are sweet with fern and rose,
 Our hills are maple-crowned;
But not from these our fathers chose
 The village burying-ground."
WHITTIER.

SORREL HILL, my dear, — your mother's and my own birthplace, — was in one of the loveliest valleys the sun ever shone upon. It was a pleasant little town, sloping gently down the hill-side to the creek's brink. A " meeting-house " was one of the first objects that caught the traveller's eye as he approached the village. It was an edifice possessing little architectural beauty, and yet its plain outline appeared as a great index pointing towards heaven. There was a mill-pond at one end of the little town, and a graveyard at the other. Not that the one was an essential adjunct to the other, for we had little sickness, and the funerals were so far apart that we almost forgot what one was like. But still there was a graveyard, far away through the meadows of green and white clover, and over the little stony mound, where we used to go to hunt for snail-shells and periwinkles, and where the sheep and kine wandered at will, cropping the blades of stunted grass and tufts of wild wood-sorrel, that grew in great abundance, and from which, I suppose, the town must have received its name, and, at its christening, its bright new dress of red and green, with flowers of May-weed for its border.

A gaudy dress was that, donned in leafy June, when all the world seemed burdened with its wealth of floral glories, and worn with becoming grace and dignity, until the sun's bright rays had faded its rich tints, and blended with them a sober, misty gray, to be succeeded by as pure and beautiful a white as was ever worn by maiden bride.

On the western slope of the hill-side, where the sun sank behind the tall tree-tops when five o'clock came, burnishing with golden glory the yellow leaves of autumn, or warming into life the fragile buds of spring, with its few silent inhabitants, lying side by side among the wild trumpet-creepers, and the dear little blue-and-white flowers that I never knew any name for. It seemed as if the angels must have planted them there, for people did not then, as now, adorn and beautify their burial-places with all that art, and taste, and affection can devise. Save a few native trees, left to grow untrimmed and shapeless, there was not an ornament within the little paled enclosure. O, I would not like my grave to be in a place too dark and gloomy for the bright flowers to live in, flowers first, pruned and tended by the hands I have clasped confidingly in my own, and then a willow to spread its green arms over me. Don't interrupt me now with your " What difference does it make?" It *does* make a difference; for it seems to me the dead can see, and know where they are lying, whether thick mists, and silence, and darkness rest upon the sod that covers them, and the place gainsays the good man's tale, that "the grave is a desirable goal," or whether over their face fall the sweet night-drops of heaven, distilled from the rose's leaf or the willow's stem. There you are again with your conjectures. " Guess spirits have something else to think about besides rose-bushes and dew-drops." Well, it may be, and you are privileged to theorize as you like; but I never lay a flower upon the graves of departed friends but I imagine it brings them to my side at once; and the simple tribute exhales a perfume sweeter than that of roses or odors of spices and

gums burned in religious rites. The offerings of the heart
are sweeter and holier than the censer's breath, and that
little heap of dust a *shrine* at which love pays homage to
departed worth.

It seems as if the flowers changed hands merely, — that
their spiritual presence can be felt and enjoyed, and that
even the thoughts of my heart can be discerned by them.
I do believe they know the thoughts we cherish of their
memory, — whether their love is the inner temple of the
soul, and none other earthly hath power to invade the sanc-
tuary ; or whether, if they could come back to us, we would
not cling to some new object, whom we have learned to love
since they went away.

Bright shone the sun upon the hallowed graves, and softer
seemed the moonlight that fell along the green mounds which
hid the loved ones from our gaze. Hushed was the voice of
merriment when the hill-top was gained ; and though the black-
berries that skirted the sacred enclosure were large and lus-
cions, they were picked in silence, or in reverential whispers,
and, as if by mutual consent, not a squirrel or butterfly was
ever chased beyond the enchanted boundary. The little
white-and-blue flowers that turned their tiny faces up to the
bright sky, were indeed emblems of the dear dust they covered — too fair and fragile for the fierce heat of midsummer,
or the chill breath of autumn, that made so merry with the
silken drapery of their less frail sisterhood. They seemed
well content to bloom in this silent solitude, where none ever
came to admire them, bending their graceful heads to the
earth as if a consciousness of the fleeting nature of all beautiful things had taught them humility. And when their lives
were spent, they calmly shrunk into their beds of dusky um-
brage ; but every year they came, testifying with their constant breath to the truth, that " if a man die, he shall live
again."

2

CHAPTER III.

THE OLD SCHOOL-HOUSE.

> " The dusky walls
> Hold the fair germ of knowledge, and the tree,
> Glorious in beauty, golden with its fruits,
> To this low school-house traces back its life."
>
> STREET.

REAMILY wound the little rivulet along, which, at this point, could be spanned by my pony's bridle. But a mile below was the large mill-pond, at once the pride and profit of our village. A strong contrast marked the two extremes; for all day long, and far into night, might be heard the busy humdrum of machinery, or the sharp click-clack of the water-wheel that propelled it. It was here where the farmers for miles around came to get their milling done; here, too, the industrious smith labored at the bellows, and the ringing sound of the anvil kept time to the lighter but none the less energetic stroke of the cooper's hammer. The cooper was contiguous to the smith, and the smith to the wagon-maker, and the wagon-maker to the carpenter and the shoemaker; and then came, in regular succession, Deacon Sloper's barn, with its great perpendicular gables, and the lightning-rod in the centre, of which we youngsters' stood very much in awe. But not so with the painted weather-cock, which, we were told, always crowed when he heard others crow! This mystery it took years to solve. Then there was " Uncle " Gilbert's cider-mill, and the widow Miller's log cabin, with its one window front, and the blue smoke from the stone chimney curling up above the green tree-tops before her better-to-do neighbors had left their downy couches.

This was "Main Street;" but farther back, under the graceful maples and tall poplar trees, were nestled many snug little cottages, with their shining coats of red and white glistening in the sun, and several there were that rejoiced in the aristocratic appendage of green blinds to their front windows. Then there were venerable-looking barns to each, hay-ricks, corn-cribs, and milk-houses, which all helped to give Sorreltown, or "Sorrel Hill," as it was sometimes called, quite an air of thrift and rivalry; at least we thought so, who had never been farther from home than Weedsport or Scrabble Hollow.

The old brown school-house — good old *Alma Mater* of us all that she was — had weathered the storms of a quarter of a century, and witnessed as many revolutions and final abdications of nearly that number of pedagogues, who were so unfortunate as to be appointed by the selectmen to assume the dictatorship of the young and rebel portion of our little republic. Sometimes their revolts amounted to actual anarchy for a whole day, especially when the snow was soft and warm, in prime order for pelting ducks and geese, or when the ice on the mill-pond lay like sheets of silver glistening in the midday sun, or the sleds had a charmed existence, wooing their impatient owners away from the dull routine of school-life. How could they work within doors, when the rafters of heaven were bending low without, with such a vast expanse of blue sky unbroken by a single cloud, and the mellow moonlight, with its soft and soothing shades calling to them in language more eloquent than "Kirkham" or "Daboll" could possibly employ? They believed, with the wise man who searched to know *all* wisdom, that "much study is a weariness," and no voice is so enticing as the voice

of nature : hers it was that often charmed them to their ruin ;
for if the master happened to be an autocrat of the old school,
woe to the delinquent subject who dared question his authority or disobey his mandates.   They were sure to " feel the
thorn pierce through their gathered flowers."   But if — as
was once or twice the case during my school-days in Sorreltown — he was a republican in feeling and principle, and
had a heart in the right place ; if his justice was tempered
with mercy ; if his ferule was swayed with less of passion
and ire than equity and humanity ; then were his subjects
loyal, and if they occasionally suffered for their follies, they
knew that it was love that corrected them.

The only blow I ever received in school was inflicted
under that roof.   It was made with a broad ruler upon my
little bare shoulder, and never shall I forget the pain, and
shame, and fright of that moment — never, though my head
should be whitened with the snows of ages !   It was for a
fault I did not commit.   My tears were of no avail, and I
was too much a child and too terrified to explain.   The
master had been whipping all day, without discriminating
between the deserving and the undeserving ; and when the
freak took him, very few were so fortunate as to escape.
His name was Whipple, — I wish I could remember the
whole of it.   He must be an old man now ; and I have
sometimes thought I would not give him a night's lodging
in my house to shelter him from the fiercest storm that ever
blew.   But a moment's thought has at such times made me
feel more hospitable, and recalled the precepts and example
of the Great Teacher.   I should not foster an unkind thought
towards my worst enemy, but spread the mantle of charity
over his faults, as I would others should do to mine.   We
heard, years afterwards, that he had married a meek, blue-
eyed little creature, whom he won away from a father's loving heart, which it nearly broke, and that, after two years

of neglect and ill-treatment, she returned alone to the ark of rest which had sheltered her sweet childhood from the waves of sorrow that had deluged her bride-life.

The old school-house stood a good distance from all the rest, within a neat enclosure; and with the time-honored structure are associated a tall " liberty-pole " and huge piles of cord-wood, arranged on either side of the door. They were obliged to splice the liberty-pole, I remember, for very large timber did not grow around Sorreltown; and (let me say to you in a whisper, dear reader), as in the natural, so in the mental world. It seems the fact got abroad, and became a maxim in the neighbourhood. We had our " selectmen," our " justice," and " pathmaster," it is true; but when a judge or a governor was to be made, or a congressman to be manufactured, the knowing ones somehow never came to Sorreltown for the timber! But some noble scions have sprung up from the old stock of home-made fathers and mothers, who have become "bright and shining lights" in the world! Many sons and daughters of intelligence and genius, who have since occupied proud and conspicuous stations in life, as mechanics, lawyers, merchants, clergymen, orators, authors, and artists, drew their infant breath among the hills and vales of old ———— county, of which " our village " formed an inconsiderable part.

Perhaps I may look with a too partial eye upon the place of my birth: if so, it is a good fault; but I would ask any wanderer from this Eden if in all his journeyings he has found a more quiet or beautiful home. It seems to me the sun never shone upon a fairer or more picturesque region.

I cannot recount to you the steps of progress made by *all* the young aspirants for fame. I will simply relate the freaks of fortune as connected with one, or perhaps two, who stood side by side with me on the lower round of the " ladder of learning."   .

They have, many of them, far outstripped their humble contemporary; and it is with a feeling of pride that she gazes aloft upon the bright stars which shed lustre upon one whose radius is smaller and dimmer than theirs.

CHAPTER IV.

THE CHRISTMAS PARTY AT SQUIRE BROWN'S.

"There is strength
Deep bedded in our hearts, of which we reck
But little till the shafts of heaven have pierced
Its fragile dwelling. Must not earth be rent
Before her gems are found?"

MRS. HEMANS.

ELCOME, Christmas, merry Christmas, the great jubilee of the Christian world! How full of joy and thanksgiving and good wishes, how incalculably rich in gifts, how replete with peace and good will to all, is this day, which calls to mind the manger and the sheepfold, the virgin mother and her divine Son, for whom there was no room in the inn!

The poor labourer, toiling for a pittance, is not so poor in spirit, or so devoid of human sympathy, as not to allow himself to share in the general rejoicing; and the man of wealth and worldly cares, whose social life is hidden during the whole busy year, now folds up the record of his accumulated stores, turns the key on his golden gains and the austerity of his nature. To-day his heart is young again; he never once thinks of the wrinkles which the circling years have furrowed upon his cheek, or of the snows that lie thin and white upon his brow. His step, though less firm and elastic, has something of youthful sprightliness in it, because he is homeward bound, to mingle in the gay festivities, the delightful scenes, to which the happy season invites him, or perchance to join in the youthful sport of those who have long since looked upon him as superannuated.

O, if there is a spark of love and humanity in the breast, let it shine out, at least on Christmas; count your saddened thoughts among the years that are gone; skip over the seeming ills which have risen to bar your entrance to prosperity or preferment, and let your spirit rejoice in the present good, and your heart-harp vibrate joyfully to the olden song of the angels over the fields of Bethlehem.

Bright and cheerily shone the morning sun upon the little village under the hill that lay embedded, as it were, in the soft, white snow. Soon the eaves began to drop their tears of joy, and the snow to settle in a compact mass upon the ground. The fleecy cones that decked the half-foliaged trees and garden shrubs had flashed their short-lived radiance, leaving brown and desolate the long boughs that but the night before had bloomed in icy whiteness. The town is all astir, the roads alive with busy, bustling youngsters. There is not one of all the jolly throng but has donned a holiday suit in honor of the " Merry Christmas."

While the fathers and grandfathers, mothers and grandmothers, maiden aunts and bachelor uncles, are interchanging social greetings, and discussing the merits of the turkeys which have rendered up their lives with a noble self-sacrificing ambition, the younger ones are intent on the more animated part of the evening's entertainment.

Lizzie Brown's party is to come off to-night, and it is full five miles to the " Corners," where Squire Brown resides. And so sleighs are being fitted up in grand style, that will hold a dozen or more; and cutters are skimming through the streets in quest of fair occupants; and bells are jingling here and there, and everywhere; and the living cargoes of youth and loveliness are soon in their respective seats, impatient to be away.

All are in high spirits, and their mingled voices of merriment grate harshly on the ear of Mark Miller, as, with folded hands, he silently sees load after load of happy, joyous hearts dash past, making the clear air ring with their united peals of laughter.

"Go it, Mark!" said one, as he gave his whip a flourish; and the sharp, ringing crack that followed sent his horses far ahead of his competitors.

"Put in your best licks!" shouted another; little thinking of the keen pang his careless words caused to shoot through Mark's heart.

"Hurra-a-a-a!" cried a third, as his light cutter dashed furiously past; and soon the ringing of the bells and the music of happy voices were borne back on the cold, still air; and then, as he turned to resume his work, tears, large and heavy, dropped on the sheaf of corn he was husking.

Mark had not been invited. Contrary to his expectations and glowing hopes of being among the happy guests at Squire Brown's, he found himself almost the only one whose name had been omitted in the list of invitations. For two days his mind alternated between hope and fear. Thinking there might be some mistake, he ventured to inquire concerning it, but was told that all the "cards" were distributed.

This was on the evening previous; and it was with feelings little short of desperation that he reached his little attic without having betrayed any sign of the distress he felt. While in his mother's presence he suppressed his agonized feelings with a fortitude worthy of a better cause. Now his high-wrought imagination pictured himself fatherless, friendless, and alone, with no one to advise him in this hour of sore trial.

"I do not deserve this," said he, mentally; "I am as good as the best of them, if I am poor;" and again the tears flowed fast, and great sobs choked his utterance. Work he could not; and he gave these harrowing thoughts free scope until the tide of grief had spent its force, and ebbed slowly back upon his heart, freighted with shame and pride.

"These tears are unmanly," said he; "and my mother must not see their traces on my cheeks. Work is only for us! Yes, we must *work!*" and he resolutely resumed his task. Again and again he found himself absorbed in thought, and the pile of corn at his side increasing very slowly. His fixed, stern gaze on the blank barn-door before him, and a resolute compression of the lips, manifested the strugglings of a strong spirit, and some mighty warfare going on within, which must soon resolve itself into action.

"Perhaps it will not always be so," he murmured, half audibly; and then an ominous shake of the head showed his thoughts, whatever they were, to be very extravagant ones.

A long time he sat thus, resolving and doubting; his changing countenance now lighted up with hope, and then the old frown and look of deep despair, proved there were obstacles in the way of his high resolve. What thoughts rioted in his heart, even his mother, — from whom no thought of his was hidden, — had she been there, could not have guessed. He felt, for the first time, the powers of manhood nerving his arm, and the strength of a determined will gradually undermining the difficulties that seemed to lie along his future pathway. A long time he sat with his head resting on his hands, his tattered handkerchief being brought into frequent use in wiping away the drops of grief which, in spite of all his manly resolves, would betray the strong emotions of his soul. The bright afternoon was passing away, and the excitement under which he labored had, in a measure, subsided, and he was able to think calmly on his future course of action.

"This is no place for me, and my poor mother works far beyond her strength. I am now old enough to do a man's work, and all last summer I kept up with the best of the field hands; but 'boy's wages' only were given me, and grudgingly, too, I thought.

"I must seek among strangers that aid and sympathy which are denied me here. I will, in the first place, get an education, independently of any other resource than what my own hands can carve out for me; others have done it, and why not I?

"There are many self-made men in the world, who, according to their own confessions, were considered no smarter boys than common — rather below par, than otherwise. Who was it? Some great man has said he always stood at the foot of his class when a boy; and that is what I do not, long at a time. There are few boys in this little 'burgh' that can outstrip me in anything, and *I'll make them take off their hats to me yet!*" Springing to his feet as he gave a strong emphasis to these last words, he lifted his slouched cap from his head, and dashed it to the ground, as if the act would ratify the treaty of peace he had made with the conflicting elements of his mind, and give an additional impetus to his resolution.

It was now about three o'clock in the afternoon, and Mark had shovelled the corn he had been husking into one of the large bins in the granary, and pitched the stalks over into the haymow, and was preparing to go home, when the barn-door was swung open, and his employer, Deacon Sloper, entered.

"Why, Mark, you at work to-day, when all the rest are at play! How's this? Why did you not go to the sleigh-ride?"

"I was not invited, sir."

"Not invited! I thought the invitations were general. I am sure that was the intention of Mr. and Mrs. Brown. Who gave out the invitations?"

"I believe a list was sent to Sam Maynard, and it appears my name was not on it; so, of course, I was not wanted.

Perhaps they thought my clothes were not good enough; but I have a new suit, as good as the best of 'em." A slight trembling of the lips, and the huskiness of his voice, betrayed to the practised eye and ear of his auditor how great were his chagrin and disappointment.

"I will inquire into this. Depend upon it, there is some mistake somewhere," said the good old man, in whose breast was a heart as warm and full of Christian kindness as ever beat.

Seating himself on some bags of wheat which leaned against the side of the barn, and motioning Mark to a seat on the half-bushel by his side, he began, in a round-about way, to elicit from Mark some information in regard to his present necessities and future prospects.

He was a large man, rough in his outer appearance, and oftentimes in his speech, but kind and benevolent when his sympathies were enlisted. He was not a Pharisee, yet strict in the observance of all the rites of the Christain faith. What he believed to be the doctrines of the gospel were the rules by which his life was governed. It was the strangest thing on earth, he said, why people could not always do right, speak right, and think right. He fulfilled the letter of the law in ordering his own household aright; was the husband of one wife, although he remembered that, away back in the early history of his Christian pilgrimage, the grave had closed over a gentle and lovely being who had borne his name and slept in his arms but two short summers.

The gentler qualities of his nature seemed to have taken their flight with the pure spirit that for five years had held his own in sweet and sacred bondage. Then, in course of time, he took unto himself another wife, who proved, in some respects, a counterpart of the first, though the neighbors all wondered how it ever came about, he was so stern and austere, while the wife was so sprightly and good-natured;

and they augured that no good would come of it. But some-how each fell into the other's habits, and ways of thinking, and acting, until in time they were quite well balanced in mind and disposition; and he would smile at her lively sal-lies of wit and humour, and she, thinking, perhaps, so much frolicking and gayety unbecoming in a deacon's wife, would check her somewhat ardent love for the ludicrous. So, as the years went by, the stern, uncongenial spirit of the one, subdued by trials in part, was softened into a sociable and pleasant companion; and the other, without her happiness being in the least diminished, was calm and even-tempered, the meek graces of the true Christian adorning her life and inspiring the respect and confidence of all who knew her. Without seeming to notice Mark's discomfiture, the deacon said, —

" And so you've been at work here all this pleasant day ! "

" I have not worked *all* day ; I *could* not."

" Where's your mother ? "

" At home, sir."

" Not been out to dinner anywhere ? "

" No, sir."

" Suppose you're going to have a turkey at home."

" No, sir ; we had only two fit to kill, and I sold both of them."

" Got any left ? "

" Yes, sir ; some young ones, for next year's brooding."

" Got any corn to feed 'em on ? "

" O, yes, sir ; plenty. You know, deacon, I'm never idle ; and as I take part of my pay in grain, we have always plen-ty to eat, and to feed our stock with. By the way, Mr. Slo-per, can't I sell you that young heifer of mine ? She will be two years old in the spring, and is as fat as butter."

" What on earth do you want to *sell* her for ? "

" I wish to raise a little money, if I can."

" Owe some little store bill, I suppose."

" No, sir ; we owe no man a dollar."

" What then?"

" I think of leaving Sorreltown in the spring, and shall want a little spending money until I can get something to do."

" What on earth put that into your head? and where are you going?" said the deacon, looking up in perfect astonishment.

" I have not fully determined as to where I shall go, and can hardly tell what first induced me to entertain the idea ; a train of circumstances which perhaps only needed the little incidents we have been speaking of, to bring my half-formed resolution to maturity. Perhaps you will aid me with your kind advice, before I make up my mind as to my future employment ; I should rely upon your judgment, and be sorry to do anything at variance with your wishes."

" Why, if you want to learn a trade, you needn't go away from home to do that.   I ain't sure but Mr. Ganyard would take you into the mill ; he was telling me, the other day, he was going to put in another run of stones, and would have to hire a man for the summer ; but whether you would be stout enough to handle so many heavy bags, or not, is a question in my mind."

" I am strong enough to do any work at the mill.   I have done a man's work for the last year, but I haven't received a man's wages ; besides, there is not work enough here to give me steady employment. You know the farmers, as a general thing, have hands enough of their own, except it may be a short time in haying and harvest."

" Yes, I know it's as much as the best of us can do to get along, and keep clear of debt ; no one feels able to hire much ; but if you could manage to putter around, and do little odd jobs for one and another, and tend mill during the busy season, I think it would be better than tramping off on an uncertainty."

" I think I should not suit Mr. Ganyard, nor he me ; be sides — "

"Well, I think you are a little too honest to go with Gan-yard; but you could soon learn to take as much toll as he does — couldn't you?" said the good deacon, ironically.

"I shall never learn to be dishonest, if I starve for it," promptly responded Mark.

"Well said, my brave boy! stick to that, and you'll do well enough anywhere. Your father was an honest man before you; too conscientious for his own good, may be. If he hadn't a' been, you might have owned that ten acres where Ganyard's orchard now stands. It's a pity he mort-gaged it for so small a sum; but then, poor man, he was taken sick just when it was the most pinching time with him. If I had been as well off then as I am now, he never should have lost it. But that's neither here nor there. You know the whole story, and it's mighty harrowing to your feelings, and mine also, to call it up. What do you say to learning the tanner's trade? There's Simms, that's made a snug little property at it. When he first came to Sorreltown, he hadn't ten dollars in the world. I think you might do worse than learning the tannin' business; and if you say so, the next time I go down to the 'Forks,' I'll speak to Simms about it."

"I am much obliged to you, Mr. Sloper; but I had an-other, and, you may think, a less commendable project in view. I wish to get an education, for the purpose of making it available for my future support, as well as my mother's when she is infirm and aged, and possess myself of some advantages that cannot be obtained in a small place like this. If I had some good friend to recommend me, I think I might find a place in the city where I could make myself useful, and compensate any one who would be so kind as to receive me into his family."

As the old gentleman looked very earnestly at Mark, and listened apparently with much interest, he was constrained to proceed.

"If, for instance, I had some acquaintance in Albany, who

was interested in my welfare, and who kept a man to take care of his horse, and sweep out his office — "

" And black his boots, and brush his clothes, and go to market," interrupted the deacon.

" Yes, even that," replied Mark, emphatically ; " I would not hesitate to do anything that is honorable and upright, so I could pay my way ; and perhaps in time I could do copying ; and who knows but I might one day be a lawyer ! and prove no disparagement to my preceptor or myself."

" Well, Mark," said the deacon, with a long-drawn sigh, " you know there's a great many ifs in the way of one's advancement in this world. If I'd had anybody to boost me up there, I'd been gov'nor by this time. I'm a smarter man nat'rally than ever Gov'nor Worth was. You see, we were brought up together, and I ought to know something about it ; our fathers' farms jined, and the houses didn't stand twenty rods apart ! Now, you may think I ought to feel proud of living a nigh neighbour to a family that raised a live gov'nor ; but he wan't gov'nor then, by a long chalk ; we've had many a ' set-to ' in our boyish days, and we'll have another if I ever catch him off his own premises, for vetoing that bill about *the canal-feeders.*

" Why, it was the most ridiculous thing I ever heard of. If I'd been in the legislature, he'd got a piece of my mind ; and he did as it was, for I wrote him a pretty crusty letter about it. And he always thought a good deal of my opinion about matters and things, though we differ in politics. Mark, just throw some corn over to those pigs — will you ? — and see if it won't stop their squealing. I never can come nigh this barn but them pigs set up an everlasting racket ! "

Mark speedily complied with the deacon's request, but was too much interested in his conversation to wish it dropped ; so it was resumed by his asking to what circumstance Governor Worth owed his exalted position.

" Well, you see," said Mr. Sloper, " his father never could

make much out of him at home. He hadn't no natural genius for farming, somehow, and hard work didn't agree with him. He'd get tired and have a headache, and his mother spoiled him ; I really believe she thought he *was weak-ly*, and I used to think so, too, in one sense. He never took no interest in things about the farm, nor no pains to learn anything but books. Couldn't hold a plough, or plant his rows straight, or top off a haystack with any sort of taste ; and so his father, after he had pretty much made up his mind that he never would amount to anything, sent him off to college."

" How did he make it go there ? "

" O, he picked up considerable after that, and, I've heard say, ' graduated with high honours,' as the saying is. I never heard of anybody graduating at all that didn't. But there I lost sight of him for several years. He took to the law for a living, and I moved to the ' Genesee country.' The next I heard of him, he was in New York. I had just then commenced taking ' The Sun,' or I never should have known it, I don't suppose. He was then candidate for judge of the Supreme Court ; and would you believe it ! he had renounced the religion of his fathers, or, what is the next thing to it, had apostatized from the true principles of this great republic, and the faith in which he had been educated, and turned democrat, and by that party put into office ! and what made me madder than all, was to hear that paper puffing him up, and speaking of him as ' a young man of splendid talents,' ' brilliant acquirements,' and all that sort of thing. Well, that's neither here nor there ; perhaps he was. I should always a' been proud of him, if he had not disgraced himself by turning democrat."

" Had he ever voted with the whigs? " inquired Mark.

" Voted? Why, no. I don't suppose he ever voted at all, until he got to New York, and looked about to see which way the crowd went. But what of that? wasn't his father

3

and his grandfather before him whigs? wasn't it his birth-right?"

The good old deacon was becoming excited, and measuring the barn floor with his rapid strides; and how long he might have indulged in a political tirade against the incumbent of the gubernatorial chair, we know not, had not Mark interrupted him by asking him quite earnestly, "Are you then on good terms with his excellency?"

"Good terms? Why, yes. I never go to Albany but he's as glad to see me as he would be to see his own brother. We agreed, the first time we met, — and that was on the day of his inauguration, — never to say a word more about politics. He owes his advancement to his party, and it would look sneaking mean for a man to desert his party, after he had fattened on the emoluments of his office. And he knows very well that I'm a regular hard-head, and it's no use talking to *me*. I couldn't help telling him, on the sly, that instead of being a gov'nor, he might have been in the cabinet, or sent on a foreign embassy, seeing we've now got a whig administration.

"He's got some good streaks about him yet; for he don't seem puffed up a bit, nor forget his old friends either; for he invited me up to his house, and introduced me to his wife, who said she felt as if I was an old acquaintance, she had so often heard her husband speak of me. And then there were so many fine ladies and gentlemen there that evening, paying their respects to the new gov'nor and his lady, I felt, somehow, as if I hadn't ought to stay; but they made me, whether or no, and I got introduced, as 'my old friend Mr. Sloper,' to all the 'big men,' who treated me with as much respect as though I had been gov'nor myself; and so, you see, I take the liberty of expressing my disapprobation when he does anything that don't exactly suit me. Says I, in my letter, when he vetoed that bill — "

"Excuse me, Mr. Sloper; but I am all anxiety to as-
certain one thing. Will you do me the favour, and a great
favour it will be — and one that I will never forget — will
you give me a letter of introduction and recommendation
to Governor Worth? I am confident, with that in my
pocket to start with, and his influence to aid me, I shall
succeed in my plans. I had not thought of seeing my way
so clear in six months as I see it now."

The deacon stopped short in his walk between the fanning-
mill and the corn-pen, and stood eying Mark with a kind
of strange bewildering stare, as if not rightly comprehending
what he had said.

Mark saw at once that he had taken his good friend completely by surprise; but as there was no manifestation of
unkindness, he was encouraged to hope his entreaties would
be successful. A slight flush passed over his face as the
kind old man hesitated in his reply. Mark sprang to his
side, and taking his hand in both of his, said in a firm,
manly tone, —

"Mr. Sloper, I can keep back no secrets from you, who
have always been a good friend to me and my mother. You
may, perhaps, have an idea that I am not capable of taking
care of myself in any other capacity than as a 'hireling.'
But I am vain enough to think that I possess sufficient
intelligence to work my way up gradually to independence. I cannot bear to think there is no higher destiny for
me than to be always in my present position, working a day
here and a day yonder, whenever I am so fortunate as to
get any work to do. According to your own story, there is
many a man who has made his 'mark' in the world, who
had, perhaps, no better foundation to build upon than I
have, and no greater advantages in his youth than I have
had: to be sure, mine have not been many, but I have improved them to the best of my ability. And it seems to me
that I ought to leave here. I am not always treated just right."

This last sentence was uttered in an almost inaudible whisper, and Mark had to choke down the rising emotion, which had well nigh mastered him.

Mr. Sloper remained silent, but had resumed his seat on the bags of wheat, and it was now Mark's turn to manifest the excitability of his nature by moving hither and thither, in a state of restless anxiety. The changed and serious expression of the deacon's countenance assured Mark that his words were not lost upon him, and he was encouraged to go on.

"I don't mind *that* so much on my own account, but it wounds my mother's heart to see her son slighted because we are poor. I care but little for respect myself, for I am strong, and can endure hardships; but I look forward to a time when it will devolve upon me to take care of my mother, who will soon be past hard work. Nobody but myself knows how many long and late hours she toils, and oftentimes when she is not able. O, sir, it makes me feel as if nothing was too great for me to accomplish. This is not the first time I have worked all day, when every other boy and girl in town were away on a pleasure excursion."

The old deacon moved nervously in his seat, and after a slight fit of coughing, took out of his hat a flaming red and yellow bandanna, and wiped away the moisture that had gathered about his eyes.

"Besides, it ain't particularly agreeable to do the roughest kind of work, and feel all the time as though I was beholden to my employers for the privilege of serving them. I know a great many little jobs — such as husking this corn, and thrashing that buckwheat — are given to me out of charity. I don't know as I can say that of many besides yourself. You are kind to us, and but for your and Mrs. Sloper's regard for my mother, I fear we should sometimes come to want."

"As long as Enoch Sloper has a peck of potatoes to call

his own, you never shall want," thought that worthy man; but he said nothing, and Mark continued, —

"Were I a few years older, I would go out by myself, unadvised and alone; but a boy of my age needs at least one friend to put him on the right track, and keep a little lookout after him, to see if he goes straight; and now I ask you again, Mr. Sloper, will you be that friend to me? I do not want a better one. I could not have one that would advise me what is for my interest as well as you. You always tell me when I go wrong, and have such a good heart. You are the only man I ever worked for who seemed to think I could get tired, or needed rest, or recreation, like other boys. You've been like a father to me, and —"

"Hold on there, Mark. I never could stand flattery, no-how, and I'm too old a bird to be caught with any such chaff! Besides, I've spoken rough to you more times than you've got fingers and toes. Didn't I scold you considerably when you left them bars down, and the cattle got into the meadow? and didn't I threaten to flog you once for breaking that new plough? And haven't I sometimes told you you was a lee-t-l-e too smart for your clothes?"

"Whenever you have reproved me, it has been for my good, and I know I deserved it. I remember I was left to watch the gap, and went off with James Waters to go in swimming, and forgot all about it, when night came; and there is no excuse for boys *forgetting*. I had rather be whipped, any time, than be obliged to say I *forgot* a thing! And as for the flogging you threatened me with, it was so long ago I was in hopes you had forgotten it. I wish I *could* forget that; but I never shall. If a boy ever deserved a good thrashing, I did then; for I went in direct opposition to your instructions; I thought my way was the best, and drove between the stumps when you told me I couldn't do it, and not to try. Yes, I remember all about it, as well as though it was yesterday — how you had to take a hand from the field, and both horses from their work, and send five miles to get the plough mended; and then the blacksmith was from home, and it lay there a week, and cost an extra journey, besides setting the spring's work back so much."

"Yes, Mark, a little accident, like that, will often make things go criss-cross all summer. There is a time to plant, and a time to sow, as the good book tells us; and if it slips by, and we don't improve it, we can't expect much of a crop. I believe mine were rather slim that year, owing to the seed being put in so late; but I never laid it up against you. Boys will be boys, and you are about as good as they'll average, I guess. I am a little cross-grained sometimes, when things go con-*tra*-ry; and the best of us have our ups and downs, our trials and grievances, and they are not sent us for nothing either. I had to live a good while before I learnt it. As to your pulling up stakes in Sorreltown, and trying your luck among strangers, I don't *know* about that. There's always two sides to a picture, you know — a shiny side and a shady side. You will find the world into which you would be going very different, in many respects, from what you anticipate, and the people with whom you may come in contact, very different sort of folks from those you've been brought up among. We are a plain sort of people down here, not much used to refinement and fashion, and all that sort of thing. There's many an honest country lad, with an older head on his shoulders than yours, who has unmoored his little life-boat, — where it lay snugly anchored by the old hearth-stone, — and pushed out into the broad stream of pleasure, or ambition, or enterprise of some kind, who was foolish enough to think he would always find smooth sailing. But I tell you what — he found his little bundle of experience dreadful poor ballast when a squall came up. He was glad enough to reef sail, and pull for home. The 'light of home' has proved a beacon light to many a man who has ventured too far out among the breakers! I've seen the time, Mark, when I hadn't as good a home to steer to as you have. You look surprised; but so it was. My father died soon after George Worth went to college, and my mother — God pity her — went crazed, and died two years after. There were seven of us left. Our farm was small, and what was that to be divided among so many? One had to go here, another there, until we were all scattered, never to be reunited again as one family. You see the light of *my* early home went down in darkness deep and terrible; and but for the star of faith that shines above the Christian's pathway, and shows his way among the reefs that lift their threatening heads as though to bar his entrance to a heavenly rest, I fear I should have been shipwrecked long ago."

The lips of the strong man quivered, and his ample chest heaved to and fro, as Memory swept her magic hand over the chords of his large heart, making it vibrate with emotions too painful for concealment.

Tears filled the eyes of Mark, and for the moment he was half resolved to abandon his project, which before had looked so feasible. His humble birthplace possessed a thousand charms, before unappreciated, and the world beyond, which but an hour before looked so bright and alluring, now seemed replete with dangers insurmountable.

For a young adventurer, like him, to cast his bark adrift on an unknown sea — as his experienced friend had been pleased to term his entrance into the more active pursuits of life — with no hand but his own to guide its onward course, seemed impossible, and his courage was sorely put to the test; but the thought of his mother's lonely, toilsome life, and his own meagre subsistence, earned by the sweat of his brow, with no prospect of a better future, again arose before him like a spectre, to fright away all these unpleasant misgivings, and he resolved once more that nothing should decoy him from his purpose. As a thought of his own weakness stole over

his heart, it was lifted in silent prayer to Him whose covenant with those who put their trust in Him is everlasting.

"The arm of my mother's God shall be my guide," said
Mark, raising his eyes to those of his companion, who had
remained some minutes silent, while these conflicting thoughts
rioted in Mark's heart. "In His strength will I go forth. I
may encounter adverse winds and threatening waves, but
will trust the 'helm' in the hands of 'One mighty to save.'"

As Mark's tearful face, beaming with strong assurance of
heavenly guidance, was lifted to that of his friend, both became, as it were, in a moment inspired with a prophetic
vision, looming up in the distant future, brightening as it
led farther and farther towards the goal of promise — a vision beautiful and glorious, beckoning him onward, with its
mystic light, away through the green fields and flowery
paths of learning, or the more intricate windings of wisdom,
or up the steeps of science, until "its vane, slow-turning in
the liquid sky," reveals the outer court ambition rears to
genius.

"Well, Mark, I will no longer oppose you, nor throw any
obstacles in the way of your noble resolution; and perhaps I
may aid you in removing any 'stumbling-blocks' which
your unpractised hand might find too hard to manage. Go
home now to your supper, and we will consider the matter
further, and conclude what's best to be done."

As Mark ascended the little footpath leading to his humble
home, the good old deacon watched him until the door
closed behind him, and hid him from his earnest gaze.
Knowing something of Mark's taste, and disposition to
acquire useful knowledge, and having long reposed in him
the highest confidence, he no longer hesitated to encourage
him in his laudable pursuits.

"He's a noble fellow! And I do not much wonder at his
being dissatisfied with his present lot. I will see what I
can do for him. If I had had some of his grit at sixteen, I

might have been a different individual at sixty from what I am. No, I guess I did about as well as I *could*. It required a good deal of real courage and fortitude for a boy to get along as well as *I* did. Only think how I have succeeded. Everything I put my hand to seems to prosper, and it would be sorter charging God with unbountifulness to say that he had not prospered me. Let me be thankful that I am what I am, and have what I have."

Thus he reasoned and cogitated while he foddered the stock and drove the sheep into their accustomed pen, and fed the poultry and the pigs, who were again importunate in their demands upon his stock of patience. He then turned his own steps homeward.

"And as your patience must be exhausted," quoth aunt Bessie, "we will pause here in our narrative until another evening."

"Just tell me one thing, auntie," said I, as she was wiping her spectacles and pinning up her curls, as if she would dismiss me for the night; "was Mark Miller any relation of ours?"

"Why, what put that into your head, child? We have no relatives by the name of Miller, that I know of."

"Well, but is it not only an assumed name for —"

"O, I shall not spoil my story to gratify your childish curiosity. So now give me your good-night kiss, and pleasant dreams to you."

CHAPTER V.

NETTIE NOT INVITED.

" The sorrows of thy youthful day
    Shall make thee wise in coming years;
The brightest rainbows ever play
    Above the fountains of our tears."

MACKAY.

SAID Mark's was the only name omitted in the list of invitations to Squire Brown's that night; but there was one other who felt the slight as keenly as Mark did.

Though why little Nettie Strange should have indulged in the vain hope of being one of the happy recipients of so much pleasure as this occasion offered, I know not, except it be for the reason that she had heard *everybody* was to be there. She had never been to any of the merry-makings, and save that her place in the old school-house was generally occupied during the winter session, she would scarcely have been known to exist. As it was, her existence was made up of the monotonous round of farm-house drudgery, and not only that, but field-labour when her in-door duties were performed: there was hay to rake, or flax to pull, or apples to be gathered.

But Nettie had received a present of a new gown from one of the work-hands, when he was paid off in the fall, with green and yellow and red flowers scattered all over it. It was made low in the neck, and with short sleeves; and with her own chubby hands, hardened by labour and browned by the sunshine, she had hemmed and crimped a white cambric ruffle, and basted it on as neatly as a seamstress could have done it. There it had lain for three months, folded up nicely, in one corner of the great chest where the Sunday clothes were kept. But she knew no Sunday, except that on that day she was left alone to tend the baby and keep the four younger children out of mischief, while her mother went to church. At such times, if she could get the one to sleep and the others out to play, she would steal up stairs and take a long admiring look at the forbidden treasure, smoothing out the wrinkled folds, and wishing that a time would come when she might wear it.

She had heard of the sleigh-ride, and the party at Squire Brown's, through John Thompson, who came to borrow her father's sleigh-bells, and said, in her generous little heart, " Now I wonder if they will think of me. O, if I could only go this once ! " She ventured to express her desire to her mother, and received a sharp reproof for her presumption.

" That would be a pretty dress for you to wear this cold weather — wouldn't it ? "

" Lotty Harwood is going to wear her green crape, and it has both low neck and short sleeves."

" Well, if Mrs. Harwood is fool enough to cut up her dead mother's clothes into gowns for her lazy girls to string out, it's none of my business, or yours either. If it wasn't for the property the old woman left her, they wouldn't hold their heads higher than other folks, nor dress any smarter either.

" What are you standing there for? Why ain't you about your dishes? Don't you see it's almost night? Talk about going to the party ! I wonder what shoes you'd wear! Them of yourn would correspond amazingly with a new caliker gown ! "

" Couldn't I have a new pair ? " modestly asked Nettie,

while she hung her head, and the tears trembled in her soft blue eye.

"New shoes indeed ! You'd better look at mine," thrusting a dilapidated shoe into notice ; and if large feet were an indication of good blood, she might have claimed to be a lineal descendant of some royal line of autocrats.

"Do you think we are made of money? and that we have nothing to do with it but to buy finery for you? Go along to your work, I say. You needn't trouble yourself about the party. It's noways likely you'll go, or have a chance to. When you've done up the dishes, get some of them marino potatoes, and cut up for the cow. What have you done with the swill-pail? Haven't I told you to let it stand by the stove? What did you set it out for?"

Nettie said the baby would paddle in it, and she had to remove it.

"Then why didn't you keep him in the cradle, or carry him about? That's the way he's got his frock so greasy and dirty."

Nettie didn't see that it was any dirtier than common; besides, he was so heavy to carry.

"None of your impertinence, miss. I wouldn't give you your salt for all the good you are to me, or ever will be, unless you turn over a new leaf."

The next day was Christmas ; but no holy joy beamed from the cold gray eye of David Strange, and no bright, happy smile lighted up the hard, uncouth visage of his wife. The large, unfurnished house reverberated to no merry Christmas greetings ; there was no fire-light dancing on the parlor walls, and no love-light in the hearts beating beneath its roof. This day was passed as all the others in the year had been. Toil and trouble, fretting and fault-finding, were the predominating influences under which the children had been born and nurtured. The light of life, if it had ever shone at all in the parents' hearts, and the sweetness of human sympathy, seemed to have long since died out, or were shrouded in the unwholesome mists of avarice and austerity. To supply the bodily wants of his family appeared to Mr. Strange the sum total of his duty as a father and husband; while Mrs. Strange imposed no obligations upon herself as a wife and mother, except to see that the most pressing necessities of life were frugally furnished them; that nothing was wasted, and that they " got ahead a little every year." The wants of the heart, the refining influences of social life, the soul's yearnings after higher and nobler pnrsuits, never once suggested themselves to her mind; she never dreamed of those immortal duties to her kindred race which would exalt her virtues and rival her brightest hopes of worldly prosperity.

All day long had Nettie's unguarded thoughts been with the gay *cortége* she had seen pass as she stood at the kitchen window. Scrubbing and churning seemed to be the hardest tasks she had ever performed. She thought the butter never *would* come, and her hands trembled, when, after sweeping and hanging up the broom, she stopped to wipe the perspiration from her heated face. More than once was the checked woollen apron raised to her eyes, to brush away the truant tears that would drop in spite of all her womanly resolves to care nothing about it. Her mother seemed to feel for her too; for the bitterness of her nature was sweetened a little, and she was less disposed to be cross and fault-finding than usual. But if there were any of the gentler qualities of woman struggling for the ascendency in her heart, she was not the one to betray them in words.

" If you'll hurry with your ironing, and bring in the oven-wood, and get supper out of the way before dark, you may go down to widder Miller's this evening. I want to get her. brass kettle to do up some pickles in; and as you've been pretty hard at work to-day, you can take your knitting and stay a spell. I s'pose Mark has gone with the others, and the old woman will be alone. And you can ask her if she has any ' turn-pikes' to spare : I'm afraid mine got froze, for this bread ain't going to rise to-day, as I see.

" There, you needn't hurry over your work in that manner ; there's plenty of time to do it well. *Do you call that dicky ironed ?* "

To tell the truth, it had been somewhat slighted ; for Nettie's hands moved swiftly over the ironing-board, and her heart was all in a flutter, in anticipation of passing the evening with her best friend. But she dampened the plats and collar of the incorrigible dicky in some clear-starch water, and in a few moments took it to her mother to show how nice it looked.

" Well, *that'll do.* I never like to see things half done. How much more have you got to do? It is time the kettle was over."

" O, there's not much ; only father's shirt, and these towels, and Benny's aprons, and the table-cloth, and a few other things ; but I will put over the tea-kettle now, and it will be all ready when I get done. Shall I fry some ham ? "

" Yes, and you'll have to make biscuit too, for them young ones have done nothing this whole blessed day but eat and waste their bread upon the floor. John, come out of that cupboard this minute, or I'll trounce you. Do you hear ? "

John reluctantly obeyed, but not until he had stowed the last remaining slice of bread into his pocket, to be divided between himself and the dog.

Then followed various demands upon Nettie's time and patience ; but she actually flew in the discharge of her varied tasks, as there was so much to accomplish within a given time. What tried her most was to have to wait so long for her father's coming, after everything was steaming on the table.

At last he came ; and a less experienced eye than hers could tell at a glance that he had not spent his Christmas happily. Something, as usual, had gone wrong; and the moody silence with which he at first sank into his chair soon gave place to an outburst of pent-up wrath. The storm of words was not exhausted until the meal was finished; and Nettie's heart was relieved of a great load when she saw him take his hat and wend his way towards the town.

"We will have to milk and fodder the cattle, Nettie," said her mother, "for father won't be back again till midnight." And again she gave way to anger, as she thought of the many similar trials she had passed through, and all on account, as she thought, of *his* bad temper. She never once thought that "a soft answer turneth away wrath;" that it was as much her own fault as his that these unpleasant jars were becoming more and more frequent every year of their lives.

"Patience brings roses," and at last it brought Nettie to the end of her allotted tasks. When she had smoothed her luxuriant blonde hair (which would curl in spite of the neglect it met with), and rolled up her knitting, and pinned it carefully in her pocket-handkerchief, she stole up behind her mother's chair to ask if she might wear her new dress; but the question died upon her lips ere it was uttered. She thought, sure enough, it would contrast strangely with the thick, coarse shoes she wore. And so, with a clean linsey-woolsey, and a neat pink apron pinned around her waist, and a faded green cloak thrown over her shoulders, and a worse-looking hood (after having received her instructions as to her errand over and over again), she sallied forth into the clear moonlight, on her way to Mrs. Miller's.

The "genii of the night" ne'er placed in Dian's 'broidered vest jewels more rich and royal than those sparkling in her deep blue robes this night. It might be their reflection on the snow-drifts that gave to Nettie's eyes their brilliant lustre, for never had they shone so beautiful as now. She waded through the fleecy whiteness until she struck the open road, her face as free from cloud or shadow as was the night's pale queen sailing through the snowy clouds above.

She passed the little stile that separated her father's broad, barren domains from the lane leading to the small ten-acre lot of his less affluent but more thrifty neighbour Smith. This was a renowned trysting-place for the youngsters of the village when the early summer shrouded it in a mass of green foliage. But now, how sad and desolate it looked, with its heavy carpet of snow, and the long grapevine, that in autumn was laden with its rich purple burden, grating harshly against the old hickory, as it stretched its huge arms abroad as if to protect it from the sweeping blast! Nettie was a brave, thoughtful girl, far beyond her years; and though in the morning of her " teens," in her heart were germs of intellectual strength and beauty, only awaiting the genial climate of love and the guidance of some stronger spirit to make them expand into womanly grace and dignity. People wondered of whom she inherited all the quiet gentleness and amiable self-possession that characterized her daily life. But Nettie was the first-born of her parents, and came into being before their hearts were quite alienated from each other, and when all that was good in their natures showed itself in their affection for their little girl. As they increased in years, cares increased, and they, becoming greedy of gain, forgot to cast their cares and burdens on the Lord, but tried to carry them alone. And so, at length, each became discouraged, and sank under the accumulated load. Nettie paused a moment by the stile, although her feet and hands were cold, for her shoes were old, and Bennie had lost the nice warm mittens Mrs. Miller had netted for her. She cast her eyes wonderingly towards the only spot in the world for which she had any affection: I should except Mrs. Miller's cottage; but she was seldom there: it was a mile from her father's house, and she never went anywhere without taking the children. But she was sometimes permitted to bring them here to play in the cool shade, for there were no trees around the tall, gaunt house of Mr. Strange; and but for a prolific hop-vine that shaded the front doorsteps, and spread its noxious leaves over the one south window, where Mrs. Strange forever sat with her foot jogging the cradle, the house might have defied any one to discover the most distant approximation to ornament or comfort. But this spot to Nettie was the one little green Eden where she led her unruly charge, whenever their teasing to be taken out to play became no longer endurable to the mother. In the hot, sultry summer days they came but seldom, for then Nettie's tasks were too many for her to spend so much time; but in the sweet spring time, when the sun shone warm and pleasant on the green earth, and there was not so much to do within doors, would they come; and while the children filled their aprons with the yellow dandelions and the pretty violets, blue and gold, and the air with the sounds of their boisterous merriment, Nettie would sit quietly apart and build " air castles," peopling them with beautiful beings and things clothed with the vesture of immortality. Strange day-dreams, and a thousand bright images, would haunt her imaginative mind. O, what beautiful dreams had she of the great unknown, as these spirit-fancies ran riot through her brain! An unseen power led her whither it listed, until her rapt vision became dazzled with its own brightness. It was here she learned of the spirit-world lying all around her, of the powers of the immortal mind, and the strength of the human will. And as the years sped away, purer and deeper were the spirit-voices that wooed her (she had no social life) to a life within herself. A beautiful little snow-peak, with a spire formed of a broken tendril, rested upon the summit of the grape-vine arbor; and as a little cloud of silver and gold rolled away from the moon's bright face, a haloed radiance played about the snow-peak, until it seemed too glorious a thing to be swept away. As Nettie looked, its foundation became undermined by the sudden swaying of the branches on which it rested, and it fell among the broken twigs.

"O," exclaimed Nettie, "that is too bad; why could I not gaze upon it a moment longer? Such is the fate of all my visions! Ere I get them shaped to my liking they fade away into nothingness. But I must hurry along, I am so cold; by and by the spring will come, and I can visit the stile, and dream under the green trees."

She quickened her pace, and soon the cheerful light in Mrs. Miller's cottage window rose to view, and she smiled involuntarily a pleasant smile; for it was a beacon-light to her, shedding a serene glory upon her lonely heart. Soon the inviting voice of Mark bade her "walk in," and her heart was put in the least little flutter in the world, for to meet him was an unexpected pleasure.

"Why, Nettie! how do you do?" and

"Bless the child!" said the mother, both in the same breath.

"Are you not 'most froze? Come to the fire, do; Mark, bring the little rocking-chair. Why, your cheeks are really purple!"

"O, no, I'm not much cold; and I've had a pleasant walk. There was a good path after I got out into the road, and I might have been here sooner only I stopped —" at the stile, she would have added; but she interrupted herself by asking Mrs. Miller to untie her hood; the strings had got into a hard knot. The mischievous tape baffled the skill of Mrs. Miller, and Mark was forced to undertake the untying of the incorrigible string, while his mother busied herself in drawing out the little round table, and placing the candle and a dish of red-checked apples thereon.

"Are they all well at home?" inquired Mrs. Miller, with kindly interest.

"Quite well," said Nettie.

Mark was so long untying the string, that Nettie said " break it; " and she was a little vexed, too, when he stood with his lips so close to hers (just a little, you know), for so good a girl as Nettie never got exceedingly cross about any-thing. Mrs. Miller thought he was looking straight into Nettie's eyes, and not under her chin, as he should have done. But Nettie never raised her eyes to see, and at length the knotty question was settled by Mark's tossing the old hood into a corner; and then, drawing a chair close to that of Nettie, he began to banter her on her good looks.

" Why, Nettie, how tall you've grown l I haven't seen you since last harvest." He did not ask her where she had kept herself all this time, for he well knew she hardly ever went beyond the dilapidated enclosure of her father's grounds.

" You have not been here in a long, long time," said Mrs. Miller ; " and as Mark says, so says his mother,—I think you have grown both tall and handsome since we saw you last. Stand up here under the notch, and let me measure."

" Is that notch there yet? That was made a year ago, and I must have grown some since then; but not all that ! " and she stepped back from under Mrs. Miller's hand, that had been placed over her head, and saw how far above the old notch on the cellar door was the new one just made.

" If I grow as much as that every year, I shall soon be as tall as Mark."

" You are nearly up to my shoulder now," said Mark, pressing Nettie to his side, and passing his arm around her waist, while he attempted to snatch a kiss from her pouting lips. Nettie turned up her saucy little nose, and retreated to the chimney corner.

" He's a naughty boy, Nettie ; I wouldn't mind him."

" I wouldn't mind it at all, only I knew you were look-ing."

" That's an honest confession. Mother, what made you look?" and a right merry peal of laughter burst from all lips.

"Nay," said Nettie, archly, "that is not what I meant;" and the laughing dimples deepened on her cheeks.

"Take an apple, Nettie, and let us be good friends. Here, this big mellow one, and I'll name it for you. I'll name it that great 'straddle-bug,' who was around here try-ing to get up a dancing-school."

"Humph! I would rather you'd name it yourself than him!"

"Just as I supposed; thank you for the compliment."

"O, you 'good-for-nothing!' you misconstrue everything I say. I meant your name was bad enough, without going away from home to hunt up 'straddle-bugs.' How can you make me blush so?"

"It is only the reflection of the apples."

"Ah, how nice they are, too! Did they grow on the tree down by the spring?"

"Yes, Nettie, they grew on the tree you helped me to set out. Don't you remember holding it up with your chubby little hands while I piled the earth around it? We have always called it Nettie's tree."

As the evening wore merrily away, Mark and Nettie thought they were never so happy before, and that it was far better than going to the sleigh ride. The jovial remarks of the one, and the sprightly rejoinder of the other, quite upset the gravity of Mrs. Miller, and the shadow of the old woe floated away from her kind spirit. Nettie was so frolicsome, and Mark so seemingly happy, it was impossible to be sad now. The last word of the sprightly repartee lay on the lips of Nettie Strange, when she suddenly thought of her own unhappy home, and the necessity of immediately re-turning thither. The bright smile went out from her face, and the sparkling light of her eye was clouded by the long, drooping lash.

The old clock told the hour of ten, and Nettie started from her momentary reverie, and with an assumed cheerfulness, said it was time for her to go.

" Well, Nettie, would you like to have a certain 'good-for nothing' see you home?"

Nettie blushed her consent, and since the disappointment of the morning so happy a smile had not irradiated Mark's face. The cloak and hood were brought by Mark, and Mrs. Miller hastened to bring the brass kettle and the "turn-pikes" for Mrs. Strange. When the cloak was properly adjusted, and the hood pinned closely about the face (Mark thought, " What a pretty face to be cased in such an outland-ish bonnet!"), by Mrs. Miller's nimble fingers, she kissed her with a mother's tenderness, and said she was so glad to see them happy! Gazing upon the children as they took their leave, the grateful tears gathered in her eyes, and she thought, as their retreating footsteps and merry voices were borne back on the night wind, she could never more feel poverty while the wealth of two such loving hearts was hers. " Heaven bless them!" ejaculated she; " in all the wide world there are none others to love me." And it was a happy hour when, alone by her silent cottage hearth, the poor widow thanked God for his great mercy. An hour after, all were sleeping sweetly beneath their respective roofs, and the pleasant smiles that played around their lips seemed to tell of happy dreams.

CHAPTER VI.

SAM MAYNARD CALLED TO AN ACCOUNT.

"To the expanded and aspiring soul,
    To be but still the thing it long has been
    Is misery, e'en though enthroned it were
    Under the cope of high imperial state."

                                    JOANNA BAILLIE.

THE morning after the party two friends met, and one expressed surprise at the other's absence.

"Why were you not there, Mark? We had a delightful time; and I heard Mrs. Brown inquiring after you, and Lizzie sent her regrets. They feared your mother was sick."

A strange, inquiring glance shot from Mark's eyes, that betrayed a momentary struggle between pride and passion; he felt that a new insult was offered him, in the shape of a seeming solicitude they did not feel. He said as much, and his friend marvelled at this unwonted spirit of resentment.

"Did they think so mean of me as to suppose I would come unasked?"

"Unasked! Certainly not; but you *were* asked."

"No, George, I was not invited; and ignorant and uncivilized as I am, I hope I have too much good sense to crowd myself in where I am not wanted."

"There is some mistake about this, Mark, for I was present when Mr. Brown commissioned Sam Maynard to write the invitations; and when Sam asked for a list of names, the old gentleman remarked, 'There is no necessity for a list; only mind and get them all.' He was particular to say, 'Ask every boy and girl in the village.' These were his own words."

Mark looked surprised, and, as if to excuse Sam's negligence, remarked, carelessly, —

"It's no great affair. I suppose he thought I had no decent clothes to wear, and wouldn't go, any way."

"That makes no difference," rejoined his friend; "he was in duty bound to fulfil Mr. and Mrs. Brown's request, as he acted for them in the matter."

Mark's next thought was self-reproachful and humiliating; but in a moment there was in his eyes and voice an expression of joy his friend could not understand, until he said, —

"Between Squire Brown's family and ours there have always existed the utmost harmony and the closest friendship. We always thought more of them than anybody else, because of their long-continued kindness to us, whether in sickness or health, joy or sorrow. How could I have been so deceived? I will never trust to appearances again, until I know the truth; and if Sam Maynard has some cause for hating me, I must know what it is."

"You do not intend to go to that conceited coxcomb and ask him, I hope. He never had but an idea and a half in his head at a time. Hate you, Mark! What reason has he to hate you, I would like to know?"

"That's just what I would like to know myself. So come with me, George, and we will try and discover the reason. He avoids me, and this affair of the party is as much of a mystery to me as to yourself."

George's only reply was a look of surprise; but he followed Mark up the street, and into Mr. Maynard's store. Sam drew his cap over his eyes, and pretended to be busy with a customer, and, without deigning to notice the twain, set up an elaborate encomium on some tobacco just received.

" Well, I don't use the weed; but you may weigh me out a quarter of tea for the old woman; and, now I think on't, I'll buy Josh a jews-harp. Have ye got any?"

" No — yes — I believe so; at least I will look and see."

And so, with the weighing of the tea and the hunting for the jews-harp, which he could not find, a full half hour was consumed.

" Sam, a moment with you, if you please," said Mark, as he saw he was determined to give them the cold shoulder. The blood rushed to Sam's face, and his eye fell beneath the strong gaze of the two boys; but assuming an air of indifference, he advanced and asked, —

" What will you have?"

" Did you give out the invitations to Lizzie Brown's party?"

" Yes, I did."

" You did not give me one."

" Did you expect one?"

" I did, most assuredly."

" And you want a reason, I suppose, why I did not send you one."

" Precisely."

" Simply because I thought your clothes unfit to wear to such a place, and the notice too short for you to obtain new ones. Is that satisfactory?"

" Not exactly; I had new clothes, and it was not for you to say who were to go and who not. I feared you had other causes; some personal dislike, or pique, or — "

" None whatever, sir. What put that into your head?"

" I have thought your manner towards me changed somewhat, since your return home, especially; you never speak to me when you meet me, and once before you have treated me with contempt."

" And so I am brought to an account for my neglect of the ' common hireling of the village.' We are not on equal footing, I take it."

An angry flush passed over his face, succeeded by a smile of insolent scorn, as he turned to wait on some customers who just then came in. Mark's heart beat thick and fast as his feet took him involuntarily from the store; and wending his way homeward, he threw himself into a vacant chair by the fire, without taking his hat off, to think. For more than an hour he sat thus, without interchanging a word with his mother, who was busy with her domestic affairs. But finally she noticed his downcast looks, and came up behind him, and peered, inquiringly, beneath the broad brim that shaded his face. It wore its usual calmness, and she thought it a handsome face.

"What are you thinking about, Mark?"

"I was thinking about you, mother."

His eyes sought hers, and, in a tremulous voice, he continned, "And something about myself — though that was a secondary thought." And he felt the dreaded hour had come when his mother must know all.

"Mother!" he said, rising and pacing the room to and fro as he spoke, "I cannot bear the idea of always remaining here in Sorreltown, to be 'the common hireling of the village.'"

These words had much significance. They comprised every kind of work that was hard and disagreeable, and he would have recalled them, for he saw, with regret, the gloom that stole over the kind mother's face. He observed the long, sad glances thrown at his retreating form, as he strode the floor; but they were spoken, and he continued, "I have looked away to the hills that shut us in here, and thought there was something beyond worth the seeking."

A sigh from his mother arrested for a moment his further speech, and he sat down by her side.

"Mother, you must not oppose me; I must see what there is outside our little home valley, though I will venture to say, nothing pleasanter will ever cross my vision. But there is something for me to do and learn that will make me a man."

" Why, Mark! you are only a boy yet," said his mother, as she thought of his few inexperienced years; " when you *are* a man, you will, no doubt, possess a man's abilities and a man's ambition. These come only with years and experience, and you are yet in your teens."

" True, mother; but if I would reap wealth and distinction in my manhood, I must sow the seeds in my youth."

" Distinction, my son, oftener eludes the grasp of those who pursue it, than those who, by patient merit, await her coming. Wealth, or at least a competency, may be obtained anywhere, if we have health and energy."

" It will be a long time coming to us here in this little nook of a place, work as we may. I believe there is a wider field for me, in some place, where my labour will be better rewarded, and " — " where I shall be better appreciated," he would have said; but the words died on his lips ere they were uttered.

" How long have you thought of this, Mark?"

" Ever since the sleigh ride," rose involuntarily to his lips; but that, too, was thrust back before the thought was framed into words, and he said, —

" It is not a resolution formed to-day. I have had a long conversation with Deacon Sloper, and he seemed to approve my plan; and if I can only get your sanction, mother, my way is clear."

" Have you asked God to sanction it?"

" Yes, mother, I have. I will never do anything upon which I cannot first invoke his blessing."

Mrs. Miller's heart rose in gratitude to that Being who has said, " As the waters of Noah shall never return to cover the earth, so the covenant of my peace shall never depart from thee." She could trust her boy in the hands of the Lord after that; wherever he might go, her faith built a bridge for his feet to walk upon, whether over the deceiving quicksands of temptation, or toiling up the long, steep " hill Difficulty," or shrinking beneath the shadows of disappointment: she felt secure in those promises which were not written in vain. While she was sitting in the shadow of the faded chintz that draped the window, her eye sought the various things arranged about the room ; and when she remembered that they were purchased by the sweat of the brow, she knew how to value them. Their real worth was known only to them, because they only knew the toil and self-denials they had cost. Every tin pan on the dresser, even the faded rag carpet that covered a part of the floor, was witness to the privations it had cost to place it there ; and though they worked ever so hard, it was as Mark had said, they did not seem to prosper very much. It was a kind, benevolent, but care-worn look that greeted Mark when he looked up from his fit of abstraction, and his heart smote him that he should ever cause another line of pain and anxiety to be written there, in that face, to him so gentle and good ; and he thought, for a moment, rather than grieve that dear, kind mother's heart by a single additional sorrow, he would forego his cherished purpose, and crush back the hopes that promised such rich rewards. He saw the struggle it cost his mother to accede to those plans ; for would it not take him away from his home and her presence? And humble though that home was, it possessed attractions for them, and associations never to be forgotten or lightly esteemed.

" There is only one thing in the way, mother," resumed Mark ; " but for your staying alone I could leave home with a light heart."

" But where will you go, Mark? We have no connections in the world who could aid you in any way ; and as for friends, I don't know as we have many outside of Sorreltown. I would not mind staying alone next summer, if it was for your good. I could go on with my spinning and weaving just the same; old Brindle generally finds her own way home, and after the garden is planted, I see but little for you to do about home, and perhaps you might do better in some other place." But the words were uttered in a tremulous voice, and a look almost doubting her own sincerity stole over her pale face, leaving traces of the heart-struggle going on within.

" Mother, if *you* could see me depart with any degree of satisfaction, and think it would be for our mutual good, then, indeed, my mind is made up. I thought of going to Albany. Deacon Sloper will give me letters to some friends there — his own sister, who, if she is any like her good brother, will take a little interest in me, for the sake of our neighborhood relations. Only let me see you cheerful, mother, and the worst is over." The tone of love and anxiety quite sealed the mother's lips, and the better to conceal the elements at war in her heart, she put the burning brands together, and filled the iron tea-kettle, and swung the trammel back, after changing the kettle on the hook.

" Don't we want a new back-log, mother?"

" No. I think this will do for to-night."

And then a thought occurred to both. Who would provide these and other necessities — which his strong arm always brought — when he was away? But remembering, if he saw traces of tears on her cheek, it might discourage him, and decoy him from his high purpose, she dashed away the pearly drops ere he marked their falling; and he, to gain more confidence in himself and his new-wrought theories, whistled a lively air as he took his mittens, and prepared himself for his evening's chores.

CHAPTER VII.

DEACON SLOPER'S MEMORIES AND ANTICIPATIONS.

"Though old, he still retained
His manly sense and energy of mind.
Virtuous and wise he was, but not severe;
He still remembered that he once was young:
His easy presence checked no decent joy."

ARMSTRONG.

IFE, what do you say to letting the youngsters have a little frolic here in our great old house; it's been many a day since there was a fire in the west end; and for once I'd like to see it all lit up with pleasant lights, and cheerful faces, and a blazing fire on every hearth. What say you to giving a grand New Year's entertainment, eh?"

"Say? Why, I say, husband, that same thought has been running in my mind ever since Christmas; only I thought I would like to see young and old all enjoying themselves together. Sure there is room enough in this great barn of a house to entertain the whole neighborhood."

"Well, then, young and old it is," said Deacon Sloper; "though I tell you, wife, it will spoil all the fun for the younger ones to be set up with their fathers and mothers; they won't enjoy it half as well; no, no, let's have one at a time."

"Please yourself, my dear; it is as well, perhaps, for New Year's is too near at hand to think of making much preparation."

"What'll you have to do to get ready?"

"O, there will be mince pies, and tart pies, pound cake, and loaf cake to make, and turkeys and chickens to stuff, and all the china to wash up clean, the silver to rub up, and the brass to scour, and the nuts to crack, and the apples to wipe off, and all the beds to be made over, and the chintz curtains to come down, and the dimity ones put up, and—"

"O, wife, wife, don't enumerate any further. Why, everything about the house is as slick as a new ribbon; and what's the use in tearing up everything, and making such a fuss over a little jollification for the young ones? Bake a few pies, cut a new cheese, and we'll have some chestnuts, and some apples and cider passed around, and that's enough."

But Mrs. Sloper, the most thrifty and notable housewife in Sorreltown, never did things by halves; and all that was enumerated in her catalogue, and much more, was accomplished between the following morning and New Year's day. The whole house was turned topsy-turvy, and by the time she was done with the airing and the dusting, the sweeping, the scouring, and the polishing, the good deacon, who was glad of an excuse to absent himself, had paid a visit to nearly every house in town, and, after chatting and talking of the weather, the crops, politics, and religion, wound up by inviting the young people to his house on New Year's night.

"And so you're going to have a party at your house, I hear?" said Mrs. Strange, as the deacon seated himself in the splint-bottomed chair, which Nettie set for him, after punching up the feather cushion, to make it soft and inviting.

"Why, yes, a little bit of a gathering for the youngsters: there didn't seem to be anything going on, and I thought I'd just like to see how it would seem to have the old house lit up once more, and hear the merry voices of song and laughter; and I guess I'll get a fiddle, and let 'em dance."

"O, Mr. Sloper! are they going to dance?" cried Nettie, whose wide open eyes and ears caught every syllable as it was uttered. "I never saw any dancing. How I should like—"

"Go about your work now, and not be begging invitations where you're not wanted.   When Mr. Sloper wants
you to go, he will say so.   Put some more wood on the fire,
pick up that bridle, and sweep them husks out o' doors.
I declare, if the floor ain't worse'n a barn floor; if them
boys fetch any more of their pop-corn in here, they'll be
sorry; and I wish *he'd* mend his bridles somewhere else.
How on airth Mrs. Sloper can keep her house looking so
decent, is more'n I can tell.   But she's no young ones to
litter up, as I have.   I'm about discouraged trying to keep
soul and body together.   But, Mr. Sloper, you're not going
yet?   Sit down a spell longer."

"I must go soon; I have to go over to 'the grove' yet,
to-night, and that is quite a step from here.   I want you to
let Nettie come without fail; I came on purpose to ask her.
I want every young person for five miles around to be there.
My sleigh will come for her about dark; and, Nettie, my good
girl," said the generous old man, patting her on the cheek,
"you must look your prettiest, though I'll lay a wager there
will be no sweeter face in the room than yours.   If your
mother could spare you, I know who would be glad to get
you for his own."

"Let's see; it's nigh on to six year since Lucy was married — ain't it?"

"Yes, almost seven; and since then the old house seems
lonesome like, with us two old folks in it all alone; but we
are getting used to it now; at first it was like as there had
been a funeral in it, when the last of seven went away!"

"And many another aged couple has felt the same, and
said the same," said aunt Bessie, the moisture gathering in
her quiet eyes.   "Thus it was in my own father's family.
'We were seven,' and it seems but yesterday when we were
children at our mother's knee; and now we are scattered the
wide world over, no two in a place.   And so the children
of her love went out into the world, one after another, I

among the rest. We have never been all together under the
old roof-tree since. The boys became men, and went off,
one to his farm, another to his merchandise. The girls listened to the soft eloquence that love pours into the ears of
blushing maidenhood, and they too went out from the old
home, leaning upon the faith of strangers. So it is, and so
it must ever be while the world lasts. But mother said she
was comforted that she had so many and such good children,
and that they were all happily married to good wives and
husbands."

"Good evening, Mrs. Strange; good evening, Nettie.
You must be sure and come; be all ready by six o'clock."

"Yes, I will," smiled Nettie; and her eyes glistened like
two diamonds at the thought of going to a party.

"What do they do at a party, I wonder! and what is one
like?" she would say to herself a dozen times a day. She
would like to ask somebody, but her mother has been so
cross all day, she dares not allude to the subject that is up-
permost in her thoughts.

Mark was invited, and so were the Maynards, and their
friend Miss Grace Pearson, who acknowledged in very lady-
like terms the happiness it would afford her to be present.
"Is it to be a quilting or a paring bee?" inquired Mrs.
Maynard, when she had learned the object of Mr. Sloper's
visit.

"Neither, ma'am, but a real old-fashioned New Year's
frolic, such as we used to have when I was a boy."

"No dancing, I suppose?" said Helen, who knew the
deacon's proclivities for long prayers and short stories.

"Dancing? Well, yes, mebbe; we don't know what
might happen. You had better bring along your pumps,
so's to be prepared, in case —"

"Why, Deacon Sloper! and you a church member! and
a deacon, too!"

But that he was a member, in good standing, of the Baptist

church in Sorreltown, the books which he himself kept gave unmistakable evidence; and since the memory of the oldest inhabitant no accusation against himself of the slightest weight could be found in their infallible records. He was an honourable man, and a faithful Christian in every sense of the word; and so he was going to give to the children and the young people of the village a little "hop" under his own roof. To be sure he was.

"What's the harm, pray?"

"*No harm*, Mr. Sloper; but what will folks say?"

"Mebbe a few will grumble, but I've counted noses around, and shall have a majority on my side; so good evening, ladies."

"Good evening."   "Good evening."

"O, delightful!" cried Helen Maynard.   "We shall have a splendid time.   Mrs. Sloper always gives such excellent suppers, and the house is large enough to hold all Sorreltown."

"It is that large house, with such a number of gables and chimneys, down by the river, I think you told me."

"Yes, that one which stands back from the road, with two great elms in front.   In summer it is most beautiful, for the yard is full of lilacs and snow-balls, peonies and roses, and vines that clamber to the eaves.   Then there is an arbour down by the spring, where the wild honeysuckles grow so thick one can hardly see through them.   There's also a swing down by that clump of poplars, and a grove of wild plum and crab-apple trees, where it's real fun to go in summer when there is no dew on the grass.   O, I think you would like Sorreltown in summer.   It was not then the desolate looking place it is now; that is, you would like it as well as you could any country place.   To be sure, there's not much society here; but I've become so accustomed to do without that, I do not mind it."

"No society!   Why, I think your neighbours very kind,

5

good people," said Grace Pearson, who was quite indisposed
to admit the truth of Helen's assertion.

"Why, yes, they are kind enough, and good enough, for
that matter; but there's no intelligence or refinement amongst
them. They dress so old-fashioned, all in homespun. Pa
hardly sells a yard of silk or broadcloth the year round.
And they talk and act so inelegantly! I almost blush for
my own mother sometimes. She has acquired their ways
by mingling with her neighbours, which she is obliged to do,
you know. I wish pa would move to the city: every time
I come home from school, the place has less attractions for
me. There isn't a marriageable young gentleman in it. And
there hasn't been a wedding in it since — I don't know when
— since poor Lucy Sloper was married and went away."

"Who was *she?* Deacon Sloper's daughter?"

"Yes."

"Why do you say *poor* Lucy Sloper?"

"Why, you see, a young student from — dear me, I can't
think of the name of the college where he graduated — but
he was going away off to some of those heathenish islands
in the Pacific, as a missionary. No, I believe it was to
Burmah, where they went, or to Greece, I don't remember
which."

"Did she go with him?" asked Miss Pearson, much
excited, and without waiting for Helen to finish her nar-
ration.

"Yes, to be sure she did! They were married, and left
Boston, with a great many more missionaries, for that out-
landish, heathenish country. I'd as soon have tied a mill-
stone to my neck, and gone to the bottom of the sea at once.
That was a good many years ago. I was not more than
twelve years old; but I remember the wedding, and how
people talked about it for a long time."

"What did they say?"

"O, they thought it was queer that she, so young and so

beautiful, should take such an odd fancy into her head; and
queerer still that he should love her, a plain country girl;
though she had been off to school somewhere in Massa-
chusetts: there's where they became acquainted; and people
said they guessed she'd repent her choice, and all that; but
what was more surprising than all, was the perfect willingness of her father and mother to give her up. They never
raised a single objection, though they knew it was as if they
buried her."

" Had they other children?"

" La, yes, a whole snarl of them; but they were all married, and a long way from home. She was the last of them
all, the little pet lamb of the flock."

" But they heard from her often — did they not?"

" Not very often: once she wrote from some little island
where they stopped to take in fresh water. She described it
as a cheerless, desolate looking place, but said it was far
pleasanter than the rolling ship. It was a year before the
letter came; and then again after she arrived at — dear me,
I wish I could remember the name of the place; but I'm so
forgetful! besides, I have no taste for these missionary enter-
prises, or sympathy for those who go to heathen lands.
But she wrote several long letters after her arrival there,
and they were published in Boston, and created a great
sensation, so I've heard say; and after she died, there was a
great deal said and written about her, as being ' a noble,
gifted, heavenly-minded woman, just such a one as the
infant missionary cause needed there.' That was all very
flattering; but what good could it do her, after she had
sacrificed her life, and was in her grave?"

The listener's heart heaved with emotion, and she wept as
she thought of the dear girl sleeping beneath the shadow of
some lone " Hopia Tree," thousands of miles from her
kindred shore; and wondered if, in the morning of the resurrection, her glorified spirit would seek among the old,

forgotten graves of Hindostan the frail tenement that once held such a godlike soul! But she was silent, and Helen proceeded.

"It was two years after her death before the old people appeared at all like their former selves; and yet no one ever heard them murmur, or say they were sorry she went, or take any blame upon themselves for consenting to it. They never like to talk about it much. Once I remember asking Mrs. Sloper if she was not sorry Lulie went away to Burmah — yes, that's the place where they went — and you ought to have seen the smile on her ashen-white face when she answered, 'Sorry? No, Helen, I am not sorry, but glad, that I had a lamb so young and spotless to offer to the Lord. We gave her to Him at her birth, and when she was eighteen He called for her. Though we little thought, when we lay our little, wee lammie on God's altar, that He would accept our sacrifice in such a way, or that one so humbly born, and so sinful, as myself, could present so pure a thing for His acceptance.' 'But,' said I, 'she might have served God in some other way, and been alive now, and living near you.' 'She is always near me,' said Mrs. Sloper; 'and though her dear body lies far away from the rest of them, it will be just the same when the dead shall rise. I am never unhappy when I think of those who have gone home before me.'"

"Has she lost other children?"

"Yes, three or four; but not until they were married, and gone from home. I believe they have but two left: one is a minister out west somewhere, and their daughter lives in Albany."

"Lives in Albany! What is her name?"

"Mrs. Lòveland. Her husband has a bank there. They are wealthy, and she sends her mother sights of nice things every year. There! I've broken my needle, and it's the only decent one I had to sew with."

" Here is my needle-book; help yourself. Does this old couple have no one with them? Are they living alone?"

" O, they are hardly ever alone. They have very nice company from the city, and their house is always headquarters for persons of note, young and old, who come out here ruralizing in the summer. Last summer there was a splendid young gentleman stopped there for several weeks; but he was very seclusive. I invited him to dinner, and to horseback rides; but he always declined with such a gentlemanly air, I could not help but like him. He was a convalescent."

" A what?"

" No, not exactly a convalescent, but a — what do you call it? He had been in ill health a long time, and came out here for a change of air: his physician recommended it."

" A valetudinarian."

" Yes, that's the word I was trying to think of. But ain't you getting sleepy?"

" No, indeed; I am very much interested in your friends, and by the clock it wants a quarter to nine. Tell me more about Mrs. Sloper. Does she keep any servant, or any one to assist her?"

" She generally has a girl to do the spinning, and another during harvest. But mercy! she is smarter than you and I both, and can do more work. You will see how nice everything will be, when you go there New Year's. I suppose Mrs. Miller will help her along with her preparations for the party. She lives close by, and is always at hand when wanted for a day's work. And I presume her son, Mark, will be at the party. O, you'll laugh when you see him. I know he'll be there, for the deacon won't miss any; besides, he is a great favorite of the deacon's."

" Who is?"

" Mark Miller, widow Miller's son. They live in that little log hut, down under the hill, just before you come to Mr. Sloper's."

"I remember it, and I think it a cosy little place, though the house is built of rough logs. Why do you think I will laugh when I come to see this man?"

" He is not a man. He's a mere boy, not more than six-teen or seventeen; but he is so queer and old-fashioned, so countrified, and demure as a parson."

" Are they very poor?"

" Poor! Yes, indeed; they have hard work to live."

" You mean, they have to work hard, to live."

" Yes, he is the hired ' help ' of the village, and his mother weaves cloth, and coverlets, and spins linen, and does a'most anything that comes along to make a living. But she is a real good woman for all that. She is so good in sickness; and she always has a kind word for everybody and every-thing."

" And is not her son like her?"

" O, yes; he's a pattern of goodness, for that matter; but he is so awkward and clumsy; not about his work, though. He is very active and smart when at work; but he has so little refinement, and dresses so shabbily; no, not exactly shabby, for his clothes are clean, and patched and repatched, until you could hardly tell the original garment; and wears such great hob-nailed shoes, and hats that have neither crown or rim." And a little laugh wound up this last sentence.

" Has he no education?"

" Y-e-s, he's picked up considerable learning, here and there; though I wonder how, for he only goes to school a little while during the winter, and the rest of the time he is hard at work. But he reads a great deal. I have heard Mrs. Sloper say there was not a book in Sorreltown that he had not read; and I presume he studies at home. Pa has often set up Mark as a pattern for us, and said, if we were half as industrious as Mark, we would get along faster. He outstripped us all in arithmetic last winter, and is a better reader and speller than any of us. What will you wear to the party?"

"I hardly know. Some warm dress will be most com•fortable, as the weather is so cold."

Helen thought the weather might moderate; and as she was quite desirous that her guest should create a sensation, she intimated that she had a choice in the matter. It took her a long time to choose for herself between her bottle-green silk and scarlet merino. At length the latter was decided upon, as being the least liable to get torn or soiled. Miss Pearson, to please her friend, decided to wear a rich changeable silk.

Long before night the deacon had forgotten he had invited Nettie Strange to his house; but with Nettie it was quite different. She was as tremulous as a young aspen all day. She hardly dared to broach the subject of the party to her mother; and whenever she addressed her, her voice seemed modulated to more than its usual gentleness, fearing, all the while, some untoward circumstance might interrupt her anticipated enjoyment. Life's stern lessons had put a wo-man's heart in that childish bosom; and so Nettie hid all her thoughts there, and was brooding tremblingly over them.

CHAPTER VIII.

A NEW YEAR'S PARTY AT MRS. SLOPER'S.

"Thou'rt like a star; for when my way
  Was cheerless and forlorn,
And all was blackness, like the sky
  Before a coming storm,
Thy beaming smile and words of love,
  Thy heart of kindness free,
Illumed my path, then cheered my soul,
  And bade its sorrow flee."
                        AMERICAN LADIES' MAGAZINE.

"Great souls by instinct to each other turn,
  Demand alliance, and in friendship burn."
                        ADDISON.

T was still and warm on New Year's night. All day long had the bright sunshine dallied with the frosted pane, the snowflakes lying on the window-ledges, and the icicles depending from the eaves, until they wept themselves away in an agony of joy, seemingly happy that their brief life had helped to make glorious the new advent. The snow lay deep upon the ground, the warm sun had spread a shining radiance over it; and now, as it glittered in the mellow moonlight, it seemed studded with jewels and precious stones.

There are lights in every window, happy earnest voices in every house, and gladness in every heart. Even Mrs. Strange has caught the infection; for she is assisting Nettie with her toilet, has done her hair very prettily, and bidden

Nettie look in the glass to see how long and nicely it curls. The pink dress and white apron are airing on a chair, all ready to be adjusted after she has put on her new shoes and white lamb's-wool stockings. There, now she is all ready, and surveying herself in the broken mirror, though it is so small she can only see a portion of herself at a time; yet by moving it around, first looking at her face, then her feet, then her arms, and so on, she scrutinizes the whole form with much satisfaction.

O, she is so happy! All the reproofs with which her ears have been assailed since morning are forgotten, or remembered as a troubled dream from which she has awakened, to know disquietude no more! The clock has struck six, and Nettie is becoming quite alarmed for fear Mr. Sloper has forgotten to come for her, when her ready ear catches the sound of sleigh-bells. In another quarter of an hour, Nettie has been deposited in Mrs. Sloper's great arm-chair by the kitchen fire, until she gets thoroughly warmed.

Rapidly over the smooth white ground come the sleighs, depositing their happy cargoes at the front door, and then off again as speedily as they came. By seven o'clock the great old house, that was flooded with light and warmth two hours before, is filled with as merry a group of young folks as ever hailed the advent of the New Year. Nettie's heart beat faster and faster, as she saw the rooms filling up with gayly-dressed ladies and gentlemen. There was a great tumult of voices, which generally dropped into silence until a fresh arrival was announced, and the new comers had been greeted by their companions, welcomed by their host, and the curiosity of each gratified by looking around to see who were there, and how they were dressed. Then the hum of voices again arose, some relating a particular adventure as happening to themselves, others laughing as though it were really laughable, while others were grouped together around the table, or in a corner of the ample fireplace, from which glowed so bright a fire, that it was next to impossible to set foot on the broad rug in front.

Miss Pearson and Helen Maynard were sitting near the door when Mark entered.

"Who is . that?" was just on the lips of the former, when Helen suddenly averted her eyes, and whispered side-wise, —

"There comes Mark Miller. I told you he'd be here. O, my goodness gracious! How sniptious he looks! — a span new suit, and a standing shirt-collar! Would you like an introduction?" said she, ironically.

"*Yes, I would*," rejoined her companion, in a tone of decision that gave her friend no room to doubt the sincerity of the words.

Helen felt a little abashed at the prompt and rather tart manner in which her attempt at raillery was cut short. She had anticipated a whole evening's enjoyment for herself and Miss Pearson, in keeping as much aloof from the company as possible, and in criticising the dress and mannerisms of each and all. She had, indeed, abundant opportunity of displaying her spirit of sarcasm, supposing, very foolishly, that one born and bred in the city, and accustomed to re-fined society, as Grace had been, could see nothing in the little circle before her but awkwardness and countrified airs. How great was her disappointment, when, a few moments after, she politely requested of Mr. Sloper an introduction to each of his guests!

"Well, I'm not much on etiquette, Miss Pearson; so I guess I'll turn you over to Mr. Maynard. Here, Samuel, please take Miss Pearson under your wing, and present her to the company. You are more used to these little niceties than I am; besides, I am wanted down stairs just now. Make yourselves at home, all of you. I want you to enjoy yourselves to the fullest extent; get up some plays — can't you?" So saying, he left the room; and Grace, under the escort of Sam, was taken around and introduced to all. Mark was sitting by the table, his face all aglow with cheerfulness; and yet there occasionally came over his heart a saddened feeling as he recollected that the time was soon coming when he would be far away from the scenes and companions of his childhood. He felt quite sure this was the last time he should see them all together. In making the circuit of her new acquaintances, Miss Pearson found many intelligent, joyous-looking faces, who responded to her simple, yet lady-like questions with a freedom and grace that would have done honor to any circle in society, however refined. At length they came to where Mark was sitting. He instinctively arose, prepared to make his best bow in his best possible style. But without deigning to notice him, Sam was passing on to the next, when Grace reminded him of Mark's presence, by saying, —

" We have missed one gentleman."

" O, he's of no account; never mind him."

" Please introduce me."

" Is it your wish?"

" Yes, I insist."

" Well, then, put on all your dignity!" But Mark, meanwhile, had walked away to hide the mortification that well nigh overcame him. He knew too well the slight was intended. He knew, too, that others saw it; but he did not know the interest he had already awakened in the heart of the fair girl, who, in after years, was to become the guiding star of his life. Why she felt so deep an interest in one a total stranger to her, she hardly knew herself; but since the conversation with Helen Maynard, and more especially since she had seen Mark, she desired to know him. His face pleased her; and once, as she encountered his large dark eyes, beaming full upon her, she became spell-bound under his earnest, mystic gaze, although it lasted but a moment. The joyous lustre, that shone out of their clear depths for the instant, faded away, and a saddened, almost sorrowful expression succeeded, as if there was a whole heartful of unhappy emotions struggling to betray themselves in his countenance. Their eyes met no more until a little accident — a serious one it liked to have been ; a happy one for both it proved to be — brought them into a close companionship, which lasted until the close of the pleasant evening's entertainment, and until — the close of life !

CHAPTER IX.

A FORTUNE-TELLER COMES TO THE PARTY.

"Then all was jollity,
Feasting and mirth, light wantonness and laughter,
Piping and playing, minstrelsies and masking."
                                        ROWE.

"WHOSE beautiful little face is this?" said Grace Pearson, as she found herself by the kitchen fire, where still sat Nettie in the arm-chair, having been until now quite overlooked, although she saw and enjoyed all that was passing till her eyes shone and twinkled like two stars set in the brow of evening.

"This?" replied the deacon, patting Nettie affectionately on the cheek, which looked as rosy as a red apple in the bright fire-light. "Why, this is my little friend Nettie Strange, as good a girl as lives in the world. Bless me! Nettie, have you been sitting here all this time? You must get up and make yourself agreeable. This is Miss Pearson, Nettie; I am sure she will love you; but if she don't, I know who does."

"I am sure I shall love her, and I know she must be good; no one can have such beautiful blue eyes and not be good. What pretty brown ringlets, and how long they are, too!" and Grace wound her fingers around them, separating the two large curls which shaded her temples into smaller ones, making them very beautiful. Then she took some little rose-buds from her own hair, and placed them in Nettie's, much to the admiration of the deacon.

Nettie's heart fluttered like a frightened bird. It was the first time she had ever heard herself called beautiful; and to be called both beautiful and good in the same breath nearly took hers away.

Grace was no flatterer; she was kind and sociable, not from a desire to be praised and petted as a favourite, but from true benevolence, and a disposition to make all happy who came within her sphere. And so she spoke kindly to Nettie, and imprinted a kiss upon her forehead, saying, "You must be my little chaperon for the rest of the evening." Grace's back was to the fire, and as she stooped to bestow the kiss, which to Nettie seemed like a benediction, her dress came in contact with the flames! In an instant the silken fabric was blazing with a velocity that threatened destruction to the beautiful form it enveloped. All was terror and consternation! Shrieks and cries of alarm rose from lip to lip, while one cried, "Bring a blanket!" another, "Where's the water?" a dozen, "What's the matter?" A stentorian voice exclaimed, "Stand back!" and a powerful arm was thrown around her, and in a moment Mark's strong hand had torn the burning garment from the terrified girl, and his foot sent it into the fireplace, where it was harmlessly consumed. All this occurred in a moment's time, and no great damage done to anybody, or anything, except the dress, the waist of which still clung to the trembling girl. Faint she did not (she did not belong to the fainting sisterhood), but she looked pale when she realized how narrowly she had escaped.

"No, I am not burned!" she said, as soon as she could command her voice; "not even scorched! Many thanks to—" And what her lips, through fear and excitement, failed to utter, her eyes, beaming with tenderness and gratitude, fully expressed.

"I beseech you, do not be alarmed; there is no occasion for alarm. I am only a little nervous; not in the least injured," said she, as Mrs. Sloper, quite agitated, surveyed the scorched waist, and removed the remnants of lace from about the neck and sleeves. "You will allow me to return home, I trust."

Mrs. Sloper reflected for a moment, and being very desirous that her young guests should not lose the pleasure which the presence of the charming stranger would afford them, said, —

"I have an idea. Come with me."

They ascended the long, front stairs that led to the "spare-room," from which opened several closets of large dimensions. In one of these hung, in orderly array, Mrs. Sloper's "best things," and from "stuffs" of various kinds and colours she selected a shining black satin, saying, as she held it up for Grace's inspection, —

"Now, we cannot very well spare you from our pleasant little gathering to-night. All, I am sure, would be disappointed should you go away. So you just get into this dress of mine, and make us all happy by remaining. My dear child, I am so thankful you were not burned!" As she spoke the tears gathered in her benevolent eyes, which made Grace's well over with gratitude.

"May be it won't exactly fit about the waist, but in length it will be just right. So please hurry, and I'll hook it for you. Come into the next room, my dear; there is a good fire for you to dress by, and I'll hunt up something for you to wear round your neck. Here's a white vandyke; but may be you will think that too old fashioned. Let me see," — opening a great chest of drawers, and displaying their various contents to the gaze of her bewildered auditor.

"Here's a nice dress handkerchief, that will, perhaps, be more becoming; or this white muslin under-kerchief; you can fold it in, and lay the pleats *just so.*"

All this time the "dear child" stood surveying the articles laid out for her inspection. The tears were dried, and an

" idea" seemed to have taken sudden possession of *her* mind, for a merry twinkle was in her beautiful eyes, and she could scarcely refrain from laughing outright.

" Mrs. Sloper, will you indulge me in a little pleasantry? I see the satin is quite too large for me; allow me to make my own selections. Now, you assist me, and I will dress myself as a gypsy. Then I will go around to the front door and knock for admittance. You can let me in, and introduce me as ' Mother Cheatem,' and I'll tell their fortunes."

" Capital! capital! I know just what you want! Ah! I thought there was fun in those snapping black eyes of yours!" And so the shining satin, not destined to be honored on this occasion, was hung back in its accustomed place; and from the bottom of an ancient chest of drawers, that helped to lumber up the rear attic, sundry articles were brought to light that for years had lain hidden in its mysterious depths. Grace helped to convey the ancient habiliments to the dressing-room; while, as she arrayed herself in them, she often indulged in suppressed laughter. Mrs. Sloper, who loved a good joke, and was always ready to help carry it out, chimed in with her low, musical voice. The gypsy's dress consisted of a yellow-silk petticoat, quilted in fine diamond-shape to the knees; over that was a white dimity short-gown reaching midway, with a fine cambric ruffle at the bottom, wide and full, starched and crimped, and the cuffs edged with lace. Over this was worn a kind of bodice of dark figured silk, with wide shoulder-straps laced behind and before, very much like the stays ladies wear nowadays (but stays were not in use then, and ought not to be now); a pair of high-heeled, narrow, round-toed shoes, with great silver buckles, encased her feet, and a couple of plain gold rings, with seals as large as a shilling, adorned her hands.

" Now a cap, if you please."

" Yes, you must have a cap! Tuck your hair nicely under the broad frill, while I lay this black ribbon over it.

There, that will do; you look charming! Don't laugh so loud, or they will hear us! . Wait a while, and I will go down for the deacon's Sunday specs!"

"But I must have a bonnet."

"Yes, yes; I'll bring a bonnet, and cloak, too." Saying this, Mrs. Sloper hurried below stairs to obtain the "specs," and gave satisfactory answers to many inquiries relative to the young lady's welfare and reappearance. On her return she again visited the attic, and brought forth, nicely folded, a scarlet cloth mantle, with a great hood at the back. As she placed it on Grace's shoulders, she said, —

"This cloak, my dear, is older than I am! It was my grandmother's, and in its time was a beauty, and the pride of the family. So I have heard my mother say. It was bought new to wear to the christening of their first child, who was my mother's eldest brother. It is a little moth-eaten on one side. That was done in my mother's time; but as I have always kept cedar shavings in between the folds, they never molest it now. Always rĕmember this, dear, that cedar shavings are the best things to preserve woollen goods from moths. Camphor is good likewise, and a little of both in the same chest will do no harm. Now for a bonnet. Let me see. There's my old, sugar-loaf leghorn; but then it has no trimming on it. But I've plenty of odds and ends, and we will pin this yellow bow on one side, and wind this bit of green ribbon round the crown, and take these strips of chintz for the strings." They both laughed heartily at their ingenuity, and at the young lady's grotesque appearance. A work-bag of large dimensions, a snuff-box, and some knitting-work were speedily furnished; and. after admiring herself in the mirror to the entire satisfaction of both, Mrs. Sloper led the way through an unoccupied part of the house until they came to a narrow, back stairway that led to the rooms below. She descended first to see that the coast was clear; and as it happened, no one saw the gypsy (she looked more like the witch of Endor) pass out. Mrs. Sloper gave her some instructions in a low whisper, and before she joined the company in the parlor a loud knock was heard at the front door — so loud that it reverberated through the whole house, silenced every voice, and set each heart in motion, every one thinking something terrible was about to happen. The deacon strode hastily forward to see what the matter was, while the rest put as wide a space as possible between the door and themselves. The little old woman entered with tottering steps, leaning heavily upon her staff, while Mrs. Sloper, with feigned surprise, hastened forward to give her welcome.

" Good evening ! "

" Good evening ! Why, its Mother Cheatem ! "

" It's a' awful cold night, Miss Sloper," said the little old fright, in a well-affected nasal twang, that would have defied her most intimate friend to recognize as belonging to her.

" I've come a long way to see ye, but I didn't 'spect yer had so much grand comp'ny, or I shouldn't a' dared to come in ; leastwise I shouldn't a' thot o' comin' without a' invitation."

Mrs. Sloper had given her husband a pinch on the arm, and she placed her finger on her lips, as much as to say, " Keep dark, and help us on with the joke." So the deacon, in his blandest manner, bade the old dame welcome, saying, as he wheeled the great arm-chair near the fire for her acceptance, —

" You could not have come on a more auspicious occasion, for you have a whole house full to welcome you."

The old lady, in the same affected tone, said it *did look a little s'picious!* Was it a weddin? or what? And wondered where they would put her to sleep, as she was quite sure every bed in the house would be full, if they " kept over " all that were present. In turn she was kindly requested to give herself no uneasiness on that score, and assured that the best room in the house, and a bed all to herself, were at her disposal.

"I wouldn't mind jinin' with some one, but yer see, it alers gives me the nightmare to sleep double, and since poor Cheatem died, — the dear soul; how I deprecate his memory! — I've never jined with anybody. I've eat alone, slept alone, talked and walked, sung and laughed, and cried all alone; and alers expect ter." And here the old lady brought out a flaming red cotton handkerchief to wipe away the drops of well-affected sorrow, which were coursing down her cheeks.

Mark had walked off to conceal his merriment, for he understood it all at a glance; and the rest were wondering much where she came from, and who she could be, having never heard — much to their surprise — of a character so replete with oddity, and so familiar as she appeared to be with the deacon and his wife.

"Let me take your cloak and bonnet," said Mrs. Sloper, bending herself to the task of untying the gaudy calico strings, at the same time bidding Miss Helen to assist her in removing the cloak. The young lady shrunk back, horrified at the thought of coming in contact with such an ugly old fright.

"She must be crazy!" whispered she to Sam. "I should not wonder if it was that old crazy woman we have heard of up at Mallowfield. I thought her eyes looked rather wild."

Her outer garments being removed, and Mrs. Sloper assured that she was thoroughly warmed, she was assisted to rise by that benevolent lady, and her chair turned around so as to make her face visible to the company. She was introduced formally as Grandmother Cheatem, and made a very low courtesy ere she resumed her chair. From her ample pocket, which hung on her arm, she drew forth her

snuff-box, and took a large pinch : then elevating her eyes,
she ventured to survey the inmates of the room.

Helen ran up to the dressing-room to acquaint Grace with
the strange and unlooked-for acquisition to the company
below stairs, and was much surprised to find the room unoccupied. After a fruitless search in all the adjoining rooms,
she was descending to inquire after her, when her ears were
greeted with shouts of laughter, as if the veritable spirit of
Momus had taken each heart by storm ! Peal after peal
arose above the incessant chattering of the old crone, who
declared herself ill used by those who were "big enough,"
she said, "to treat old age and deformity (she limped dread-
fully when attempting to walk) with greater respect."

Helen soon saw how matters stood, declaring she "knew
it all the time," elevating her little pug nose by way of
emphasis.

"Have done, I say ! Will ye's be after putting an old
woman's eyes out?" exclaimed the old lady, changing her
voice from a coarse guttural to a rich Irish brogue. "Ye'r
an unmannerly dog ! Get ye from forninst me, ye spal-
peen, or I'll be afther persuading ye with this sprig o' shil-
laly !"

The person addressed was none other than the veritable
Samuel Maynard, Esquire, who had attempted to snatch her
spectacles, but came off minus a handful of hair, which
clung tenaciously to the taper fingers of the insulted dame.
Another tried to possess himself of her cane ; but the possessor, asserting rights of property, declined surrendering
it, declaring it was "agin Scripter" to covet a neighbour's
goods ; and though one seized her cap, another begged a
bow therefrom, and a third put her wig terribly out of
crimp, she succeeded in maintaining her rights, until she
had convinced all who attempted to trespass on those rights
that it was no child's play with her.

"*Do* let me hold your cane,"

A punch in the ribs forbade further familiarity.

" Give us a pinch of snuff."

She helps herself, and replaces the box in the reticule, saying, —

" It's not for youngsters to indulge in such delicacies; only poor old addle-brains like meself should take snuff."

" Well — tell us a story."

" Yes, a story ! a story ! "

" No ; I am no story-teller ; but if it pleases you, I'll be a gypsy, and tell your fortunes."

" Good, good ! " " Better yet." " Here ! let me tie this bandage over your eyes ; fair play ; no cheating, Mother Cheatem. There now."

" Lead them up, one at a time."

And so the palms of each were successively laid in those of the prophesying gypsy, who foresaw their good or ill, as her fancy dictated. Some she sent on exploring expeditions after the philosopher's stone, telling them they would never be satisfied until they had found it. Some possessed extraordinary musical talents in embryo ; others, wonderful mechanical genius, waiting only for some unforeseen accident to develop itself. Some she dubbed knight-errants, the honor of whose chivalrous deeds would shed lustre upon their descendants until the latest generation. Some were placed upon the pinnacle of the temple of fame ; others suffer martyrdom at the hands of some heartless coquette. One will pay homage at the shrine of beauty until he finds himself approaching old bachelorhood, and then he will marry a perfect Xantippe. Another is told that if he will never use tobacco, his wife will be beautiful and sweet-tempered ; and though the chimney might smoke, and the children be cross, and he be in the sulks, yet she would be calm and good-natured, and even smile over his deliuquencies. This one was clothed in a coat of mail, impervious to anything ignoble. That one might one day govern the

nation; but he must first learn to govern himself. There
was some great good for each to attain, some moral excellence for each to strive for.

As for the young ladies, there was not for them such an
extended sphere of usefulness. They need never expect to
do any one great act that would immortalize them. They
need not wish to become heroines. It was a woman's glory
to walk in a separate sphere from man's. Though humble,
it rested with herself to make it happy and useful. "Woman's life," said the gypsy, "is made up of small every-day
experiences, and every little kind act, every generous and
noble impulse, tells largely for her future well-being. It is
hers to bestow charities, to visit the sick, to comfort with
kind words and deeds the aged and infirm; to give to
infancy its first great thought, to guide its first pure prayer,
and shape its little heart like unto her own. She need not go
out into the world's great arena to seek for fame and power.
It was hers to excel in all those gentler qualities which
make her life of more importance than man's. To her
belong truth, humility, tenderness, fidelity, and a forgiving
spirit; and love, holy and fervent, lends its rosy hue to
brighten her existence. She need not sigh that her sphere
is circumscribed, if she have but her own heart to care for;
and 'though to itself it only live and die,' she will find a
lifetime well spent in fitting it for higher spheres than this.

"But you, my dear child," she continued, taking another
by the hand, "have a large field of usefulness to labor in.
The sunny dreams of girlhood are fast passing away; you
will, if you live, soon be a woman. You wish in your heart
it were now. You think you will be happier then; but
believe me, you are now seeing your best and happiest days.
Remember what the old gypsy in the red cloak tells you;
this very night will be like a little green Eden in your life.
Though your feet may press the turf of other lands, and
your ear listen to the sweet cadence of strange voices, yet

amid .all the beauty, and splendor, and luxury that may
or can surround you, your heart will murmur, 'In life's
sweet spring time were my happiest days.' You will become a great and good woman — great because you are good.
You must henceforth cultivate all those Christian graces
which will fit you for a life of usefulness. Your destiny is
a serious one. Set yourself steadily to work to learn some
new thing every day that will help to perfect your character
as a woman and as a Christian. You have much to learn
of yourself, of your motives for generous action. Let not
pride, or a wish to become famous for goodness and benevolence, have aught to do with your charities or kindnesses.
Charity, in its true sense, is not lavish alms-giving, but a
heartfelt sympathy for those who are in affliction ; and more
than all, a disposition to put the best construction upon the
conduct of others, and a thousand little nameless acts of
kindness so cheap to ourselves, but so precious to those upon
whom they are bestowed. As silently you receive grace
and strength from the Almighty to perform your duty, so
ought you silently to dispense to others; 'and the Father
who seeth in secret shall reward you openly.'"

Mark offered no resistance when his turn came. He was
led up to the fortune-teller who had so successfully divined
the future destiny of his compeers. A something told him
she would know his hard, brawny hand from the rest; and
so it was. After a moment's hesitation, as if to collect material wherewith to pave another pathway to the goal of
fame, she said, " This hand will work out for you a noble
future ; for it will labor for others' happiness more than your
own. You have an ambition to emulate the great and good.
It is a laudable ambition ; and, unless the gypsy's vision is
obscured, you have a goodly amount of stock in bank, which
will win you success. Industry, honesty, integrity are a good
capital to start out with, and their profits will accumulate on
your hands. But you have other qualifications which will

materially assist you in your not altogether newly-formed desires. You do not act from impulse; you have the power to consider before you act, and this is what we are not all blessed with. You have firmness, with a will to do; but your pursuits in life will give you many an occasion to measure your *will* with your powers to accomplish. Be not discouraged should Fortune frown darkly on your early efforts; heroic spirits will one day win her smiles and don her favours. If *you* wear her livery, it will be nobly *earned*— not *purchased with the stain of dishonesty* upon it. If you would sit in the councils of the wise, remember Wisdom, unlike Fortune, never seeks her votaries.

> ' The clouds may drop down titles and estates,
>   Wealth may seek us, but wisdom must be sought;
>   Sought before all, but (how unlike all else
>   We seek on earth!) 'tis never sought in vain.'

" The *intent*, however dearly nursed, will never gain you preferment. Action and energy, well directed, steady, and persevering, are the two great propelling principles which will bring you success. Sloth finds too many lions in the way, and shrinks at what its own inaction makes impossibilities. Your path is onward and upward; but, like poor Pilgrim, you will find yourself often fainting under your burden, as you ascend the long, steep ' hill Difficulty;' and, like him, you will persevere, until the day dawns that sees you knocking at the ' wicket' for admission into an extended field of usefulness and honour."

To Nettie she said, " The possessor of this little hand has a warm, affectionate heart. She is kind, and gentle too, and will always be good, and do good, because she wishes to do what is right. She has little selfishness in her nature, and her faults will be easy to correct. She knows that to be strong to do the right, she must ask of God daily for those helps which the best of us need to keep us from doing what is amiss.

" His blessing will always attend your every effort to be patient and persevering in the path of duty. You will find many things that will teach you the necessity of cultivating a patient spirit, a gentle voice, and a cheerful manner. These will be everything to yourself, and much to others. Though to do good may often involve a sacrifice of our own personal ease and comfort, yet will our sleep be sweetest, our dreams rosiest, when our heads repose on pillows made welcome by sharing the burdens of others. ' Be not weary in well-doing. Ye shall reap if ye faint not.' "

CHAPTER X.

NETTIE'S ASPIRATIONS.

"White-winged angels meet the child
On the vestibule of life."
MRS. E. OAKES SMITH.

S may be supposed, the kind, make-believe fortune-teller spoke at random, having had little opportunity to study the characters or dispositions of her young friends. A word dropped here and there, together with the expression of Mark's countenance and his general appearance, which prepossessed her altogether in his favor, enabled her to judge somewhat of the bent of his inclinations. That he possessed strong perceptive faculties, with a mind to grasp knowledge, and a will to succeed in whatever he set about to do, his fine, manly, open countenance would have given abundant proof to one less skilled in the art of testing the qualities of mind by outward appearances. She had little thought or care about jeopardizing her reputation as a prophetess; she wished only to contribute to the general amusement of the little circle around her; and she succeeded admirably, interspersing her graver counsels with many little pleasantries, which provoked frequent peals of merriment.

None of the virtues were overlooked by the dear old gypsy. All were told to emulate the good, the great, the godlike. And if she aroused dormant energies in some youthful heart, which, until then, dreamed not of its own inherent powers, it was because it caught her inspiration, while with glowing enthusiasm she contrasted the pleasures of virtue and Christian piety with the miseries of ignorance, vice, and sin.

One there was who felt within him a spirit to do and dare anything, that her words might be fulfilled.

Nettie's master-thought was, as she gazed admiringly upon her dear stranger friend, "O, how much I would like to become what you are! When I am a woman, I will be a good woman. She has told us that to become wise and good men and women, we must begin early; and I am sure I shall from this time be gentle." And then her heart sank, for she remembered how her ears were daily assailed with harsh epithets, and that she was "the worst child that ever lived." She had heard this repeated too often to have the least doubt of it. Ah, could she but hope for the attainment of but half the virtues with which her friend had endowed her, how arduously, how perseveringly, would she labour in her little home-sphere! Beyond that sphere she felt humbled to think she might never be permitted to go. She knew her own littleness, or thought she did, as compared with others, who had different homes and different influences to mould their characters. She brushed away the tears which gathered under the long lashes and swept her cheeks, and with those last words of the noble lady, who was to be thenceforth her oracle, — "in due season, if ye faint not," — there came, laden with a host of soothing influences, a sweet and holy faith, which shed its serene and rosy light over her struggling and unquiet spirit. She knew it not by its true name, but she felt within her heart a presence of something good and great, strong and courageous. A kind angel was thenceforth to walk forever by her side, the glory of whose countenance reflected brightness, and dispelled the shade of gloom that rested upon her own. She folded her white wing about her, and whispered softly in her ear of brighter

days to come. " Fear not," said the voice within; " I am
with you; my rod and my staff they comfort you;" and
like the " pilgrim to the Holy Shrine, who sees Oriental skies
from amid alpine snows, and plants his staff with a firmer
hold upon the icy verge of the precipice," so she took God
at His word, and bade despair flee her presence.

While Nettie sat apart thus musing, the rest were by no
means idle: a spirited conversation was kept up; and suddenly, above the din of happy voices, rose a bewitching
strain, that set everybody's spirits a-tiptoe; and the possessor
of each fluttering heart was made happier still when Mr.
Sloper said, —

" Children, I want to see you dance a few times; and, as
one of the young gentlemen has volunteered his services as
musician, you may now, as many as can, take possession of
the west room, and form yourselves into a set."

This was instantly responded to by an unusual commo-
tion and a rush for partners; and ere ten minutes elapsed,
thirty or forty of the older ones had arranged themselves for
a country dance. The walls of the capacious rooms were
lined with those who did not participate, but who seemed to
enjoy it as much as the rest, hoping their turn would come
next. And come it did to all who were disposed to indulge
in the pleasant amusement.

Mark stood as remote as possible from the dancers, envy-
ing those who excelled in easy grace, and despising one who
was the cause of his embarrassment. This one took upon
himself the office of " master of ceremonies," and insisted,·
with mock politeness, that Mark should dance with the lady
whose graceful form seemed like some powerful magnetizer.
His eyes involuntarily followed her wherever she flitted
through the mystic windings of the " opera reel," or the
more intricate mazes of " money musk." But he declined
the honor with a freezing air, though it cost him an effort
to refuse the pleasure.

CHAPTER XI.

GRACE PEARSON AND MARK HAVE A QUIET CHAT.

"Dire was the clang of plates, of knife and fork,
That merc'less fell like tomahawks to work."

WOLCOT.

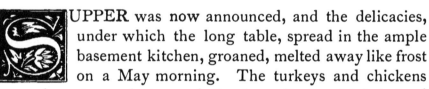UPPER was now announced, and the delicacies, under which the long table, spread in the ample basement kitchen, groaned, melted away like frost on a May morning. The turkeys and chickens were done to a nicety, and the ingredients which helped furnish the other goodies might have come from the four quarters of the globe, to mingle on this proud occasion. There were nice fresh rolls, which looked like patted snowballs, so soft and white were they, and the warm mashed potatoes, pyramid-shaped, and dotted with pepper, looked very like a volcano in miniature, while the melted butter, as it rolled down its side, represented the lava. Then there were mince pies and apple pies, tarts and salads, which no one knew how to make better than that notable housewife, Mrs. Sloper. Cakes, whose frosted crust glistened so purely white it seemed a pity to mar their beauty; and jellies so varied in color and transparent in substance, that, as the light shone through their cone-shaped forms, they fairly quivered under the gaze of so many bright, admiring eyes.

Miss Pearson was led down by the veteran host himself, and placed on his right, while he took the head of the table, behind one of the huge turkeys. Mr. Maynard resigned his post at her side, very much as a boy would resign a large piece of gingerbread, which a hoarded sixpence had bought. The deacon saw by the disappointed look that followed hard after the retreating fair one, that he had committed an egregious blunder; but he had the prize so safely under his escort, and she clung so lovingly to his arm, that he was in no wise inclined to surrender her, now he was fairly under way. And so he thought to purchase indemnity for his fault by begging this young gentleman to assist in doing the honours at the other end of the table. Sam's first thought was one of pride, that his host had given him this preference above the others, and he accepted the post of honour with much graciousness. But by the time he had helped his half of the company to turkey and chicken-pie and other et ceteras, he found to his cost that serving others was not eating himself. One would thank him for " another slice of the breast," another, " a little more stuffing, if you please," a third, some of " the nice cranberry," and so on, until he came to the very unpleasant conclusion that he was working for his dinner.

The look of resignation that stole over his face, after the twentieth attempt to taste a mouthful, would have done honour to a king when he saw his throne in the possession of an adversary too powerful to cope with. He wiped the perspiration from his brow, as he again bent himself to the task of carving and serving, fully resolved that he wouldn't eat a mouthful that night. He would let them see what a martyr he was making of himself. Thus he sat, carver in hand, surveying with assumed coolness his voracious customers, as much as to say, " Now do your worst; I'm a match for you!" and they, perfectly unconcerned, to all appearances, as to whether he ate or not. That the " Fates " were against him this night he fully believed. There was his " bright particular star," who, having doffed the *bizarre* habiliments of the gypsy, shone resplendent in her original character, and others basking in its radiance. Why couldn't she see that he was miserable? And Helen, too, was gormandizing, as if she feared there would be even a drumstick left for him to nibble at. And Mark — did his eyes deceive him? — was actually seated next to Grace, and presuming to indulge in a mirth-provoking repartee, with that feminine divinity. How happy they all were! All but he! He could, perhaps, have borne it all on a full stomach; but to be victimized thus when combating with these internal elements, whose yearnings would not be silenced, was absolutely unbearable: so, when coffee was served, with the cakes and sweetmeats, and his services as carver for the numereifully fastidious appetites he had vainly endeavored to appease were no longer required, he was preparing to leave the room, when a voice from the farther end of the table arrested him. Had it been another voice, it would, I fear, have fallen upon ears deaf to its entreaties. But when Miss Grace, in her blandest tones, bade him "come and pull a wish-bone," he could not refuse without compromising the self-sacrificing reputation he had so dearly earned. By the time the "merry-thought" was divided between Grace and himself, — he getting the larger share, — his wonted suavity had gained the ascendency. "What nonsense," thought he, " to go without my supper! There's enough left to feed a hungry regiment." As the deacon had not found time to replenish his first plate, he concluded Sam was no better off than himself. As the rest were leaving, he begged him to remain, as he had a few words for his private ear.

"How did you get on with your carving? I haven't eaten a dozen mouthfuls!"

"I haven't tasted a thing!" said Sam, in his surliest tone.

"Just as I expected. Hallo! Sara! bring us some hot coffee, and everything nice. I'm as hungry as a bear after a six months' fast. Bring a clean plate. Come, wife; come, Mrs. Miller."

Sara, who was the " help " for the time being, hastened to rearrange the head of the table, and a cup or two of the steaming, delicious beverage, a large quantity of " every-thing nice," and Mrs. Sloper's lively conversation, soon put Sam in the best possible humour ; and when he joined the company in the great " west room," no one was the wiser for the many and terrible emotions that warred so furiously in his — stomach.

During the evening, Grace and Mark fell into a quiet chat. She included him in the general courtesy extended to all, and, as if by accident, was seated by his side. Her easy and graceful manner won his confidence, and he surprised him-self by indulging in a vivacity of spirits and an elevation of thought almost foreign to his nature. He actually questioned the propriety of uttering sentiments which she might con-sider artificial, or at least inconsiderate, in one so vastly her inferior in intellectual culture and solid acquirements. On one or two occasions his opinions were adverse to hers, and once he corrected her on some incident in history, where she was forced to yield the palm to his superior memory. For the first time in his life he found himself *vis-à-vis* with an educated, accomplished, elegant, noble-hearted young lady, who sought, rather than shunned, his society. The effect was congenial to his mind and feelings, instead of mortifying and dispiriting, as on former occasions, when he had too often been made the victim of ridicule and unkindness.

How intensely such sensitive minds suffer at the hands of that assumed superiority that delights in harassing those whom they consider beneath them! Many a fine mind is debilitated, if not utterly paralyzed, and many an affectionate heart wounded and rendered sorrowful in the morning of life, or broken at its noon, through such treatment.

Grace, who never permitted her friendship to be biassed by the preferences or dislikes of others, saw beside her a young man of respectable talents and scholarship, joined to

an extremely sensitive temperament, which unhappy peculiarity had been forced by depression and the ill-natured superiority to which he had been subjected. It required a whole
battery of tender glances from her spirited eyes, and much
gentleness and perseverance, to draw out his strong points
of character; but she, being an admirable tactician, succeeded beyond her hopes. Both were interested, both were
delighted.

"You are quite monopolizing Miss Pearson, Mark. Suppose you trust her to me a while : I will take good care of her."

"Certainly, sir. Excuse me, Miss Pearson : I fear I have
trespassed upon your goodness ; but I am so pleased to find
one who appreciates me, and thinks it no disparagement to
herself to treat an awkward boy with kindness!" A rich
flood of happiness swept through his heart until it overflowed, betraying itself in a smile so radiant, that in the eyes
of the fair girl at his side he seemed beautiful and manly,
with a mind too noble to be raised or lowered by circumstances. Her heart beat a tender response to his, when she
assured him the pleasure was mutual.

A circle was formed for "hunt the slipper." Miss Pearson acted as prominent a part in this as in "hurly-burly"
and "run-the-thimble," that preceded. There were no
forced spirits in that joyous social circle. All were children
in deed and in truth. The nimble feet that tripped so lightly
to the sound of the witching viol were none the less fleet,.
when circling round the room in anticipation of the kiss that
followed the catching. The scarf, which answered for the
slipper, was lying at Mark's feet, dropped by Grace, none
of the others deigning to notice him, and probably not wishing their rosy lips to come in contact with his. He sprang
to his feet, nothing loath to accept the challenge from so fair
a competitor. Round and round they circled, dodging and
doubling, amid the reiterated cheers of the company, who
thought the prize well worth the contest.

7

" Go it, Stubbs ! " sang out an unruly little wretch, who had not the fear of the deacon before his eyes. However, a well-merited rebuke, given in a whisper, from that horrified worthy, forbade further attempts at ridicule.

At last the twain came to a halt, Miss Pearson receiving on the forehead the chaste kiss so perseveringly won. She took her place in the ring, amid much merriment, and Mark went round and round, at a loss as to who should be the recipient of his ungracious favor. There was evidently a collapsing of crinoline, — though " extensions " were an absurdity unheard of in those days, — and Mark could see, with half an eye, that none would feel flattered by his preference. He threw the scarf to Nettie, who was only too happy to join the increasing circle. He suffered himself to be easily caught, and Grace made room for him at her side. All were so interested in Mark's growing favour with Miss Pearson that they paid little attention to Nettie, until they descried the deacon's streaming coat-tails hard in the chase after that little nymph. The uproar that followed this discovery made the old house ring. No one could recognize his own voice, or tell who laughed the loudest, or longest. Tears of delight rained down each fair cheek, and handkerchiefs were saturated with the excess of their merriment. The deacon was not to be outdone in gallantry ; but he might as well undertake to catch a rabbit in a cornfield as that fleet-footed little puss. When he thought he had her just within his grasp, she was half way round on the other side, urging him to renewed effort. Though the deacon walked with no snail's pace, Nettie's nimble feet were more than a match for him, and when she thought his strength and patience about exhansted, she became a willing captive, returning his " smack " with a seeming relish.

Thus passed the pleasant evening until the old clock on the wall struck the hour of three. Could any body believe it was so late. It must be too fast by many hours.

But the knowing ones began to whisper, and then others talked aloud about its being time to take leave of their host and hostess and one another. All united in saying they had had a " splendid time," and each buttoned in with his cloak and overcoat pleasant memories, that lasted a lifetime.

Grace folded Nettie's faded shawl around her, imprinting a parting kiss upon her lips as she bade her good night.

" Shall I never see you again?" sobbed the child, as her arms clung to the dear friend who had encircled her in her own.

" O, yes, I mean to come and see you before I go home. Where do you live?"

" Away up over the hill, that way," — pointing in the dircetion of their house. " Do come. I would like my mother to see you."

" I will certainly come, Nettie; so good night."

" Good night," and " good night," were reiterated and responded to until the door closed upon the last retreating group.

In taking leave of her host and hostess and Mrs. Miller, Grace expressed herself happy to have made their acquaintance, and hoped it would not be long before she would again visit them.

" I have been happier to-night than I ever remember to have been in my life."

" Yes, it don't do city people any hurt to give their manners a good country airing once in a while," replied the deacon, shaking her warmly by the hand.

" My city and country manners are the same, sir. I fear I do not inherit more dignity than is meet for me. Come and see me in my father's house, and judge for yourself whether I forgot to pack up my ' airs' with my travelling outfit."

This and much more pleasant badinage passed, while the last load was being shawled and muffled. Miss Pearson

was one of the last to take her departure.   The house was ·
at length left to its inmates and its wonted quietness.

That never-to-be-forgotten dream of happiness was over;
and Nettie crept to her bed, in the great unfurnished chamber, with no light to cheer its gloom but what the sinking
moon afforded.   The wind shook the crazy old windows,
and the snow drifted in through the cracks, and Nettie
thought of the warm fire in Mr. Sloper's house, and the
cheerful, happy hearts in Mrs. Miller's cottage, so unlike her
own home; but such sweet thoughts came crowding in upon
her heart, that she almost forgot the cold, and sank to sleep
while planning little reforms and improvements for the
future.   And then she dreamed beautiful dreams.   May we
not believe that over that innocent head the guardian angels
dropped a tear of pity?

CHAPTER XII.

LITTLE JANE FALLS ASLEEP.

" Weep not for those
Who sink within the arms of death
Ere yet the chilling wintry breath
      Of sorrow o'er them blows;
But weep for them who here remain,
The mournful heritors of pain,
Condemned to see each bright joy fade,
And mark grief's melancholy shade
      Flung o'er Hope's fairest rose."

MRS. EMBURY.

HEN Nettie entered her mother's room early on the following morning, anxious to give a detailed account of all she had seen and enjoyed, she was greeted with moans, and a hard, dry cough from her little sister. Her mother's voice arrested her ere she gained the bedside.

"Nett, go and build a fire quick, and warm some water; I fear Janie has the croup! She's been wheezing all night; hurry yourself, and get the kitchen warm, so I can get up."

For two hours Nettie and her mother sat by the cradle, doing all in their power to relieve the sick child. She was restless and impatient, and complained continually, until Mrs. Strange, becoming alarmed, succeeded in arousing her husband, who went immediately for a doctor. To Nettie the time seemed long before the physician arrived. The breathing became more laboured; and when he came he looked grave, and said it was " a doubtful case."

In twenty-four hours little Jane was with the angels.

Nettie had never seen death before; and though it came
in its mildest form and softest transition, yet it was death,
and bore away upon its dark, receding wing the little head
that had so often nestled on her heart. While life remained,
she, of the twain, was the more assiduous in her efforts to
relieve the suffering child, moving from room to room, as if
its dear life depended upon the alacrity with which she
warmed the flannel, or mixed the mustard, or prepared the
medicine. The mother was nervously excited, giving vent
to her tearless grief in hysterical sobbings; the father weeping in unrestrained agony, as he beheld his little helpless
one in the iron grasp of the " king of terrors." On Nettie
and the doctor devolved the task of nursing. It was her
hand that applied the draughts and chafed the contorted limbs,
and her arm that pillowed the little head when the medicine
was administered. As long as life remained she could do
this, and much more if need were; but when the struggle
between life and death was over, and she saw the face grow
whiter and the limbs become cold and rigid, an awe crept
over her heart, and an indescribable terror nearly paralyzed
her faculties. The colour forsook her cheeks, and the face,
which an hour before was flushed with anxiety and hope,
became pale and rigid as the little one that slept so sweetly
in its peaceful unconsciousness. She could no more pillow
that little head on her breast, now that death had left its
solemn and awful impress there, than she could restore life
to the little body lying so silently under the white sheet. A
shudder ran through her limbs as she was bidden by one of
the women, who assisted in the " laying-out," to go into the
room where the body was, and get some article that was
required. For a moment she sat gazing abstractedly into the
woman's face; then a faint realization of the purport of her
words came to her, and she attempted to rise, but clung to
the chair for support, and would have fallen; but the woman,

seeing her bloodless face and large, dilated eyes, caught her and replaced her in her chair.

"Why, Nettie, how cold you are! Are you ill?"

"I don't know — yes — I feel sick."

"She has had no sleep for two nights," said Mrs. Strange. "You had better go up stairs and lie down."

"No, no! I could not sleep! Let me stay here."

She thought of the dear lady who had spoken so kindly to her on New Year's night, and wished — O how much she wished! — she was here. The colour came slowly to her lips, but she dared not express her desire, until some mention was made of the making of the shroud, when she ventured to ask if she might go for the dear young lady. Mrs. Miller, who was present, immediately seconded her proposal, but thought her father might go, as Nettie was too ill; and added, "As there will be the muslin to buy, you had better let your father go, or some of us."

"No, no! do let *me* go. The cool air will do me good, my head aches so!"

"Go," said her father; "and as you come back you can stop at the store for the muslin. How much will it take?"

The number of yards was decided upon, and as silently as she could Nettie passed the outer door, and hurried through the gathering shadows. Overcome with excitement and terror, and a multitude of confused thoughts rushing through her mind, she scarcely remembered how she came there, the moments seemed so few since leaving her father's door.

The reverberation of the heavy knocker on Mr. Maynard's door startled her; and not until "Nettie, dear Nettie" fell upon her ear, and she found herself clasped in the arms of Grace, did she fully realize where she was, or the purport of her errand. She stopped as Grace drew near a sofa, and drawing Nettie down by her side, pressed her hand very affectionately between both of hers.

"You are very pale, Nettie, and cold. You have worn nothing around you but this thin shawl, and are without gloves or mittens. But you do not feel the cold, I presume, your poor heart is so sad. Yes, I know what it is, Nettie, that makes you tremble so; we heard of your bereavement this afternoon."

"And will you come?" cried Nettie, in imploring accents, though in a tone so agitated as to render her words nearly inaudible.

"Come? Who wants me to come?"

"I do. I came for you to make baby's little shroud, — the little white dress that she's to be buried in. Mother told me to, and father says we are to stop at the store and buy the muslin."

"Certainly, I will do both. Thank you, dear Nettie, for thinking of me in this your day of trial. When we are in trouble, darling, we think of our dearest friends first;" and she drew the little yielding head closer to her breast, and spoke words of sympathy and consolation.

"Your little sister is now an angel in heaven; she will never suffer more, nor sin more. The Saviour sent beautiful angels, all robed in white, to bear her soul away to never-ending happiness. She has not gone far: a few years and you shall see little Janie again; you will follow her through death's dark valley, but you will find the loved and lost in the regions of eternal day. Her pure spirit knew no sin; she had no stains to wash away to fit her for her passage to the skies. Jesus died that He might prepare a glorious home for little innocents like her; and for us all, if we will but have faith in His name. This is faith, to know that He is God, and that He cannot err. He sunders the dearest ties, the sweetest bonds, the holiest love, that bind our hearts to earth. O, how we cry out in anguish of soul when our loved ones are torn from our embrace! But Faith looks up and says, 'Father, thy will be done.' Faith questions not the justice of the Almighty. No 'why?' nor 'where-fore?' should issue from our lips."

" O, it is so dreadful to see her lie there dead!" sobbed Nettie, her tears, the first she had shed, raining on the gentle bosom that supported her.

" It is not little Janie that you see lying there so cold and white. It is only the little casket, without sense or feeling, that will be borne away to the silent house appointed for all things; the priceless gem which was but yesterday en-shrined in it, is now a beautiful jewel in Jesus's crown. Its brightness can never become tarnished, and throughout all eternity she will be enjoying more and more of the blessed-ness of heaven. If she had lived, think how much she might have suffered, and perhaps sinned. Another thing: remember the body of your sister will one day be raised from the dead, and shine like Christ's glorified body."

Nettie looked up with eager, inquiring eyes, and over her sweet, thoughtful face there seemed to shine a glorious faith, imparted from Him who afflicts not willingly the children of His love.

" Your words have made me very happy. I will try and not weep any more for little Janie. I only wish I was in heaven, too."

" No, Nettie, you must not wish that; that was a sinful thought. In God's own appointed time the beautiful angel, Death, will summon you away; and what though his touch be cold, and the shadows of the grave lie along his pathway? It is Death's hand that unlocks the golden gates of the beau-tiful city, and restores our loved ones to our gaze. There they will watch and wait for us until we are all at home in the Saviour's fold."

" O, how my tears flow! Indeed, I cannot help it, Miss Pearson."

" Do not try to help it, Nettie; let them flow freely. It is a blessed luxury to weep when the heart aches. It is a stoic's nature that disdains to weep; and we do violence to our own when we force back the hot tears upon our stricken hearts. Tears are welcome when the strained eyeballs burn, and the heart's emotion is too intense and powerful for utterance. Jesus wept for His friend Lazarus, and He will not condemn the broken-hearted when their tears flow in anguish, not in sinful murmurings and rebellion against His chastisement. For only a few weary years they are hid from our view, and we lose their society and sweet companion-ship, and sweeter counsels."

" O, I do love to hear you talk so : you have taught me what I never knew before. It makes me very happy, and very sad; happy, to know that the heaven which you have pictured so beautiful and bright is now my little sister's home; sad, when I think of my own sinful heart, and how much better and holier it must become before I can look up to Jesus as my Saviour." As her voice trembled, and she hid her face on the young lady's shoulder, Grace was her-self affected to tears. Presently she said, —

"Nettie, do you feel the need of a Saviour's love? Would you have God for your Father and Friend? one to whom you can always go when your heart is oppressed with a weight of sorrow grievous to be borne? one on whom you can lean, with a sweet, clinging faith, when your own strength is too feeble to meet the exigencies of a moment like this? "

Nettie lifted her swimming eyes to the face of her friend, but she hesitated to reply; and Grace proceeded : —

" The Bible teaches that Jesus hath borne our sins and sorrows in His own body on the cross. He died a sacrifice for our transgressions. Perhaps this very affliction was sent to draw you closer to the pierced feet of the Crucified One. O, Nettie, now is the time to seek the Saviour, in the days of your youth, before your heart becomes engrossed with the cares of the world, or hardened by sin. O, seek Him who was sent into the world to bind up and heal the broken-hearted."

" I should so like to become pious and good!" sobbed Nettie. " Teach me to become what you are."

" Make Christ not only your sacrifice, but your pattern, my dear child. He is without sin, pure and holy. He is more worthy to be imitated than the best of us. I would have you better than I am, Nettie, for I have a very sinful heart."

" You?"

" Yes, darling; my heart is sometimes light and trifling, and prone to set too great store by the pleasures of this world; and sometimes I find my religious duties irksome. I felt last summer that my Sabbath school class was becoming tiresome. The weather was warm, and I had a good way to walk, and my duties as a teacher were not as solemnly impressed upon my heart as they should have been. And I often have a desire to dress in a style unbecoming a Christian. I never could reconcile gay and costly dress with a meek and humble spirit. Still my heart rebels sometimes, when I see this and that to admire, and think how becoming it would be to me. It is only a strong effort of the will, and urgent, earnest prayer, and the grace of God, that keep me from becoming a vain, worldly-minded woman. The world has many allurements for the young, and the heart, unregenerated by the Holy Spirit, is apt to seek its pleasures in things present, impatient to be held in check by a prohibition of what would eventually be its ruin."

Nettie's tears ceased to flow, but a deeper sadness lay upon her heart. She thought if the angelic being at her side, from whose sweet lips dropped such gentle admonition, such heart-felt sympathy, and who held up virtue and goodness in their fairest light, and gave to sin its most hideous aspect; who practised self-denial that she might add to the happiness of others; who so nobly exemplified the Christian's character in her every-day life; who, she felt sure, was as spotless as an angel, — if she, with all her strength and purity, had struggles and heart-trials to encounter and overcome, what must her own be when contending with more and severer trials than would fall to the lot of her friend? She thought of her own darkened home. A spirit of evil seemed ever brooding over its portals, as if to preclude the possibility of a change for the better; and now that death had been there, and robbed it of the only little sunbeam that gladdened her existence and brightened her gloom, she shrank from contemplating what the future might be, and then, as if determined to master the tide of painful thoughts surging around her heart, she answered less despondingly when questioned upon the subject of her home and its associations. Although the questions were delicately put and as delicately answered, enough was gleaned by Grace to give her an insight into Nettie's family relations, and her large heart sympathized deeply with her in this her first bereavement.

She discovered in Nettie a mind capable of receiving and retaining strong impressions, and she felt assured that the good seed dropped now would fall upon a fertile soil. She saw also that she had taken a strong hold upon Nettie's affections, and resolved that hers should be the hand to mould that pliant mind to a divine likeness. She raised her heart in silent prayer to Him who seeth and heareth in secret, for strength and guidance in this her heavenly undertaking.

Mrs. Maynard just then came in to see if the parlour fire needed mending, and expressed surprise to find Nettie there, and her unreserved astonishment when informed of her errand.

"I am quite surprised that your mother should send for Miss Grace to do up her sewing, perfect stranger as she is, and I presume unaccustomed to jobs of this kind."

"My mother did not send me," interposed Nettie, tearfully; "she said nearly the same words herself when I begged to come. It was at my own earnest entreaty that she consented."

"It is presuming upon her very considerably, I think."

"I assure you, my dear Mrs. Maynard, it will afford me the greatest pleasure to go. I had thought of proposing it to Helen, and asking her to accompany me, even before Nettie came. I am not unaccustomed to scenes enacted in the chambers of the sick and dying. It involves no sacrifice on my part, when I assist in the last sad duties in the house of mourning."

"I advise you to marry an undertaker, and live in a graveyard," sneered Miss Helen, who had followed her mother into the room, but had remained silent during this strange colloquy.

"Why didn't your mother send for Mrs. Miller, or Mrs. Selden, or some of the other neighbours? They can any of them make a shroud good enough for a child to be buried in."

Nettie's voice trembled as she informed them of her mother's almost distracted mind, and that Mrs. Miller and several others were already there. "But," added she, winking the tears from her eyes, "I would so like to have this dear young lady go with me, if you please. I thought little Janie's memory would be pleasanter, if *her* hands made the little dress in which I shall see her for the last time."

"Quite romantic, indeed!" laughed Helen.

"You can bring the stuff here, and we can help to sew it up, without the 'dear lady' tramping away up there in the snow. Have you got the cloth?"

"No, ma'am; it is not bought yet; we are to call at the store for it as we go home."

"Did you bring the money to pay for it?"

"No, ma'am."

"What an absurd question to ask! If your father would—"

Nettie's ear did not catch the unfinished sentence, as the door closed with a loud bang just at that moment; but Grace heard it, and also the inquiry relative to the money, and it smote upon her heart like a knell. She begged Mrs. Maynard to give herself no further uneasiness on her account, as she had made up her mind to go, and thought possibly she might remain all night.

"I guess you'll change your mind when you get there."

"Let her do as she pleases, mother. She is such a philanthropist, she won't mind a little dirt or tobacco smoke."

This unfeeling remark was made as they were leaving the house, and Grace hoped Nettie had not heard it.

They walked silently side by side until they came to the cross-roads, one of which led to the village store. Nettie paused as though a sudden and painful thought oppressed her.

"No, no, I cannot; I will let father come for the muslin. He must have forgotten to give me the money." And she knew Mr. Maynard never trusted her father.

"Give yourself no uneasiness, dear Nettie. Come with me to the store. I wish not only to make your little sister's shroud, but to purchase it. That was a sweet thought of yours, Nettie, one that I shall forever cherish in my heart; and to-day has been one of the days that will live always in my memory."

"O, you are too kind, dear Miss Grace. I did not think of asking so much of a stranger."

"We are no longer strangers, Nettie. Something tells me that we shall know a great deal of each other, and perhaps contribute largely to each other's happiness. Our two natures are very much alike, and we will do each other good. What a comfort it would be to me, if all the secret thoughts, interests, hopes, and desires of your heart could be poured unreservedly and fearlessly into mine! I have

few confidants, Nettie, but I would not fear to make you
one. It does me good to come in contact with a true heart,
an unsullied nature, when there are so many proud, soul-
less persons in the world; it raises me farther from earth,
and brings me nearer to heaven. But here we are at the
store."

"Let me look at some fine jacconet, if you please. Yes,
that will do. Cut me two yards. Have you some white
merino?"

"Not any."

"I am sorry. Show me some book muslin. Not quite as
coarse as this. Yes, this is finer. Three yards, and two
yards of narrow white ribbon."

"Anything more?"

"Nothing more to-day."

"Nine and sixpence. Thank you."

And the twain left the store without further compliments
or embarrassments, the one thinking, —

> "How cheap
> Is genuine happiness, yet how dearly
> Do we all pay for its base counterfeit!"

"Nine and sixpence! what an insignificant sum to pay
for the train of beautiful happy thoughts which come like
a shower of sunshine to my heart! Nine and sixpence! so
little to purchase joy for two; the greater, because shared
by another. How true that beautiful sentiment I read this
morning in Young's Night Thoughts! —

> ' Nature, in her zeal for human amity,
> Denies or damps an undivided joy.
> Joy is an import; joy is an exchange;
> Joy flies monopolists; it calls for two;
> Rich fruit! Heaven-planted! never plucked by one.'"

The other was wounded and distressed at heart; for upon
their entrance, Mr. Maynard senior had riveted upon Nettie

his sharp gray eyes, as much as to ask, " What do you want
here?" At least Nettie thus interpreted his keen inquiring
gaze ; but her friend came instantly to her relief; and now,
thank Heaven! she was once more out in the free air, trying
to overcome the choking sensation that made her throat ache.
She took long respirations, until the pain subsided. Then,
in a voice scarcely audible, she interrupted her companion's
revery by saying—

"This is the only thing I shall ask of you, Miss Pearson,
except it is your forgiveness for putting you to so much
trouble. It is too bad that you should be obliged to dis-
please them to serve me. It will never occur again, I
hope."

"Nettie, do you really hope *that?* Do you sincerely wish
you may never have another occasion to test my friendship?"

"No, no, not that. I love you so dearly I can never forget you while I live ; but I fear you will gain the displeasure
of your friends by doing us this great kindness. Do not
come again to our house, if they object. I will not be selfish. I had rather not see you again, if you have to be
scolded for it."

A smile passed over the placid features of Grace, as she
replied archly,—

"Do not let it trouble you, Nettie. You were never farther from right than when you imagine their regards or dis-
regards, likes or dislikes, can influence mine. Where were
my independence or strength of character, if I permitted
myself to be swayed by the caprices of others? We often
come in contact with those who do not perfectly harmonize
with us, and I am convinced it is best to avoid a collision,
if possible ; taking care, however, that they do not jostle us
out of the right path. I know I am doing right now, and
doing that which pleases me ; and the happiness conferred
upon myself, to say nothing of others, will more than com-

pensate me for their peevishness and ill humor. They are only a little too careful of me. Give yourself no uneasiness as to the scolding."

Grace could not help laughing at Nettie's fears. Nettie caught the smile, and happier thoughts took possession of her heart as soon as the subject was purposely changed.

8

CHAPTER XIII.

A ROMANTIC WALK TO REAL LIFE.

"How oft, upon yon eminence, our pace
　　Has slackened to a pause, and we have borne
　　The ruffling wind, scarce conscious that it blew,
　　While admiration, feeding at the eye,
　　And still unsated, dwelt upon the scene!"
　　　　　　　　　　　　　　　　　　Cowper.

"Make not one child a warning to another; but chide the offender
　　apart,
For self-conceit and wounded pride rankle like poisons in the soul."
　　　　　　　　　　　　　　　　　　Tupper.

THIS is quite a long hill to climb, and I think the snow is deeper up here," said Grace, pausing to take breath.

"Yes, this road is not as much used as the main street. There is hardly ever any sleighing past our house, and but for one of the neighbours hauling wood, would scarcely be broken. Sometimes, after a heavy snow, I am the first to make a path."

"O, I almost envy you the sport. I love the snow, and always hail its coming with delight. There is a strange beauty in its fleecy whiteness when it lies soft and warm on the hills, under a 'rosy flood of twilight sky,' or when the bright moonlight 'sleeps upon its banks.' I never see the white flakes fall without their seeming fresh from the spirit-land, sent on angelic missions. They awaken thoughts and feelings pure as themselves. See how soft and white it lies on the stern face of yonder mountain! I would like a scramble up there among the rocks and evergreens."

" It is very beautiful in summer, when the moss under the cliff is green and soft."

" I rather like it as it is now, in its stern, cold grandeur, jutting out bold and strong in its bleak, sterile majesty, without the added grace and loveliness of summer. I like things best in their wild state, animate and inanimate: their characteristic simplicity and my heart have a strong affinity; so soon as they become polished, and glossed over with artificial impressions, they lose half their interest to me."

" Then you would like our hills less if they were clothed with grass and flowers, instead of rocks and evergreens, and ignorant people better than those who know a great deal."

" I do not mean to say that a mind uncultivated is more to be admired than one polished by education and refined associations, or that some pages in great nature's history might not be embellished with much that would please the eye and charm the mind; but to me it is a moment of inspiration when I see something untouched by the hand of art, or differing from its fellows in some peculiarity. A summer landscape, richly shaded with light and dark green foliage, gorgeous with varied and many-coloured floral beauties, is really to be admired; but it fascinates the senses for the moment only. The pleasure it evolves is nipped with the first frost; and, like the foliage and the flowers, it is mostly dependent upon a sunny day and a clear blue sky. That barren hill-side yonder, on whose bald visage the storm-king of to-day heaps the snow-drifts, may to-morrow be unmasked by him. Calm and unresentful it stands, and the clashing elements affect it as little as though they warred not. Beautiful type of noble manhood — is it not? Dim miniature of greatness absolute! Like, and yet unlike; like in individuality, stability, stamina, and dignified repose; unlike, because inactive and unconscious. How do you like the comparison?"

"A very homely one, I should say, if all hills are like ours."

"Homely, say you? I did not think our tastes differed so much. Do you see no beauty in your native hills?"

"Not much. I've often wondered why they were ever made. I know they are awful hard to climb. I get very tired when I go for the sheep and cows, and wish, sometimes, there never had been such a thing as a hill; and that big one yonder, which you think so beautiful and grand, is the worst of the whole. It grows nothing but sorrel, and mullein-stalks, and thistles, and such like."

They both laughed a little, pleasant laugh, and by this time had reached the upper cross-roads, one turning off towards Mr. Strange's house. Miss Pearson said she feared Nettie would not make a very good Highlander, and, after a short pause, added, —

"I wish my birthplace had been in some cosy nook among the Alps, or, to come nearer home, among the Highlands of Scotland, where the heather, with which I invest their snow-capped summits, blooms for its own sweet sake, and 'the whispering air sends inspiration from the mountain heights.' But were I a peasant-girl, and obliged to herd my father's sheep and goats, the poetry might be simmered down into the dullest kind of prose."

"The novelty would soon wear off, I think."

"The novelty of being a shepherdess might; for it must be tiresome to climb steep hills, and hunt for and follow truant flocks; but a home among those wild mountain scenes, far away in some secluded haunt, with the brooklet's gentle music, and the sweet noise of the waterfall creeping by my door, would be delightful. I do not mean a simple, old-fashioned herdsman's cot, although in such a one I might be very happy; but one fashioned after a model of my

own making — one which my matter-of-fact brother Frank
would call an 'air castle.' He thinks me quite famous for
building 'castles in the air.' But, indeed, I am not the dreamer
he supposes me; it's only now and then that I explore the
realms of fancy. Then I not only build castles, but whole
towns and cities, provinces and empires, and people them
with beings and things according to my liking. Now, when
next I get on my thinking-cap, I shall have some new faces
and names for my fairy kingdom; and, Nettie, if you say so,
I'll not build any rocky hills around your home. It shall be
a beautiful summer landscape, such as you like, and you
shall flit among the flowers, the brightest of them all; only
you shall come to see me in my mountain eyrie," — and the
arm under the warm shawl that encircled both tightened
around Nettie, and the two hearts seemed as firmly knitted
as though but one pulse told the number of their beats.

"Do not separate our homes, dear Miss Grace; you can
build a castle large enough for us both."

"But you would not like to live so far up among the rocks
as mine would be."

"O, anywhere, so I might be with you."

"Then I'll not divide the estates, and you shall be the
little nymph of the grove, and I will always paint you good
and beautiful, as you are. But, Nettie, this of course is only
ideality, and may never be — at least not in this world; but
somewhere in the great universe our souls will live, and there
we may know and love each other. We may give our fancies
boundless scope, and our creative genius transform the dullest things of earth into a shower of gold; with this we may
build palaces glorious to the mind's eye; but 'eye hath not
seen, nor ear heard, neither hath it entered the heart of man,
the things that are prepared for them who love God.'"

They had now reached the footpath which diverged from
the road. Nettie pulled down the bars that let them into the
field of stubble, in the midst of which stood the great,

gaunt-looking house of Mr. Strange. Grace at once remarked its cheerless and almost desolate aspect, a heavy
sigh escaping her heart to think that this was Nettie's home.
Her eye wandered over the unbroken waste of snow. Save
a large, misshapen oak, at the back of the house, neither tree
nor shrub was within the enclosure ; and the dead cornstalks
and grain-stubble, standing close about the house, showed
there had been no flower-garden in summer to relieve its
gloom. A small barn, and some hayricks, enclosed by a
rude rail fence, and a long well-sweep, were the only signs
of improvement. " There must be an orchard somewhere,"
thought Grace ; but it was not in sight. A dead tree had
been hauled up to the door, and a man was chopping off
some of the limbs for firewood.

"You've been a long time gone, Nettie. It's almost dark."

Not until these words were spoken had they noticed the
evening shadows creeping stealthily up from the dark ra-
vines, and settling quietly upon the hill-tops. They took
no note of time, and had walked leisurely, even slowly, that
they might enjoy their walk the longer. As Nettie entered
the house, a troubled look was on her face. Grace saw it,
and took upon herself the blame, if any blame there was, for
being detained so long.

The interior of the house presented even fewer attractions
than the exterior. It was scantily furnished, and the family
room made a receptacle of much that ought to have been in
the barn.

Grace sat down on the side of the bed, where lay the
mother of the dead infant in almost hysterical paroxysms,
and having apologized for their long delay, saying the fault
was entirely her own, she, in her own sweet way, tried to
speak words of consolation to the afflicted woman.

" O, she's dead ! she's dead ! she's gone ! There's no use
trying to persuade me it's all for the best. I shall never see
my darling baby again. I have nothing more to live for

now she's taken away. I shall never be myself again —
never, never! Did you fetch the cloth for the shroud, Miss
— what's-your-name?"

"Miss Pearson," said Nettie.

"Yes, I ought to remember, for I've heard Nettie speak
it often enough for the last day or two. Are you any related
to the Pearsonses in Cranesville?"

"None that I know of. What are their given names?"

"Well, there's 'Lijah, and Timothy, and Joshua, and I
b'lieve one or two others. 'Lijah is a carpenter, and built
the meeting-house at the 'Corners,' and a mighty poor job he
made of it, I've heard say. I b'lieve the other two are farmers, and pretty well to do, though 'pears to me I've heard
Tim was a shoemaker; hows'ever, they're all very likely
folks — none that you need be ashamed of."

"They are not related to me, I presume. My father has
but two brothers, and they have different names from the
ones you mention."

"O, my poor baby! my precious baby! the only comfort
I had! O, dear! O, dear! I little thought it would die so
sudden. You'll never know anything about it, until you've
had one and lost it."

"I have lost friends who were very dear to me," replied
Grace; "and I know how to sympathize with you. I have
felt all the anguish which you now feel. I know how dark
and insignificant the world appears to you; but the consolations of the gospel dispel the gloom of the grave, and time
allays the poignancy of our grief. We shall meet our loved
ones again, and that very soon. Death is like our passing
from this room into the next, so very short is our stay here.
It is not worth while to spend the time in weeping for those
who have crossed the threshold of heaven before us. Our
dear ones will be there to receive us, not as we lay them
away in the grave, but improved and glorified, until they
become as the angels."

Mrs. Strange was evidently comforted by the kind words of the gentle being who strove to impress upon her heart the power and sublimity of those precious gospel promises, written expressly for her, said Grace, who tried, in a simple, plain way, to picture the beauty and brightness of a soul casting off its mortality.

"God sends us our trials, and in His own good time and way He will send the Comforter, if we only believe these afflictions are sent us for our good, and have faith to say, 'Thy will be done.' Let me assist you to rise."

"Thank you, miss; I'm quite accustomed to helping myself; but I think I will feel better to get up. I am most wretched; my head aches terribly."

"Benny, don't do that: it makes mother's head ache," Nettie said, in a mild tone; but the wilful boy persisted in pounding on the floor with a hammer; and when gently removed beyond his reach, he commenced kicking with his heels and screaming at the top of his voice.

"Look here, Benny; see what I've got for you."

"You hain't got nothing."

"Yes, I have. I've got a nice red apple. Come and get it."

"No, I shan't. I'll have the hammer. Give me the hammer."

"No, the hammer makes a noise; and you must keep quiet."

But little Benny was not to be bought off, or bribed into silence, as his stentorian lungs fully demonstrated.

"Ben, get up this minute, and stop your crying. If you would let him alone, he wouldn't be half as bad as he is. You're always worrying him; and you know, when he gets a-going, there's no let up to his screaming. Go into the next room, and get me a clean cap."

Grace saw the colour becoming deeper and deeper on Nettie's cheeks, and the drooping of her grave, quiet eyes told of the meek spirit within. Nettie went quietly into the room where the body of little Janie was, in obedience to her mother's command, while the obstinate child climbed to the top shelf of the dresser, and took possession of the disputed hammer. His descent was rather precipitous, accompanied by a crash of crockery and ear-splitting vociferations. The voice of Mrs. Strange rose painfully above the key-note in the conversation just then commenced between Grace and another lady present. They were speaking of the funeral, and Grace was asking her opinion relative to the making of the shroud.

The mother testified, in language not to be misunderstood, that hers were the worst-behaved children that ever lived, intimating that her trials were not to be spoken of to mortal ears, and that her sudden outbreak was quite unusual. She adjusted her clean cap before the small mirror, and was proceeding to settle herself comfortably in the arm-chair by the fire, when another and similar accident happened to one of the children, which quite upset Mrs. Strange's self-control and Grace's gravity. A large oaken chest adorned one end of the room, over which was suspended a monster bunch of red peppers; and to get at a piece of twine, occupying the same nail, another boy — and Benny's senior by two years — had climbed to the top of the chest, using for a ladder an old chair, minus the splints, which, at one time far back in its eventful history, it might have possessed. The little piece of board answering for a bottom — for the present generation's use — had been removed by the uncompromising Benny while his brother was reaching after the twine, and, as might have been expected, his descent was as ungraceful as precipitous.

"Heavens and airth! what's the matter now? Served you just right! You're always in some mischief, and if you're hurt I'm glad of it!"

Grace smiled in spite of herself; not because the angry

mother laid violent hands on the child, thereby augmenting the confusion, instead of staying it, but because of the unique and perfectly ludicrous position of the little hero of the domestic drama which was being enacted. The tableaux presented a scene which, at any other time, would have provoked a smile upon graver faces than those who witnessed it. Grace felt constrained to laugh at the boy's misfortunes; but her risibles were held in check when she remembered she was in the house of mourning instead of the house of mirth. The young offender lay doubled up in a very undignified and uncomfortable attitude — the frame of the chair imprisoning his limbs as effectually as though he were in the stocks, his hands and feet only showing themselves above the top round. It required the assistance of two or three to extricate the unfortunate lad from his uncomfortable quarters. He clamoured loudly for help, using various expletives to enforce attention. Then followed loud and passionate cries, to which Mrs. Strange paid little or no attention, such events being of too common occurrence to alarm her.

Grace was beginning to expostulate; but she restrained herself, wishing to become better acquainted with the influcnees surrounding her young *protégée;* for such she would fain consider Nettie.

" Will you never have done with your screaming? Stop this minute, or go out o' doors."

" It's the pepper in my eyes, I tell you ! "

And the voluble notes, all strung in the key major, rose from grave to acute without intervals or semitones. Then followed quick and sharp demands for water and towels, which Nettie hastened to bring; but the bathing and wiping process only seemed to irritate instead of soothe, and the passionate child screamed and shrieked for a full half hour before the paroxysms ceased.

A cloud settled on all present, while Nettie looked as though all the warm blood had left her heart, and was concentrated in her face. She gazed earnestly at Grace, as if to read her thoughts. Then her eyes sought Mrs. Miller; but with what sadness did she raise her eyes to the face of her mother! That face which never, in its pleasantest aspect, possessed anything very attractive, now, with cheek burning and eyes flashing under the strong excitement of the moment, was terrible. The sharp, thin features wore a discouraged look, and their usual gravity assumed a settled, hopeless despondency.

The uproarious urchin, after much resistance on his part, and various and sundry threats and remonstrances on the part of his mother, was trundled off to bed with a wet bandage over his eyes, being assured by Mrs. Miller that this was the only way to cure them.

The other children had suppers of bread and milk served in little porringers, and were (after the same process of urging and threatening in case of disobedience) sent whimpering to bed.

" There, thank goodness! I hope we shall have a little peace now. I don't know what it is to have a minute's rest when my children are in my sight. I shall be glad when summer comes, so I can turn them out o' doors once more; and then I shall have no little Janie to comfort me with the little pleasant ways she had!"

Tears were gathering in the woman's eyes, and sobs choked back the lamentations she would utter. She paid little regard to the " Now come, mother," " Don't fret, mother," with which her husband frequently addressed her, but, at his urgent request, seated herself in the chimney corner, and in a few moments, seemingly unconscious of anything but her pipe, was smoking away vigorously.

Another hour, and all were seated around the ample family table. Smoking viands, plain, but cooked nicely, and dished under Mrs. Miller's supervision, were bountiful. Nettie had brought from the bottom of the old chest up stairs, a clean table-cloth, somewhat yellow from having lain long unused; but the silver, and the best knives, and the shining tea-tray, together with the blue dishes, taken from the top shelf in the pantry, and washed until they looked like new, made the repast really inviting.

Mrs. Miller said an impressive "grace," and poured the tea. Mrs. Strange thought it — the tea — a little too strong, but, after the third cup, said, " It's done my head an amazing sight of good."

CHAPTER XIV.

MISS PEARSON IN THE HOUSE OF MOURNING.

"A gloomy home for one like this:
So pure, so gentle, and so fair,
Must her sweet life in weariness
Go out for lack of human care?"

ANON.

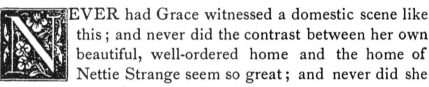EVER had Grace witnessed a domestic scene like this; and never did the contrast between her own beautiful, well-ordered home and the home of Nettie Strange seem so great; and never did she so humbly thank God for all His blessings, vouchsafed to her and hers. This unhappy household possessed few of the blessed influences that rendered hers so bright and cheerful. The sweet recollections of her happy childhood brought tearful tributes; and the deep gratitude which welled up from her heart, blending with the sweetness that always rested there, made her almost angelic. All these scenes, and many more left unnarrated, new and painful as they were to her, had not the power to quench that little spark of affectionate regard which glowed so brightly in the breast of Grace. A sweet smile said, as plainly as words could have said, " I love you, Nettie, and nothing shall ever separate our hearts."

A small fire is burning in the " spare room," where lies the little shrouded form which will ere to-morrow this time lie in even a darker and more desolate home. The room is cold and cheerless, and scantily furnished, in keeping with the rest of the apartments.

Grace, after measuring the shroud and shaping it properly, folded it carefully and laid it away until the family should retire. She had signified her willingness to remain through the night as watcher, if agreeable to Mrs. Strange. The afflicted woman, in her own peculiar way, expressed her thanks.

" I'm much obleeged to you, young woman, but I'm sorry to trouble the like o' you with watching all night in this cold barn of a house ; though, if you'll sit quite near the fire, perhaps you'll manage to keep warm. It was one of my girl's whims a sending for you to make the grave-clothes : she's always some queer notion or other in her head. I presume you're not much used to hardships, by your delercate looks."

" I am far from being delicate, and by no means consider it a hardship to watch with the sick, the dying, or the dead. It is a Christian's duty, and should be a pleasure, not only to sympathize with those whom death has bereaved, but to aid in those kind offices which, ere many days, we may need for ourselves."

" I didn't mind sitting up of a night when I was young, but nowadays it comes mighty hard on me if I am broke of my rest. When you are the mother of a family *like mine,* may be you'll be tired enough with their fretting and teasing, through the daytime, to want your rest when it comes night."

" Very likely. As our years increase, our cares increase, and I do not expect to pass through life without my share of its vexations and trials. I do not ask for myself perpetual sunshine and pleasure ; I would not fold my hands and dream away life's golden hours. I would rather know something of its sterner realities, its sorrows, fatigues, and perplexities. By these we gather strength for future usefulness, and learn how to appreciate our blessings, and to meet with fortitude any reverses or misfortunes that may befall us. Shall we receive good at the hand of the Lord, and not evil? Rather let us rejoice that we receive not all our good things in this life — that there are some in reserve for us in a life to come."

"For me, happier and better ones, I hope."

"Yes, better and happier, if that hope be well founded. Who can estimate the value of the Christian's hope? — a hope which can raise the soul above the trials of earth, and fill it with joy and peace in the dying hour."

Mrs. Strange lifted the corner of her apron, and wiped away the drops of genuine sorrow that coursed down her cheeks. And when Grace inquired affectionately concerning the hope of the Christian in its relation to her own heart, she responded tearfully, —

"I fear I am without it. Once, when I was no older than you are, I thought I got religion at a quarterly meeting, and joined the church. It was an easy matter for me to live religion then to what it is now. I had a good mother, and we allers had prayers in the family; but after my father died, I had to go away from home to live, and sometimes not among the best of folks either. I was married the second year of my living out, and I soon forgot all about my religion. I had so much to do, and the young ones began to multiply, and I became so cross and fretful I was ashamed to say I was a Christian, — Nett, go along about your work; you're allers a listening, — and then I thought there was no use trying any more to be good."

Grace improved this opportunity to impress upon Mrs. Strange the importance of the religion she once professed. Especially as a mother she needed grace and the guidance of the Holy Spirit to enable her to train for heaven the little immortals intrusted to her care.

"You left the cross, my dear Mrs. Strange, just where you

ought to have taken it up ; and just when you needed most the sweet consolations of the Christian's hope, you suffered it to die out, and an indifference to and a disregard of God's holy law to take its place."

Mrs. Strange bowed her head in silent acquiescence. She knew Miss Pearson was right.

"And as for these sad and sore trials," Grace continued, "God knows that uninterrupted happiness here would not prepare us for our future destiny ; and so He mercifully sends affliction. O, I well remember when the first dark shadow fell upon my sunny world. To my stricken heart it seemed as though the sun of my life had gone down never to rise again, and that a dark night, rayless and hopeless, in which I was to walk forever alone, was to be my future. But I sought for faith where faith was never denied ; and now I look back with many tears of gratitude, not because my mother was taken from me, but because the severe dispensation was made the means, under God, of bringing me to seek His grace, which bringeth salvation. I was favorably disposed towards religion, and felt the necessity of professing it, and promised myself at some future time to make preparation for a dying day ; yet eighteen years of my life glided away without a saving knowledge of Christ. God employs various ways to bring sinners to the foot of the cross, and there is nothing in them that is unreasonable. In kindness and mercy are our loved ones taken from us. Believe this, my dear friend : it is meant only for good ; and let me ask you to make this sad occasion a time for solemn thought and heart-felt repentance. Weep not for your dead baby. It lives with the angels ; but weep and pray for the living, for they are still subject to sin and temptation."

"O, what shall I do?" sobbed the poor, heart-broken woman, while tears chased each other down her cheeks.

"Do this first : return to that slighted Saviour, and lay a contrite heart upon God's altar ; so shall your peace be as a river; and when death again visits your household, and troubles come heavier and heavier, you will have the beautiful and holy religion of Christ to aid and comfort you, and His precious promises to bind up the broken heart."

Grace sat with one arm thrown around the weeping woman. She had become strangely interested in her, and out of the fulness of her sorrow and sympathy tears had come; and yet they were tears of joy, for a light seemed dawning in upon that darkened, sin-stricken conscience, and Grace prayed for the cloud to be rolled away.

Nettie had taken no part in the conversation. She dared hardly hear it, after her mother's sharp reproof; but how could she help it? She glided noiselessly about the room, assisting with the work after supper, and listened earnestly to the sweet words that dropped like honey-dew from the lips of the angel friend at her mother's side. They came to her like a new gospel, like good tidings of good: to her lonely heart they were new life; to her timid, shrinking nature, faith, and strength, and hope.

How beautiful religion looked to her! and how she exalted those who, like Grace, practised what they professed! O, if her mother were only a Christian, what might she not hope for herself! Then she might hope all things. Then — ah, what a well-spring of happiness seemed opened in their dwelling at the very thought.

There were tears, too, in the father's eyes. Nettie saw them drop, as he buried his head in his hands, and listened silently to the words of their young guest. He remembered with sorrow his own estrangement from the path of rectitude, and with something of the old bitterness did he recall the indignation and contempt with which his first deviation from that path was met. There was small sympathy between himself and his wife. They had ever few thoughts or feelings in common. An indifference and coldness — to

9

call it by no worse name — had long since succeeded the
attachment of their early life. They had loved mutually;
the estrangement that followed was mutual. Their few
joys had been mutually shared, but until now they had never
had any great grief to share together. Now, as they stood
by the grave's brink, and the shadow of their mutual sorrow
gathered darkly around them, the iron that entered their
souls was forged into links, to bind their hearts together
again, and both to Christ. Their hearts were softened, now
that death had crossed their threshold, and as they sat together in the gloom. Each hoped the other would feel and
understand the sorrow, and speak words that were comforting and forgiving. Each felt there was now a stronger
tie of sympathy than otherwise they could have known in
their whole existence. Aside from their present affliction,
memory was busy at the heart-strings of each. Memory
took them away back, and unfolded to their gaze a little·
altar reared beside their humble hearth-stone, where they
had offered, in child-like faith and simplicity, their morning
and evening sacrifice. At their setting out in life, a little
" grace " had been said at their table; but as the meals came
three times a day, and were always eaten in a hurry, and cares
multiplied, and the days grew too short for the accomplishment of their allotted tasks, it was sometimes neglected, and
finally omitted altogether.

Work and toil, fret and scold, from morning till night,
and from year's end to year's end, was the order of their
individual existence. But somehow, with all their united
industry and economy, they went forward very slowly. It
is true, the mortgage of five hundred dollars, which covered
the place when purchased by Mr. Strange, had been lifted,
and not a penny was now due thereon. He thought he had
done remarkably well to pay for his land, to say nothing of
the improvements. The first two or three crops of grain
were as good as the best, the young orchard yielded a small

income, and altogether they were prosperous. But for the last three or four years things had sadly changed. The step of either was no longer elastic, and any amount of wrinkles and gray hairs had taken the place of the roseate hue of youth and health, and an everlasting expression of care and discouragement settled upon the brow of each.

There had no great affliction visited them. Their cattle increased, and their crops were as good as their neighbours'; but they had overtasked their energies, and their ambition had died.

" He never found time to fix up the house, or make a garden, or do things, like other folks," so Mrs. Strange would say; and this gave abundant occasion for reproof and a settled habit of fault-finding, until ill temper became a part of her nature.

No one in Sorreltown knew that there had ever been a family altar in Mr. Strange's house; the ruins were left in their early home, where the shrew tongue of Mrs. Strange took its first lessons in reproach. Their neighbours only knew them as they were now, save that each year matters had gone on from bad to worse, until they were well nigh as bad as they could be — as Mrs. Strange frequently asserted.

No one thought of them, or spoke of them, as Mr. and Mrs. Strange: it was "old Pete," or "Uncle Pete Strange;" while Mrs. Strange was hardly known other than as "Aunt Eunice." Not that they were so old, but they "were such *queer* people," folks said.

CHAPTER XV.

THE WATCHERS IN THE DARKENED COTTAGE.

"Hers was the brow, in trials unperplexed,
    That cheered the sad and tranquillized the vexed;
    She studied not the meanest to eclipse,
    And yet the wisest listened to her lips."
                                        CAMPBELL.

HE wind moaned and sighed, as it surged around the silent old house all that long, starless night, shaking the loose clapboards and the rickety window-frames, and sometimes making the whole house tremble, as some long, low wail, more dismal than the rest, sent its dying echoes to the heart, filling it with a nameless dread. There was neither hill nor forest to inter- cept the moanings of the winds.

The house was left to the two lone watchers, who sat by the dim firelight — Mark and Grace; and though a shadow lay upon their hearts, it was a sweet and holy awe, a sad but pleasant duty, and each felt a secret pleasure in having none others near.

Nettie had sobbed herself to sleep in Grace's arms, after many fruitless attempts to shake off her drowsiness; but she was so tired, poor thing, and the night was so long! Mark drew up the long family cradle close to the fire, and made her a little bed, covering her with Grace's warm shawl. She begged to remain with them. She could not bear to go to the cold, dark attic alone; and not until the little white shroud was finished and laid away did she show any signs of weariness.

Grace drew her gently to her side, soothed her sad heart to rest with her low, sweet, musical words, such as might drop from the lips of a dream-angel; and, indeed, Grace was the angel of her dreams for many years after the sweet Eden-vision of that night had fled; and the spirit-deeps revealed to the woman-dreamer something of the mysterious power of sympathy and love.

Grace was the first to break the silence that was becoming protracted. She drew her chair nearer the fire as Mark piled on the fagots, and while the blaze lasted a quiet smile might have been seen on their two handsome faces. The goodness of their hearts illumined their cheeks like russet roses, and a close scrutiny would have disclosed a look of extreme satisfaction that they two were at last alone. And yet the form sleeping at their feet seemed in some way a connecting link in the chain of thought, which led them onward over life's uneven pathway, always together, they three, until, in the vague future, where white hairs blend with love's endearments, and tottering footsteps walk thoughtfully the silent, solemn shore, they recall the past as a pleasant dream.

Each offers a voiceless prayer for the well-being of that sleeper. "Whatever be my fate, may she be blessed," is the burden borne by the recording angel to the book on high.

"I know not why it is, but I have taken a strange interest in that child," said Grace, musingly, and with her eyes fixed attentively upon Nettie as she slept. "Never in my life have I known one so young and yet so thoughtful, and possessing intelligence and graces that would qualify her for a different sphere than the one which she is likely to occupy. I shall be very happy in having so loveable a friend as she is."

"She is very sweet-tempered and amiable, and you will become more fond of her as you know more of her, poor thing,' said Mark, lowering his voice to a confidential whisper. " She seems so unlike the rest of the family! There is none of their rudeness and selfishness in her disposition. There is such a difference in her sweet, pretty voice and the harsh tones of the others! It always makes me very happy when I hear any one praising her."

" You are a great favourite of hers, I think."

Mark's face brightened, and he looked gratefully towards the young lady for saying so much; but he never thought she regarded him as a favourite.

" My mother loves her very dearly, and I have often thought how happy I should be had I a sister like Nettie. You will think of her sometimes when you are gone?"

" Very often," answered Grace, bending over the cradle, and imprinting a kiss upon the unconscious sleeper.

" A few days and I shall be at home again; but my thoughts will often find a resting-place within these walls, and I fear they will not be such as to afford me much pleasure; but I shall pray the good Shepherd of Israel to feed this little lamb, and so to temper the winds that they visit not her fair cheeks too roughly, or blast her earthly happiness. You will see her often, and I hope you will speak such words of encouragement as will cheer her onward in the path of duty. I envy you the happiness of living so near her. Were this privilege mine, I think I could sometimes soothe and strengthen her when her heart fails her; and perhaps," she added, hesitatingly, " I might benefit them all. What an unhappy family they are!"

Mark responded thoughtfully, almost tearfully, when alluding to them; but when he came to that part of a long sentence which told of his own contemplated absence from the home of his boyhood, he quite broke down, without having given Grace any definite idea as to the expediency of his departure.

He felt uneasy under the gaze of those large, lustrous eyes, which seemed to read to the innermost every thought of his heart; and yet he appeared to be watching eagerly for a reply. He told his story in few words, and Grace became an interested listener. When he came to speak of leaving his mother, her face lost much of that ready sympathy which at first so inspired her with a hope of his success.

She was dissatisfied. He could see that by the ominous cloud gathering on her serene face. The averted eye, the look of pensive sadness, and the plainly perceptible frown which followed, all gave evidence of her disapproval.

A pang shot through Mark's heart, and his face, too, grew dark and thoughtful. For the moment he felt, rather than incur the displeasure of the dear lady who was so interested for himself and Nettie, he would forego his cherished purpose. She did not know nor dream of the power and influence a look or tone of hers might exert, or the pain and anguish it might cost another.

Grace mused a few moments, seemingly absorbed in earnest thought. Then her eyes roved abstractedly about the cheerless room, as if to give the doubts that pressed hard upon each other ample scope. At last they assumed an expression of deep and earnest pathos, as they sought, inquiringly, in the face before her, to know whether her thoughts were not vastly extravagant ones. There was something in that shining eye, which, to Grace's comprehensive vision, said a fire might slumber there, even the fire of genius, were it not extinguished ere it was fanned to a flame.

Both were aroused from their fit of dreamy abstraction by the blackened forestick snapping in twain. The charred ends, having cleared the broken andirons, forced themselves into notice by rolling half way across the homely and uneven hearth. Mark's skill in fire-mending was put to the severest test, for the only implement at hand was an iron poker, and the incorrigible brands persisted in tumbling about at will.

At length, after sundry awkward manœuvres, he gained his point. The obstinate fagots were made to lie precisely as Mark wanted them to, his own pertinacity being more than equal to theirs. Soon the struggling blaze circled around and high above the smouldering logs, shedding cheerfulness and warmth through the darkened room.

They sat silently a while, both busy with their own thoughts; and then Grace said, in a glad, certain tone, —

"Success and a prosperous future should be yours; you deserve it. You have a determined will, I see; and if the mending of that fire be any proof of a brave spirit, yours would not quail before almost any obstacle. With only that old crooked poker to work with, not one in a thousand would have accomplished what you have in so short a time; and see the cheerful sparkling light which those blackened brands emit! It is a good omen, Mark."

"And I suppose you sat there laughing slyly at my awkward attempts; though you should not have done so, for, as you say, I laboured under extreme disadvantages."

"Therein lies the merit. I could have done it myself with a good pair of tongs, and — "

"A little assistance," interrupted Mark. "Those great brands would have been heavy lifting for you alone."

"You deserve credit for your perseverance, at least," said Grace, pushing back her chair from the blazing fire.

"Well, I knew I could do it; but I might take hold of something else with less experienced hands, and yet a greater energy. There is not half the zest where there are neither doubts nor fears as to the result."

"Said like a true, brave heart!"

"The easiest path does not often lead to the goal of our hopes. Our aspirations may be ever so great, but if we turn aside from every shadow, or are scared away by the frowning rocks on the top of which our feet must be planted firm and strong, our lives might be spent ere we caught one bright flash of the shining light far beyond us. It were better, I think, to be forever striving and toiling for some good unattained, than to have no ambition and no energy, content to toil on in the daily treadmill of life to which society confines the ignorant and the unaspiring."

Mark never raised his eyes from the fire during this speech. He seemed to be climbing a mountain path without pausing to take a parting glance at the boon companion by his side, who had shaded it so fearfully, and yet so hopefully. His thoughts went on and on, until he dreamed over again his old, wild dreams, and the cloud in which he had hitherto been lost was now rolled away, or silvered over so beautifully as even to light his way onward. He would not be the one to dream idly at the foot of the cliff. Whatever work there was for him to do, must be commenced. Now was the time; delay might blunt the keen desire to rise above his life of poverty and mere bodily labour.

"I am poor in heart as well as in means," thought he. "I have no society. I want the companionship of the good and the intellectual. Why can I not have it? I can! and I will!"

There was a half-resolute, half-doubting look on Mark's face, and a tear stood trembling in his eyes — at least Grace thought so. They shone and glistened so like two stars! She broke in upon his protracted reverie by asking, "Does the picture, over which you have been dreaming for the last quarter of an hour, appear like some visionary sketch? Before we adopt a plan we should consider its feasibility. I confess I should make a very inefficient guide, though I could say, 'Go on,' and 'up;' yet to lead the way over many difficulties is quite a different thing. You spoke of making Albany your starting-point. Have you any definite plans formed? If I could aid you in any way —"

"It is the starting-point that troubles me. I have no acquaintances in Albany; but Mr. Sloper will give me letters to Governor Worth, who is an old friend of his, and to his daughter, Mrs. Loveland; and since I know you," said he, hesitatingly, " I shall not feel quite alone."

" May I ask of you one favour, Mark?"

" Yes; a dozen! a thousand!"

" But I want you to promise that you will grant what I ask."

" Put the question first."

" No, the promise first."

" Well, then, yes. I am not afraid to promise you any- thing, so it does not interfere with my leaving home."

" No; it is not that. I would go if I were you; but it is this: Will you call on me immediately on your arrival in the city? I will give you my address, and if ever you see the time when you are in trouble, or in want, — if you fail in your expectations, and should need a friend, —will you come to me, as you would go to your mother, or a sister, if you had one?"

" What an angel you are!" was just on Mark's lips; but he checked the words in time, and said, —

" O, Miss Pearson! You are too kind; but I fear you would not be very proud of your newly-found country ac- quaintance. I shall occupy but a very humble position in society. If I can only find something to do, I shall not come to want; never fear that—"

" But remember, I have your promise."

" It shall be sacredly kept."

CHAPTER XVI.

MARK LEAVES HOME.

"Gird your hearts with silent fortitude,
. Suffering, yet hoping all things."

MRS. HEMANS.

HE funeral was over. Time passed, and Grace, after having made to herself many warm personal friends within our little community, had returned home. Helen accompanied her, to remain another term at Madame Devine's seminary, and Sam was at his old post behind his father's counter.

It was now spring. The snow began to melt, the ice on the pond gave signs of a general " breaking up " of winter; so there were no more sleigh-rides, or skating frolics, or parties; and all declared the spring was coming in early.

Soon the woods and plains were laden with their usual floral wealth. The peach-blossoms, like generous emotions in a large heart, had burst into fragrance and beauty; the daffodils, peonies, and snow-balls were in full bloom. The bees were the first to make the discovery, and were hard at work improving the hours of sunshine, bearing home upon their well-laden thighs the rich treasures of these earliest heralds of approaching summer.

Mark was just as busy as they, preparing to leave home as soon as circumstances would permit; and every beat of his hcart, and every stroke of his hand, conspired to this one end.

His mother seconded his noble purpose, and from her own scanty means supplied him with several small bills, which would relieve him from immediate want should he fail in his expectations. The vague apprehension, the painfully anxious look, with which that purpose was first recognized, were now no more. Mrs. Miller was even cheerful in Mark's presence, as she sewed industriously, or assisted in those lighter out-door labours which would the sooner hasten his departure.

His scanty wardrobe was packed by his mother's careful hand in a little valise, which his good friend Deacon Sloper had given him; the promised letters, " sealed and signed," snugly tucked in one corner, wrapped carefully in a bundle of linen, for fear of their being crumpled, or soiled by the few cakes which comprised a part of his outfit. He had taken leave of that excellent man and his wife, who gave him their blessing and many friendly warnings, interspersed with kind advice, such as was most likely to encourage the young adventurer in the way of right-living and sin-shunning.

The pledge, long ago given, that his mother should be as one of their own household, was renewed with much earnestness, and all three wept when the parting moment came.

" The recollection that I left my mother with such good friends will be my chief source of happiness during my long absence, and the trials that may overtake me," were his last words to them. " God bless you, sir."

" God bless you."

" Very little could Mark say to comfort his mother; indeed," said dear aunt Bessie, tearfully, whom, for many evenings, I had not interrupted with questions, seeing they were prohibited, " we will say as little as possible about their leave-taking. They kissed many times, and wept and prayed together; and Mark, with his heart well nigh broken, started on his journey."

"I shall not be so far away but a letter, in case of sickness or any trouble, will bring me to your side at once. Be cheerful, mother, when I am gone; and my father's God protect us both until we meet again."

He was gone! gone out into the early daylight, which just began to cast its brightness in at the windows — gone out into the great world alone, with only his own feeble arm to battle with stern fate! Alone! God and he only!

Early inured to a life of toil and privation, educated to rely solely upon his own efforts as a passport to independence, his was the very nature to cope manfully with the foils of Fortune. That same Fortune had bequeathed to him a glorious dower — health, energy, and ambition, with all those higher faculties, honor, integrity, Christian virtue, and an intellect daily strengthened and enlarged.

If ever there was a nature free from the taint of selfishness and arrogance, — if ever one utterly void of that cold, calculating, worldly wisdom which robs the heart of all its generous impulses, and checks its nobler and holier aspirations,— it was Mark's; kind, sensitive, truthful, with a hand open to every distress, a heart full of kindness and charity to all.

As Mark was not ignorant of religion, he believed there was a Being above who cared for him, and who would direct his footsteps in whatever path it was best he should go; that He alone could bless this present undertaking, and he thought it worth while to ask that Being's blessing upon it; he knew it were vain to put forth his strength unless aided by Him to whom all power belongs, — that those "powers of acquisition and giving were direct mercies from Heaven."

Disappointments he might have, and did have, but they

were only such as nerved a brave and cheerful spirit to greater self-reliance and more heroic action. Of sorrow he had had his share, but not those deep sorrows of the heart which blast a man's ambition, and leave him helpless at the foot of the long, rugged hill over which his pathway lies. And though he did not lay claim to much knowledge in the school of experience, still he did not feel quite like the school-boy sallying forth, Primer in hand, to con over his first letter of the alphabet. The first page had been well learned, and the lesson had left its sad impress upon his young heart. A new leaf was now turned over, and Mark was elated that the chapter commenced so fair. God would dictate the conclusion, and he gave his life into His hands, as unto a wise Father, believing that all things would work together for his good.

The strong current which wafted him towards new objects did not carry him away from the early lessons of piety he had learned at his mother's knee. These were they that still softened those other stern life-lessons, and made them, if not pleasant, at least endurable tasks. She had taught him on whom to rely for strength when a dark hour came, and these early remembrances, he felt sure, would not be effaced by new thoughts and associations; and he prayed the God of his youth to be the God of his manhood.

To part with an only child for a length of time is indeed a trial for any mother; but to Mrs. Miller it came with more than ordinary bitterness. She thought not of her increasing cares; she thought only of the loneliness of each. She knew Mark would suffer as much alone in the great world outside, as she by her desolate hearth-stone. Alone at table, alone at the morning's worship, alone at the twilight hour, when he always came (his merry song heralding his approach) with a pleasant word to greet her ear, or an eager hand put forth to lighten her daily toil. Ah, she felt there were sorrows deeper than those of poverty or insult.

The thought of meeting, after a long separation, brought a painful throb with it. Would Mark be the same gentle, pure-minded being when the genial atmosphere of home no longer surrounded him? Would his face be the same? And his heart — now in her keeping — the same trusting, confiding heart, beating only for her? Would his sympathies, principles, tastes, and habits, which she trained and watched with such tender care and solicitude, be the same when he should be once more an inmate under his mother's roof? There was agony in the thought that time, which brings change to all, might bring change to him. And Heaven was besought with earnest importunity to spare and bless her child.

How beautiful, how sacred, is the tie that binds two lone hearts as one! Neither can enjoy or suffer apart; neither is united to aught on earth, save the one heart shrined within its own in the bonds of constant affection. Each sharing the same hopes, aspirations, intentions, dreams, and views of life; each, without reserve, pouring out his whole heart to, and having full faith in, the other.

And Mark was worthy of all this prodigality of love; intense as it was, it came not between a mother's heart and a Saviour's cross. She had but this one earthly tie. Strong as it was, it drew her not away from that Friend who loves with "a love far exceeding that of kindred." Since they had laid the clods above the heart of the one being who made her life an earthly paradise, his only was the love that made all these weary years peaceful and contented ones. Theirs had been no divided life; one current of affection ran through both hearts; an undissembling confidence knit both souls, and both had learned in the school of poverty that ready, tender-hearted sympathy for others which affliction generally teaches.

The mother stood pale and trembling where Mark had left her, striving in vain to stay the tide of painful thoughts

which rushed unbidden through her heart. Her face
was very white and calm, as she again knelt at the
Saviour's feet, and implored grace for herself and guidance for Mark. A voice whispered sweetly to her soul:
" Lean here, my child ; my arm is all poweiful, and will
uphold and shield both ; trust thy heart's treasure to my
care ; even as a father pitieth his children, so the Lord pitieth
them who fear his name."

Bending low, she pressed one kiss upon the place where
they had last knelt together, and in her heart arose an
earnest trust, attended by such peace as true faith alone can
give. Then she arose, and proceeded calmly, and even
cheerfully, with her work.

Time passed. It took days and weeks to accustom
herself to Mark's absence. She lived contentedly, worked
untiringly, and slept peacefully, but would often start
from some sweet dream, thinking Mark's dear voice
called to her, or his footstep sounded along the garden
path. She lived very much alone, as usual ; the cottage
was very quiet, the stillness almost oppressive, relieved
only by the busy shuttle, or the soft hum of the spindle.
Mrs. Sloper came every day to inquire after her, or take
her home with her to share their evening meal ; and Nettie would sometimes steal away at twilight to pass an
hour with her, which was a great happiness to both.
They were true, faithful friends, such as the widowed heart
could rely upon. Save these three, she had no confidential
friends ; but the rude walls became her confidants, the trees
and flowers her companions, her Bible and her unwavering
trust in Christ her greatest comfort.

*   *   *   *

The summer has waned, the flowers have breathed their
sweet lives away, and the autumn winds are scattering
their brown and withered leaves in every direction.
These things make the poor widow weep, for she re-

members how the winds of fate have scattered her dear
heart-treasures, and how the last remaining one is now
made the sport of the rough gale, which had shipwrecked
many as brave a heart as his. Sad thoughts would often
cross her mind, and even tears would sometimes well up
from their deep recesses in the heart; but there always
succeeded that calming, soothing confidence in the Lord's
protecting care, known only to those whom the Holy Spirit
has taught to trust Him.

10

CHAPTER XVII.

THE WANDERER PLAYS THE GOOD SAMARITAN.

" When forced to part from those we love,
    Though sure to meet to-morrow,
We yet a kind of anguish prove,
    And feel a touch of sorrow.
But O, what words can paint the fears
    When from those friends we sever,
Perhaps to part for months, for years, —
    Perhaps to part forever! "

                                    ANON.

ARK strode hastily through the village street, turning neither to the right nor left, until he came to an angle in the road, a little beyond which the view of his old home would be obstructed. Here he paused, and cast one long, lingering, loving look on that home, which, humble though it was, had been to him an ark of safety, where the dove of peace forever nestled. It was like severing his heart-strings for him to turn away from all he held dear, and seek new friends and new ties among strangers. But he felt that necessity required the undertaking, and so, summoning all the courage he was master of, he turned and walked rapidly away. No one was astir. The busy villagers still slumbered in silence, and but for their dogs' half-knowing bark, the early pilgrim might have passed on without a salutation. While ascending the long hill, — at the top of which, but away from the road, stood Mr. Strange's house, — Mark hoped to catch one glimpse of Nettie; and if so, he would climb upon the old stone fence at the stile, and wave an adieu. But she was there before him, watching eagerly for his coming. She hastened to meet him, and for several minutes neither spoke; but the audible emotion of each told how lasting would be the impressions of this hour.

"Nettie, I hardly hoped to meet you again. I am so glad you came!" And Nettie replied between her sobs, —

"I could not bear to have you go away without saying good by. Good by, Mark; and here is something I wish you to always keep to remember me by. It is my little Testament — the best little treasure I have in the world, but I will give it to you. And these violets, pressed between the leaves, will remind you of the place where they grew. I have just plucked them here by the stile. And here is another bunch for dear Miss Grace. They will wither, and be not as blue and fragrant as they are now; but I have nothing else to send. Tell her how very much I love her; and, Mark, when you are in the great city, where you will see and learn so much, don't let it make you proud, and heartless, and wicked; think of your dear mother and — me."

This last little monosyllable was uttered in a tone so low and tremulous as almost to escape the listener's ear; but he thought he heard it, or it might be but the echo of his own thought.

Poor Mark, he felt his heart had given the last great throb when he looked on the old roof-tree under the hill; but not so; it was still beating violently, and his lip trembled as he took the little brown hand held out to him.

"Nettie, I thank you for your kind, tender, loving counsel; and while it grieves me sore to part from you, it makes me, O, so happy to know that, when I am far away, you will think of me, and love me as a brother! You think it strange, perhaps, that I leave my home and my mother; but some time you will better understand the reason. Pray for me,

Nettie, that God will direct me aright; and whether my life be long or short, happy or sorrowful, I shall ever think of you as the one being, whom, next to my mother, I love best on earth."

They were both silent for a moment, and Mark had turned to go; then he came quietly back again, and stood by Nettie's side.

"You have your own troubles, Nettie; but you must be patient and cheerful, and bear up bravely under them, and you will grow strong to endure all things, and be a comfort to yourself and others. And now I must say good by to you. I intend to go as far as Edenton to-day, and that is thirty miles from here, and I may have to walk every step of it. Good by, and God bless you, Nettie."

He imprinted a soft kiss on her silent lips, and then turned suddenly away.

Nettie put out her hand, called him by name, murmured a faint farewell, and prayed the Lord to bless and protect him.

Mark was happier for having seen Nettie. From that hour there was a tenderness connected with the thought of her unknown before; a sympathy and solicitude always dwelt with her memory, framing itself into kindliest wishes for her happiness.

The old stone fence closed behind the light form of the young girl, while Mark walked on rapidly, as if every moment was precious.

He soon arrived at the narrow pass between the hills which fenced in the valley below; then, for some distance, they were steeper and harder to climb. But his step was firm and elastic, and at length their heights fell behind him, and a dense forest spread before him on either hand, with only a narrow opening sufficient for two waggons to pass. Before entering the forest, he turned to look his last upon the beautiful valley that still lay shrouded in the shadow of the mountain; but now that he was alone, not a muscle quivered as he gazed upon the loved spot. Nettie's tears, his mother's voice, and Jowler's impetuous whine followed hard after him; but, like "Pilgrim," he had set his face against his native city, and not all the luring sights or sounds should tempt him back.

His heart grew strong under the intense love which he bore to the home of his childhood, though circumstances had made it no longer a place for him to abide in.

"If I come again," said he, "I will come as a man, and no one shall be ashamed to take me by the hand, and call me friend."

A glow of manly pride and joyous exultation lighted up the face of Mark, and without another emotion, save an inaudible benediction upon his kind mother, he sped on his journey.

The last clearing was soon passed. A few scattered trees stood forth, like the advanced-guard of an army, and then Mark was alone in the deep forest. Although he had often traversed their dark recesses, and knew every withered tree and blackened stump by the road-side, yet he felt as if he was entering unknown solitudes. Here the wild-brier flourished in native luxuriance; the sassafras boughs interlocked with the thorn-apple and blackberry; the mandrake, the fern, and golden-rod disputed every foot of ground with their neighbours of still lesser pretensions; while the tall oaks and maples sheltered all, losing none of their grandeur and exceeding beauty by the contrast. The thick growth of the trees and unpruned shrubs shut out the sunshine, save that now and then a soft ray would gleam through an opening made by the felling of a tree or the lopping off of a bough. Mark was sometimes thoughtful and abstracted, and then he wished for no companion to break in upon his reveries. Gloomy as the place was, no look of dejection was on his face, and the elastic step with which he reached the end of the darkened road was in keeping with the swift flight of fancy's pinion, bearing his mind onward over the future.

As he emerged from the forest, the shadows grew less and less, the sun swept the dew from the grass that skirted the road-side, and every breath he inhaled was redolent with the sweets of spring. It gave him fresh courage, for now all is bright and cheerful; the damp and darkness that lay along his path at first are now far behind, and his young heart beats faster as he thinks it an earnest of his success.

That beautiful May day was delightfully serene; the blue skies bent low, as if to curtain in the green earth from the too glaring sunbeam; the well-trodden road was fringed with luxuriant green; golden butter-cups and dandelions — those prodigals of childhood's wealth — peep out from every fence-corner, nodding a graceful recognition, as the traveller passes their rural retreat. Well-tilled fields, covered with the dark, rich green of the young corn, and orchards in full bloom, are on either hand, while distant meadows and verdant pastures, where cattle are grazing the tender herbage, glowing in the bright morning sunshine, stretch far away to the blue sky beyond. Neat cottage farm-houses nestle cosily amid the flossy foliage, their latticed verandas overrun with the sweet-scented brier, honeysuckle, or morning-glories, while the flower-gardens, with their leafy labyrinths and variegated hues, are enough to set a stoic's soul aglow with sentiment and poetry.

Mark's eye noted all, as one scene after another rose to view and passed in quick succession. A love of the beautiful was as much a part of his nature as the pulse that told by its rapturous beatings

" How deep the feeling, when the eye looks forth
      On Nature in her loveliness."

He was not much given to dreams and musings. His had been a life too real for that. He had learned fact long

ere fancy became his interpreter. And all unconscious of
the spell this witching fairy was now throwing around him,
he gave loose rein to

> "hopes that beckon with delusive gleams,
> Till the eye dances in the void of dreams."

It was eleven hours nearer sunset than when he started on
his journey over the hills of his native county. It seemed
as if they were steeper and more difficult than formerly, and
that he was advancing wonderfully slow. Edenton was still
eight miles in the distance. He could hardly reach the village that night. He was very tired. His early breakfast,
for which he had no appetite, and light luncheon of cakes,
had but illy supplied the nourishment nature demanded, and
he was just thinking how acceptable would be a good supper, and wondering where he should get it. Inns were
"few and far between" in those days; but every roof sheltered hospitable hearts, and —

> "Every house was an inn, where all were welcomed and feasted."

A kind Providence, or good luck, as some would say, led
his footsteps in the right direction — to a place where he obtained food and rest, and a memory of things more to be
desired than even these.

Half a mile farther on he came to where the road forked,
and as the guide-board was down, he paused irresolute as to
which he should take. The one to the right seemed the
more travelled, but it led down into a ravine between two
hills, and the gap was narrow, and the shadow of the foliage
too deep for him to see beyond. The other was rocky and
uneven, and as far as the eye could reach, no house was to
be seen. Altogether it looked the more formidable of the
two, and Mark chose the right. The right one it proved to
be, for the other led to a small Quaker settlement four miles
distant, with scarcely a house between it and the place where
the bewildered traveller stood.

This was the first time Mark had lost his reckoning. Though the road over which he had walked was neither straight nor altogether familiar, yet until now he had known when to turn off and when to go ahead.

Now he had emerged into the great world, sure enough! That monstrous bugbear, which so many have slandered, abused, and feared, his good friend Deacon Sloper among the rest.   Thenceforth all would be new and strange — new faces, new customs, and strange varying scenes.   What though he should get lost occasionally? —

> " The world 's a wood in which all lose their way,
>   Though by a different path each goes astray."

What cared he that thousands had been there before him? It was a new world to him, and would, doubtless, use him quite as well as it had done.

Descending into the little glen, which, dark as it appeared to his dilated optics, proved to be the " golden gate " of his brightest hopes, it led the way to the goal his mental vision had long seen in the distance.   The " open, sesame " which folded back the glittering portal was almost as miraculous as though the " genii of the lamp " had spoken it.

At the foot of the glen Mark found a clear, sparkling stream, spanned by a rustic bridge, on which a man was leaning, waiting for some cows to drink.   They seemed quite indisposed to hurry themselves.   The day had been warm, the water is cool, and their sleek sides shrink and expand with every respiration of the cool air that sweeps down from the mountain, or silently steals up through the dark green depths of the shady glen.   The man halloed in a half-persuasive, half-authoritative tone to the cows; but they were loath to leave their invigorating half-bath, and were just beginning lazily to climb the opposite bank.

A lad of some ten or eleven summers was putting up some bars through which he had just led a pair of fine large horses in harness. The lines were thrown carelessly down, and while taking the last bar from the fence against which it leaned, an end struck one of the horses' heels, and in an instant the poor lad was lying insensible upon the ground. Mark sprang down the road, and was by his side in a moment; he saw with horror the lines coiled around the boy's foot, while the horses, darting forward, had plunged into the stream, where they would have dragged the still insensible youth, had not Mark's powerful grasp on the bit at that instant stayed their course. His strong arm held the refractory animals in check, while the father, pale and trembling, cut the reins and extricated his darling son.

"O, God! my boy is dead! my poor child! my son! my son! Help ho!"

"Let the horses go, young man, and lift me up; lift *him* up; raise his head; help, I say! don't you see he is bleeding? Great God! see the blood! it flows! Run! fly! fetch help!" And the distracted father drops his head on the bosom of his child, almost as lifeless as he.

Mark's less excitable nature better qualified him to judge the matter correctly. It was but the work of a moment to lead the panting horses back to the road-side and fasten them to the fence. He thought they might be needed. Then he hastened to bring water from the creek, to revive the lad, if living, and stanch the blood oozing from a frightful wound in the temple. The father required water quite as much, for the strong man had fainted.

Mark's hand was steady, his nerves firm, his touch light; and soon the man revived, started up with a strange, bewildered stare, fixed his gaze first on Mark, then on his son, and in a sad, plaintive tone, asked, "Is he really dead?"

"No, he is not dead, only stunned; and if you can assist me in dressing this ugly wound, I think he will soon revive."

A faint moan from the lips of the beautiful boy verified

Mark's assertion, and put new life and strength into the father's arm.

" Speak, Robert! speak to your father!"

" O, father!" he faintly murmured.

The gentleman — for such he really was — again addressed his son, calling him by name, and linking with it the most endearing epithets; but to all his questions and caresses he was answered by a lengthened groan.

The darkened circle around the eyes, quivering muscles, and unnatural respiration, all told of intense suffering. Mark remonstrated with the agitated father, warning him against excitement and its consequent evils. He raised the head gently, bidding the father sit quietly on the turf and support it, while he hastened to bring from his small stock of linen a shirt and some handkerchiefs. The former was quickly torn into bandages and scraped into lint, while the latter served for compresses, and to wash the wound ere they were applied.

" Raise him up a little more. Let his head rest against your shoulder carefully; there, that will do, sir."

A prolonged groan and the shrinking of the delicate nerves told of more acute pain, and they thought it a good omen, for now he could realize that he suffered. The dressing was soon accomplished, if not as skilfully it was as speedily, as though done by a more practised hand, and, so far as the staying of the precious life-current was concerned, answered just as well.

" You are a surgeon, sir, I perceive," was just on the lips of Mr. Newell, when he remarked the youthful appearance and toil-hardened hands of this young scion of the Æsculapian art, or one whom present circumstances had made such. Instead of this he said, —

" But for your timely aid, my young friend, — always my friend, whoever you are, — my poor boy would not have been saved. I am henceforth your debtor, and —"

"Spare your thanks, sir; at least for the present," replied Mark in as gruff a voice as he could assume; for he saw that the man's gratitude was nearly choking him.

"The next thing is to get him home."

"My house is just over the hill yonder. If you will oblige me further by driving the horses, I think I can carry my boy in my arms."

"Permit me to reverse your proposition, sir. I am stronger than you are in your present excited condition. I will carry your son, and I would advise you to ride forward and send for a doctor as speedily as possible."

Without a moment's delay, Mark raised the lad in his arms, and bore him gently to the house. The father galloped past him ere he gained the hill-top, and after answering Mark's inquiries relative to the direction he was to take, darted hastily forward, leaving Mark alone with his pallid and inanimate burden.

It was now nearly dark, and the road so thickly studded with trees and bushes that he could scarcely see a yard ahead; but he saw there were no turning-off places, and it would be difficult to lose the way. A few minutes' walk brought him into a smooth, open road, and presently he entered, as directed, a large, rustic-looking farm-gate. He wended his way up a broad, gravelled path, darkened by wide-spreading maples, their dense foliage forming an arch so sombre and solemn that, for the moment, a feeling of awe crept over him. He thought a still darker shadow might be brooding over the place whither he was bearing his precious load. Groans and heart-piercing cries saluted his ear before he reached the house, the bold outline of which was just visible through the mazy shades that surrounded it. He was met at the threshold by a frail, delicate-looking lady, three or four weeping children, and an aged granddame leaning upon a staff.

"O, my child!" groaned the mother, through her pale

lips, whose ashy whiteness was clearly visible in the deep-
ening twilight.

"Is he dead? O, Roby! speak if you are living."

Not the least murmur of response told that life remained;
and the poor, half-frantic mother, as she bent over her son,
gave one heart-piercing shriek, and was borne fainting from
the room. The children cried aloud, the aged grandmother's
weak limbs refused to support her trembling frame, and she
too sank into a chair, and sobbed piteously.

All was consternation and confusion; in fact Mark seemed
to be the only one with his senses left.

While he thus stood, wondering what was to be done with
the body (he himself feared the boy was already dead), a
door opened and there floated into the room a vision of
superior loveliness; and withal it seemed ethereal as it glided
silently past, without uttering a syllable or betraying the least
emotion.

Had Mark been superstitious, he might have thought —
and that, too, without tasking his imaginative powers too
severely — this beautiful being an angel sent from heaven
to bear back the spirit of little Robert from its earthly tabernacle. But Mark was not superstitious. Besides, the
silver-white wings were wanting; though the rustling of
celestial pinions could not be more noiseless than that airy
tread. It was an angel face, a form of exquisite beauty
and sylph-like grace, robed in pure white, with hair of a
pale golden hue, falling like a silken canopy over a neck of
ivory whiteness, and eyes full of heaven's own blue, raised
in meek submission to their native element, as if imploring
strength and firmness wherewith to meet the exigencies of
this trying hour. Such the vision, and such the thoughts of
Mark, as his eye unconsciously followed the fair form through
an opposite door whither it had vanished.

"Lay him here, sir," said the young girl, in a voice
sweet and tremulous, as if it took its music from her face.

" O, Roby! my angel brother! can it be that you are gone?"

Mark pressed his fingers on the pulse, discovered a faint fluttering of this index of life, and conveyed the joyful intelligence that the dear brother still lived, but that his life depended mainly on his being kept free from excitement.

Domestics began to crowd the apartment, evincing their grief by tears of sincere sorrow. Mrs. Newell had so far recovered from her swoon as to appear at the bedside, supported by her husband, her violent grief in no wise assuaged, as she looked upon her unconscious son, whose features were every moment assuming a more death-like appearance.

" Has a doctor been sent for?"

" Yes; but it is eight miles to a doctor, and I fear his coming will be too late."

" O, Lor, a' massy! Yes, I guess it's no use. He's done gone a'ready!"

Mark, with his sternest look, reproved the speaker, a stout, buxom colored woman, whom he afterwards knew as "Judy," or " Aunt Judy," as she was more familiarly called.

Addressing Mrs. Newell, he said, " Let all be as composed as possible until the doctor arrives. I entreat you, my dear madam, to be calm: your son is living, and much — everything — depends on his being kept perfectly quiet."

Mrs. Newell was prevailed upon to retire from the room, and in an undertone Mark reprimanded the thoughtless servant.

" Keep such thoughts to yourself. Don't you see they distress your mistress?"

" The Lord bress the dear chile! Yes, it's onthoughtful in me for to go to aggervate her; she's sickly, poor thing! and if Rob's dead, why, there'll be two funerals to 'tend — that's all."

While Mark was giving instructions to one, words of hope

and comfort to all, he was by no means an idle spectator of the scene.

He had laid the lad upon a divan of dark, rich velvet, removed a portion of his clothes, and in a low, calm tone, called for pillows, water, towels, and a fan, which the little " angel in white " hastened to bring. With light footsteps, and lighter touch, she assisted in administering the restoratives.

" Give us more air, if possible: the room is close," whispered Mark.

Mr. Newell sprang to the windows, raised them, and tore from their gilded fastenings curtains of exquisite texture, and creeping vines of rare beauty and full luxuriance, whose dark, green leaves, expanding and folded buds of glittering gold and purple, formed a tapestry of regal magnificence.

The trampled flowers, on which the evening dews are falling, breathe freely their sweet perfumes; the cool night-wind takes up their scattered fragrance, and wafts their invigorating, life-giving influence to the young sufferer's pallid features. The fluttering pulse is quickened, the eye-lids part, the lips move as if to speak; but a sharp, expressive moan tells of the intense pain which the effort costs.

" Keep very quiet," was Mark's constant admonition to the invalid, as consciousness slowly returned, and to the family, who, with hearts so full of sorrow, could not refrain from audible grief.

CHAPTER XVIII.

THE YOUNG STRANGER AT MR. NEWELL'S HOUSE.

"I love a devious path that winds askance,
And hate to keep one object still in view;
The flowers are fragrant that we find by chance;
And in both life and nature I would rather
Have those I meet than those I came to gather."

THE BRUNSWICK.

HE next two hours passed in restless anxiety and feverish expectation. Never had moments seemed so long to Effie Newell, never so replete with wretchedness. The uncertainty as to her brother's fate left an expression of deep sorrow upon her beautiful face; but her eyes were tearless, her hand quiet, her voice sweet and gentle, while endeavoring to alleviate the sufferings of her brother, or soothe her parents and the younger children, who were by no means as composed as the occasion required. She never left the bedside unless to fetch something needful to keep the almost exhausted life-powers in motion, or to convey to her poor distressed mother intelligence of every cheering symptom. She proved an efficient help to Mark; but of whom she inherited that distinguishing quality, presence of mind, was to him a mystery.

The invalid is lying very quiet, breathes more naturally, and is apparently asleep. Mark feels the need of food and rest, and for one moment turns away for fresh air. He is met at the door by the old negress, who, seeing him looking pale and weary, expresses surprise at his haggard appearance.

" Lor', sir, you looks a' most as white as de rest ob 'em. Is anything happened? "

" The symptoms are rather cheering than otherwise. I think the boy is asleep. But I am very tired. I have been travelling since daylight, and feel faint."

His head swam with a strange sensation, but the cool air revived him. A light step approached him. It was Mr. Newell's. Through the open window Mark's words had reached him, and he came hastily forward, put his arms around him as if to support him, and led him to a seat in the open air.

" Forgive our seeming thoughtlessness, my young friend. Our great sorrow has, I confess, nearly turned all our wits out of our heads. You have travelled far to-day, and perhaps have not supped."

" I have not, sir. I was just beginning to think I had walked about far enough for one day, and was looking for a house to stop at, when I came up with you."

" Thank God for sending you to me at that moment. And now I wish to know to whom I owe a debt of gratitude, such as I can never repay."

" My name is Mark Miller, sir. But speak not of gratitude : my assistance was purely accidental ; besides, I have done no more than you or any other man would have done in the circumstances."

" Very few *could* have done what you did, had their will been ever so good. I am very nervous and excitable, and my thinking faculties seemed nearly paralyzed. You would have been most welcome in any circumstances, but now doubly so ; and I hope you will make my house your home until your departure is a thing of necessity."

" Here's a glass of wine for you, Massa Miller. Take it. It's mighty good for anybody what's faint like."

" Thank you, Aunt Judy ; but I never drink wine. I will take a glass of water instead. A little on my face and hands will be quite as acceptable."

Judy filled a large tin wash-basin at the pump; and while Mark was performing his ablutions, Mr. Newell said, —

" Now make haste, Judy, and get the young gentleman some supper. A cup of good tea, and rest are what he needs most."

" O, Judy's ears ain't stuffed wid cotton ! She knowed that long afore any of yer, and it's all a-smokin' on de table ! "

Mr. Newell led the way to a small breakfast-parlour, in the centre of which stood a round table, laid with exquisite taste and neatness. After seating Mark, he excused himself, and withdrew. A small silver tea-service stood on a salver of the same material, glistening in the soft rays of an astral lamp, which stood in the centre. From the urn's spout gurgled the steaming, amber-coloured beverage, its savoury odour sending forth a soothing, revivifying influence ere it was sipped. Before him was a nice veal cutlet, fried in golden batter ; an omelet done just to his taste ; a little pyramid of mashed potatoes, browned crisp on the top; golden butter, and soft, white bread, just like his mother's. Then there were sweetmeats smothered in rich cream, and other delicacies, which Mark declined to partake of, although Judy insisted they would not hurt him after his long walk. But Mark was quite satisfied with the more substantial part of the edibles, and before he left the table was much refreshed.

" I can't imagine," said Judy, in a low tone, half soliloquy and half inquiry, " what possessed that hoss to up and kick poor Bob ! He was never knowed to do sech a thing afore ! Which hoss was it, I wonder?"

" I believe it was the sorrel horse," answered Mark, although he did not feel himself particularly addressed, or called upon for a reply.

" Yes, it was ' Fairy,' just as I 'spected ; she's alers frisky. But I never knowed her to cut up any shine like this ere one. Poor, dear Bob ! so gentle and so good ; just like Miss Effie

and Master Hal. Dem's alers good, but dese oder young
uns is a heap wus'n the wust I ever seed; though I shouldn't
say it, p'raps, seein' you are strange, and 'ud never a' knowed
it, if it warn't that you was told. But that boy Bob is just
the smartest, gentlest creatur eber did live; he's got more
larnin', too, than many a grown-up man I've seed; and now
if he dies, — and I'm sure he will, — secin' it's him, it'll jest
kill poor Missus Newell — no mistake!"

"Mrs. Newell seems in quite ill health," observed Mark,
who noticed Aunt Judy's inclination to be somewhat talka-
tive.

"Yes, poor dear chile, she's been onhealthy dis two or
three year. We used to live in New York; but the doctors
ordered her into the country, where she could get whole-
somer air, and clar cow's milk to drink; and so we come
here. Ah, me! little we thought we was a-bringin' that
blessed chile here to be kicked by a hoss! But la's a' me!
your tea is clean out, and I never noticed it! Take another
cup."

"No more, I thank you."

"Do. I alers manage so's to have the last cup the best."

"The first and last were both excellent; you must excuse
me from taking a third. I had a slight headache, but your
good tea has completely cured it."

"I'm glad of it. But hark! I hear the doctor's hoofs
a-comin' up the road. I tell you he makes that hoss of his'n
spin, when there's a mergency!"

Mark resumed his watch by the bedside, and in about ten
minutes the doctor entered. All stood silently regarding
him, as if life or death hung upon his lips. A moment
longer, and they would know whether their darling would
live or die. Every eye was fixed on the doctor, expecting to
read in his countenance the realization of their hopes or
fears. He asked several questions in a low tone, passed his
hands rapidly over the several limbs, found no fractures or

sprains, and no wound, except the one which Mark had so successfully dressed. "That is an ugly wound," said he, taking from a small case of instruments a silver probe, with which he proceeded to examine it. Suppressed groans ran through the room at sight of the instruments, and the doctor advised all to retire except Mark, who, he said, might be of some assistance.

After the lapse of half an hour the doctor joined the family, assuring them there was nothing more serious than a slight concussion of the brain, and some contusions about the body, which were not of sufficient importance to cause any alarm.

A cry of joy burst from all hearts. "Then he will be saved! My boy will live!" exclaimed Mr. Newell, grasping the doctor's hand with much warmth, while Mrs. Newell wept her thanks upon her husband's breast.

Effie sat silent for several minutes, as if struggling with powerful feelings; then she arose and left the apartment. Buried in the dark solitude of her own room, she breathed forth, in broken accents of gratitude, a deep and fervent prayer, asking of God strength and submission to whatever His will might be, and thanking Him for His great mercy. Nor need we wonder if, while she thus prayed the Lord to raise up one on whom He had laid His chastening hand, another's name was mingled with that of her brother. In sweet, low tones, modulated by new thoughts, she craved a blessing for the young stranger to whom she felt they were, in part, indebted for that brother's life.

The doctor gave hopes of a speedy convalescence, but said he would watch with Robert until morning. Mark was urged to retire; but to every entreaty he uttered a gentle remonstrance, until he saw the patient was again sleeping quietly, and apparently free from pain. It was now twelve o'clock, and Mr. Newell insisted that he should retire. He no longer hesitated, for he remembered the long journey before him, and felt the need of rest. Mrs. Newell held out her thin hand to him, and the tearful tributes of gratitude that bathed her white cheeks told more than words how heart-felt and lasting that gratitude would be. Effie pressed his hard, brown hand in both of her little, soft, white ones, and looked so unutterably gracious, and said, " Good night, sir," in such sweet, musical tones, that Mark's face assumed a half-mortified, half-vexed expression to find himself an object of such favour for doing an act of common humanity, and one which he would have had to run a long way around to avoid. He noticed, too, that the doctor eyed him closely as he left the room, but did not wait to hear if he had anything to say.

He followed Mr. Newell up the broad staircase, glad to escape a scene which left its burning influence on his cheek, to say nothing of the terrible cataract of emotions over- whelming his heart. The room into which the too indulgent host inducted his young guest was large, airy, and furnished with simple elegance. Mark cast a quick glance around him ; but that glance was sufficient to reveal to his bewil- dered senses the many beautiful articles with which the room was adorned. If he could have had his choice, he would have preferred a much plainer room. He felt awkward and constrained, but knew not whether it was good manners to express his reluctance to occupy one so magnificent. It was not in Mark to asssume an easy, careless air, as if not at all surprised with these many evidences of wealth and refine- ment, or to accept them as though accustomed to their use. Perhaps Mr. Newell noticed his embarrassment ; for he said, with much kindness, while his arms were locked around Mark in a fatherly embrace, —

" My dear sir, there is in my heart a gratitude to you that words cannot express ; rest you here to-night, and to- morrow I would know more of you. I hope you will rest well. Do not rise early ; take a good long sleep in the morning. You look fatigued and feverish; but I hope the care and anxiety which you have imposed upon yourself, or rather which we have imposed on you, will result in nothing that will survive a night's repose."

The kind, familiar tone in which this was uttered seemed to invite Mark's confidence, and had the effect of overruling his scruples about making known his wish to occupy a plainer room. "One more home-like," said he, smiling, "and a bed where I can toss about at will."

Mr. Newell's bland features grew serious, if not stern; and fixing his eye steadfastly on Mark, while he still held him by the arm, he said, —

"Mark Miller, I have no second-best room to offer to the preserver of my boy. This, our guest-chamber, is the room you will occupy to-night. Please make yourself at home in it, and when I come here to pass a twilight hour alone, as I sometimes do, it will be pleasant for me to remember that you have slept in it. The memory of this night is for a life-time, and I would not add to its painful reminiscences the thought of having treated my benefactor with less attention than becomes a gentleman and a host, or with less courtesy than the time and circumstances demand."

And Mr. Newell felt what he said. In that hour, when it seemed impossible that a greater affliction than the loss of his son could befall him, when he was convinced that the event he adverted to would have surely taken place but for the manly arm that saved him from mutilation or death, when despair and grief were exchanged for rapturous thanksgivings, could he do less, or feel less, than he expressed?

After Mr. Newell's withdrawal, Mark's eye roved involuntarily around the spacious apartment. All sense of weariness, or desire for sleep, had vanished. Rich lace curtains draped the windows, their soft azure folds contrasting beautifully with the dark-green background of creeping vines overshadowing them, and the leaves of the silver poplars and acacias whispering dreamily outside. Two or three portraits adorned the walls, and on one side was a bookcase filled with a choice selection of books. Some were lying on the table on which his lamp was set. His hand involuntarily opened at random the one nearest him, and from the page on which his eye first rested he read, —

" To seek a competency of this world's goods is not only wise, but the duty of every one who has the ability to think, or the strength to labour; but this hasting to be rich, this feverish impatience after great wealth, may be counted as one of the saddest sins on earth, and over which angels weep. For the yellow dust men will forsake the dear delights of home, leave swelling hearts behind them, brave the scorching plains or the foaming main, sacrifice health, happiness, honour, hope! Yes, even a hope of heaven! And yet upon what a frail thread hangs the rich man's possessions! They may in a day, in an hour, be swept from him, or he be taken away from them, and a grave, far away from the loved ones who would strew flowers thereon, be all that is allotted him. Dives was not richer than Lazarus on the day of his death, and certainly his fame was the less enviable. How hardly shall they that have riches enter into the kingdom of heaven! The prayer of Agur contains the greatest aspiration of a noble mind, and one that will wing the priceless soul to realms of light and life."

He closed the book, asking himself, " What am I here for? Why have I left home, and ' swelling hearts behind,' to brave an untried world, to ' sacrifice, perhaps, health, happiness, honour '? No, not honour, nor hope. These are my inheritance, my capital.

The world shut out, his heart turned to the only one in whom, next to God, was his soul's rest and comfort, his best of earthly things. He thought of Nettie, too, and her last words. Her sweet, sad face was haunting his memory, and the wild dream-angel lingered long at his side, this night, loath to depart. Before retiring, he knelt reverently, while faith and hope awoke with renewed strength within his heart. Sleep, that most welcome friend to the weary, was never more welcome to Mark. Morning found him refreshed, and able to resume his journey with light steps and buoyant spirits.

CHAPTER XIX.

MARK PROLONGS HIS STAY.

"Men will praise thee when thou doest well to thyself."
                                        BIBLE.

THE morning was beautifully calm and still, the rising sun touching with rosy tints the tops of the far-away hills, and gilding the leaves that were yet sleeping beneath Mark's window. His was a confused waking. He saw, instead of the bare rafters in the old home attic, a large, handsome room, and wondered if he was still dreaming. By degrees it all came to him, and he sprang out of bed, thinking of the beautiful boy below, and wondering if he was living or dead. He gazed one moment through the clustering foliage that draped his window's lattice, out into the broad fields of brightening verdure, ere he descended the stairs. Nature had a clean face that morning, and seemed clothed in the vesture of eternal spring. A slight shower had fallen during the night, and the little drops hung like silver on the freshened foliage. The air was redolent with a thousand sweets, exhaled from wreathing vines and flowering shrubs, and balmy incense rising from the earth. The place was beautiful, and Mark strained his wondering eye to take in the whole at a glance. It seemed to him that no fairer scene could be drawn by Nature's pencil. He crept softly along the great hall, listening for the faintest sound from the sick room. None came, not even a murmur, to tell there were living occupants within. With nervous hand he slowly turned the door-knob, and walked in. The lad still breathed. Thank God! his suspicions were groundless. Mr. Newell sat dozing in an arm-chair by the sleeping invalid. Effie reclined on a sofa by his side. She started up on seeing Mark, and inquired, with tender solicitude, how he had slept. Mark's great anxiety was somewhat relieved when told how well " dear little brother" had rested, and by observing how naturally and sweetly he was sleeping.

"The danger is past, I hope. I think he will know us when he wakes."

"I trust as much," answered Mark; "though it may be several days before he is restored to perfect consciousness."

While he was speaking, a door opened, and Mrs. Newell came towards the couch. She took Mark's hand, giving him a very warm and tender greeting. They sat by the bedside a few moments, then glided out as noiseless as they came, leaving Effie to her tireless vigil, and Mr. Newell to his unbroken slumber. A complete stillness and something like an oppressive silence reigned in and around the house; objects animate and inanimate seemed to partake of the general gloom. Every voice was hushed to a whisper, the morning occupations incident to farm-life being performed in almost unbroken silence. Mark stood upon the broad piazza, surveying the scene before him, which was one of surpassing loveliness. Away to the east rose a range of low, billowy hills, the white fog still lingering around their summits; but between the hills, and over the sweet, luxuriant meadows and newly-ploughed fields, the broad sunshine had spread a " golden fleece."

At the left of the house was a magnificent flower-garden, filling the soft air with the sweet odours exhaled from a thousand swelling buds and bright blossoms just bursting into new life and beauty. At the right, " winding at its own sweet will," and separating two broad fields of pasture-land, ran the streamlet which he had crossed the night before, fertilizing and refreshing with its clear waters the tranquil landscape through which it flowed. A rustic bridge, spanning the flowing creek higher up, united these fields of dazzling green, affording a safe passage to the kine then crossing. The house was a large, gothic cottage, with tall chimneys, high-arched windows, and wide piazzas, "flower-crowned." It stood amidst a grove of symmetrical native and ornamental trees. The oak, the elm, the maple, and the beautiful horse-chestnut cast their cooling shadows upon the ground, while the ailantus, acacia, mountain-ash, arbor-vitæ, and other evergreens and flowering shrubs, filled up the interstices, making a scene of unrivalled beauty, though with less pretensions to art than nature. Here were the beauties of art and nature combined, each enhancing the grace and loveliness of the other. It seemed to Mark the fairest spot in all the earth. And yet his heart felt that it owed allegiance to his own dear native hills, and that he was not so soon to be bribed into forgetting them.

Anxious to resume his journey at the earliest possible hour, he informed Judy that such was his intention, though very much against his inclinations. Judy pleaded hard for "young master" to stay until he should learn the fate of "poor Bob." She hastened to spread the cloth, and ere many minutes elapsed, Mr. and Mrs. Newell and Dr. Mason entered, and they all sat down to breakfast. There still lingered traces of anxiety on the countenance of each. The doctor spoke encouragingly, but admitted only the possibility of a serious and protracted unconsciousness. "I must return to town this morning," added he, "and will again spend the night with you. In the mean time I will leave such instructions as are necessary; but the most depends upon his being kept quiet and free from excitement, should he awake."

"And is it absolutely necessary for our young friend to

take his departure also?" said Mr. Newell, fixing his fatherly eye upon Maık. "We would like you to remain with us, if at all practicable."

"I had thought of proceeding on my way, but my business is not urgent," replied Mark, promptly; "and if I can be of any assistance, I will remain with pleasure."

Expressions of gratitude and glad surprise passed from lip to lip, until all had said — even the faithful Judy — how pleased they would be could he remain.

"My conscience would not permit me to decline an invitation so hospitably given, even were my stay of less importance. I have had a good night's rest; and if the doctor will give me his instructions, I can relieve you all from present attendance at the bedside of Robert, and so you can take the rest you so much need."

"Excellent young man that you is!" exclaimed Judy, with a look and tone that were meant to be expressive.

"Many thanks!" said Mr. Newell. "It is not altogether your services that we are anxious about; though perhaps you will pardon a little selfishness on our part, if we seem more importunate than consistent."

"Rather let me thank you, sir, for the honour you confer upon me, a stranger, in thus admitting me to your hospitality and your confidence."

"All in good time, young man, when I merit or desire them. For the present, you owe me no thanks."

The doctor had gone, and Mark was the lone watcher at the invalid's couch. "Poor boy!" he said, compassionately; "if he should live only to be a helpless imbecile the rest of his life, how sad! how terrible! Better that his young life end here. God's will be done." He lifted his heart in silent prayer to that Being who holds the universe and the life of the smallest insect in His hand. "If it be Thy will," prayed he, "restore this child to his parents, ' clothed in his right mind.'"

It was a little past noon when the faithful negress came to
relieve Mark of his tireless and not unpleasant watch.   He
felt he was doing good, and that brought happiness with it;
besides. it gave him time to think.   Judy " knowed he was
clar wore out 'fore this time, but she'd a heap o' things to do
'fore she could come.   There was a nice lunch for Massa
Mark in the dining-room : then he must take rest, and Judy
would stay with poor Bob."

While Mark deliberated whether to yield to the persuasive
eloquence of Judy, or remonstrate against her authority, the
door opened cautiously, and Mr. Newell entered.   He found
Robert as he had left him — still unconscious, though apparently free from pain.

" No, Judy'll stay with poor little Massa Bob ; jes' you
two go 'long and take some rest: you'll be wanted for to-
night," was that faithful serving-woman's remonstrance when
urged to retire.

After luncheon, Mr. Newell invited Mark to a cool seat
under one of the great horse-chestnuts, then in full bloom.
This quiet spot was a favourite retreat with all the family.
Here, when the labours of the day were done, and the setting
sun cast his golden beams upon the soft greensward, when
all nature seemed to partake of the peace and happiness
reigning in their own hearts, they would assemble to while
away the twilight hours.   Here the two conversed on subjects
familiar to each, talked gravely of farming and stock-raising, haying and harvesting, the capabilities of the soil, — if
sandy or loamy be better adapted to the culture of turnips,
and whether mangel-wurtzel, or ruta-baga, or sugar-beet be
best for sheep and cows.   Having exhausted the various topics
relative to farming and fencing, ditching and draining, cropping and stock-raising, — in all of which Mark proved himself the greater adept of the two, — Mr. Newell questioned
him relative to his journey.   He drew from him a clear
statement of all he wished to know concerning his home,

his early life, his aims and aspirations, his plans of operation when in the city whither his footsteps were tending when arrested by the scenes in which Mr. Newell's family played so conspicuous a part.   Had Mark been gifted with the eloquence of a Demosthenes, he could not have found a more attentive auditor.   Mr. Newell was a " self-made " man, and had — like thousands of our noble American gentlemen — risen by his own merits to the honourable position he then occupied.   Remembering his own early aspirations and discouragements, his heart ever warmed with sympathy towards young men who sought to rise above obscurity, — who felt within themselves the power and will to do and dare, to brave all obstacles to their success.   This good man smiled approvingly to the truthful earnestness of Mark's concluding words.

" I hardly hope to have all my golden boy-dreams realized. I should be disappointed were I to find ' smooth sailing.' I expect to ' row against the tide ; ' but a long pull and a strong pull tests the strength of the oarsman's arm, and ' reverses give force and boldness to a man's character.' I have only moderate abilities, and no extra amount of talent or shrewdness ; but for all that, I have set my heart on becoming a man of bril—— ordinary attainments."

Mark must be pardoned a little egotism : he spoke what he thought, and spoke truth.   His friend felt the same, and finished the word Mark had begun.

The interview lasted for an hour or more ; and at its conclusion Mr. Newell had thrown himself completely into Mark's affairs, becoming intensely interested in them.

A few hours elapsed, and Robert awoke from the sweet natural sleep that had lasted several hours.   His eyes opened with a dreamy, half-conscious expression in them, then turned, with a slow, rational look, towards his father.   A smile passed over his pallid face, and all wept with joy, but silently, well knowing that the recovery of the little patient depended on his mind being kept perfectly at ease, and the injured brain in absolute repose.

A month passed, and Mark was still at the farm. Mr. Newell had said, " If you could help me a little with my tardy spring's work, without interfering seriously with your plans, you would greatly oblige me, and perhaps I can be of some use in helping you to perfect them. It will be necessary for me to be in New York in June, and I have ideas of my own, which, if carried out, will perhaps somewhat modify yours. *I wish you would stay*." So Mark tarried; and under his supervision the work progressed rapidly. And they went to New York together.

CHAPTER XX.

WHAT IS PASSING AT SORRELTOWN MEANWHILE.

"Troubles are often the tools by which God fashions us for better things."   BEECHER.

 YEAR has not made many changes in the little society of Sorreltown. Sam Maynard has been duly installed as junior partner in the firm henceforth to be called " Maynard and Son; " Helen has graduated with becoming honours, and sustains the dignity of the sect " fine ladies ; " and Mrs. Strange is confined to her bed with a lingering, hopeless disease. Nettie's home grows darker and more cheerless, and the neighbours pity her unhappy condition. Unloved, alone, with none to cheer and strengthen her, what young heart could beat with life and hope amid such scenes? And yet Nettie's never faltered, so far as she was concerned. It was only when she saw her mother's step grow weaker, her voice feebler, and the cough more alarming, that her courage failed. The same kind heart and noble soul are hers: time and sorrow have no power on these, save to exalt and chasten, to purify and gather strength, as the years roll away. Aside from the household duties, now devolving entirely upon her, Nettie is her mother's only nurse. Her hand administers to her wants, her pillow is smoothed by the faithful child, who is now, as ever, the joy and consolation of her mother's life. She strives to bring sweetness out of the bitter ; for it is wormwood to see her mother sinking rapidly into a decline.

Mrs. Miller is cheerful, and even happy. The weekly mail always brings a letter from Mark, and her friends the Slopers are friends in the true sense of the word. " Mark is growing so tall and stout you would hardly know him," wrote Grace; " but he cares for nothing but business and your dear letters. He is still an inmate of our family; but all day long, and until after dark, he is engaged in writing letters and posting ledgers; but his heart is light, and his face wears its wonted cheerfulness; and when evening comes, we all watch anxiously for his well-known footstep hurrying along the walk, and as he bounds up the steps, my little cousins are always at the door, to greet him with shout and song and smiles of glad welcome. It is to us all the happiest hour of the day." The tears in the mother's eyes told better than words how happy these letters made her.

* * * *

Spring once more puts on its glorious bloom, and " the warm sun, that brings seed-time and harvest, returns again." All are busy with their gardens, or making improvements within doors. Nettie often glances about the rough-looking apartments, — affording such a striking contrast to the neat cottage of Mrs. Miller, — at the stained walls, dusty furniture, and smeared, curtainless windows, wondering if she cannot, without giving much offence, suggest some improvements. " O, mother," said she, one day, " I am going to be so smart this week! I am going to wash all the windows, and if we could get some lime, I think I could whiten the walls."

" They need it bad enough, goodness knows; but I believe we might wade in dirt up to our knees before *he* would lift a hand to help us. I don't know whether them winders could be taken out or not: they never have been since the house was built."

" O, yes, they can; see how loose this one is! We can pry off the casing on one side, and it will almost fall out. If father would only help me a little! and I think he will if we ask him." She found it no very difficult task, after getting her father interested; and so before Saturday night came around, the old house had quite the appearance of thrift and cleanliness. The ice once broken, and meeting with no violent opposition, Nettie resolves on further improvements. The stubble, over-grown weeds, and noxious hop-vine are rooted out, and small trees, flowers, shrubs, and vines planted in their stead. Her father seems to have awakened from his dreamy, lethargic existence, and occasionally stoops to lend her a helping hand when she is performing some task which requires her utmost strength. She always has such a sweet, pleasant smile to repay his kindness, that he goes away thinking he will help her more when he has time. His fields and fences are looking better this spring than they have for years.

Mrs. Strange often speaks of Nettie with more affection than she had ever been known to speak of any one, confessing that she is " a great blessing to her." There is less fault-finding, and the dear child works with more heart. Her mother's eye never wearies in watching her movements, now and then a smile of approval lighting up her pale face. She is afraid Nettie will kill herself with hard work; she reproves the younger children for making her so much trouble, and once she actually chastised Benny for crumbling his bread over the floor just after Nettie had swept. Nettie never wearies of weeding, and watering, and training her flowers, or of putting things to rights in-doors, flying about from room to room, with broom and duster, until the whole presents an aspect so changed that it has become one of the seven wonders of the village. " It is singular, too," they say, " how Nettie has improved."

* * * *

Another year has passed. Another form has been borne away from the cheerless old house. There is another new-made grave in the church yard on the hill-side. Nettie

12

misses her mother sadly, and weeps tears of heart-felt sorrow; but she is comforted when she thinks of the change
the last year·has wrought. She feels that her mother did
not cross the dark Jordan alone.

Nettie is still the same patient, industrious Nettie of old,
not handsome, when compared with some others, but a
truthful, loving soul, with one absorbing passion to stimulate her, — the happiness of her household, the well-being
of her brothers and sisters, whom she loves with a pure and
holy devotion; and they are paying it in their way, for they
are generally obedient to her wishes and pleasant to one
another. They live in the same old brown house, but it is a
far less unsightly place than formerly. Indeed, it is looking
beautiful now in the pleasant summer time, when the grass
is green and the flowers in full blossom. Nettie only wishes
Mark and Grace could see it. Ah, if they did but know how
hard she toiled, day and night, their hearts would ache. Mr.
Strange has once more become a well-to-do farmer, — a
sober, industrious man. When the health of his wife failed,
and he saw her passing away from his sight, he seemed to
awaken from his old life of slothfulness and dissipation, and
from that time to the present was all that a loving husband,
a devoted father, could be. He is now redeeming the wasted
years, laboring harder, if possible, than in his younger days.

Nettie has become accustomed to rely upon her own judgment in matters of economy and expenditure, her father
seeming to have more confidence in her than in himself. At
first she shrank from this self-reliance, and longed for some
strong arm to lean upon — some mature judgment to counsel, some pleasant voice to say, " Well done." Every day
saw her more necessary to her family: the little ones were
growing; and this fact impressed her deeply with her ineffi-
ciency and inexperience. Did they not, as Grace had said,
teach her patience and the need of a gentle voice and cheerful manner?

She would often say, " Soon my brothers and sisters will be too large for me to control : God help me to exert a good influence while I may, — to think of them and my father *only*, when all beyond seems so dark that the shadows frighten me." And then she would pray for light to walk by, and would leave her all in the hands of Him who could brighten or darken her pathway, as He saw was for her good.

Little time as there was for romancing, there were awakening in the bosom of Nettie new and happy thoughts, which even the stern duties of life did not help to banish. Those duties were performed cheerfully, and with no thought that they were praiseworthy, or that others would esteem her the more for them. She would sometimes dream of Mark and Miss Pearson, far away in the great city, and of " dear mother " and " little Janie," sleeping over the hill yonder in " God's acre," when her father's voice left her morning's dream unfinished, or the children's noise broke in upon some charming reverie. She would often compare Mark's busy, active life in the great city, doing good and getting good, with her own insignificant sphere and daily tread-mill existence. *He* would accomplish something ; but *her* hopes, *her* plans, *her* prospects, what were they ? Futile, worthless, nothingness. And yet hers was an ever-active life, — busy, busier, busiest, every day, and all the time. Little as she thought it, hers was a brave spirit ; though there were times when the worn-out physical nature sunk under an accumulation of care such as might discourage one twice her age. She sometimes longed for a different home, — a different life, — with some little pleasure in it, and not all duty ; but her dead mother's last appeal, — her dying injunction, — that she would " be as a mother to the children," these little ones dependent on her, and her father's lonely life, always reproved her for such thoughts. And so she toiled on, and dreamed on ; but the dear ideal of what she would like to have, and what she would like to be, seemed too far beyond her powers of accomplishment. The spirit was indeed strong; but the strength to do was weak, — O, how weak!

One day in the sweet spring-time, when the gardening was nearly done, and the old house had gone through a thorough process of renovating, and Nettie had just seated herself on the " new porch," to take a long breath, she was surprised to see the mail-coach come up the road and stop at their place. It was so unusual a thing that it quite upset Nettie's equanimity, and put her heart in the least little bit of a flutter. She sped down to the gate, hoping, fearing, she knew not what. She thought only of Grace and Mark. But the coach was empty; and but for the pleased, half-laughing expression on the driver's face, she would have foreboded evil tidings. There could be nothing serious lurking behind that jolly, good-natured face, she was quite sure. So after the usual salutations were gone through with, the man said, —

" I've got something for you, Miss Nettie, — brought it all the way from Albany. It's mighty heavy; but if you will lend a hand a bit, so I can shoulder it, I can manage the rest."

" It surely is not for me : there must be some mistake," answered Nettie, as the man was about shouldering a box of large dimensions, nearly filling the whole boot of the stage.

" No mistake at all. Just read thim letters on the kiver, and then tell me if you're not the young lady it manes."

There it was — the great box — marked, " Miss Nettie Strange, Sorrel Hill, N. Y.," in bold, legible letters, not to be misunderstood.

" What can it mean?" murmured Nettie, following the garrulous Irishman, as he staggered under the weight of his great burden.

" No, indade, bless your dear heart! there's niver a cent to pay on it, either. Asy, now; for don't ye see it says, ' To be handled with care'? There it is, now, fernenst the piazza; and you must just sign this resate, as tells how I delivered it ' right side up with care.' "

With a trembling hand Nettie wrote her name at the bottom of the paper, and for the first time in her life felt that she was of some little consequence. For the first time in her life she felt her womanhood; and we can pardon her if she assumed a little air of importance. Was not that great box with its contents hers? Had she not signed a paper to that effect? And had she not been addressed as Miss Strange?

" You will surely accept something for your trouble. I will bring you a cake and a bowl of cool milk: they will refresh you. The day has been warm for this time of the year."

" Yes; and my horses are tired and thirsty, and I must hurry on. I have no doot your cakes are very nice: I hear you are a famous housekaper; and by the looks o' things hereaboots, some deevil o' a fairy must have been at woork on the ould place. I tell you, little lady, you are a posy, and I hear the folks a-talkin' of how nate and smart you're gettin'."

The least perceptible blush of pride dyed Nettie's cheeks, for she was now a little bit proud of her home. Only there were so few who ever came to see and admire it, that this man's words made her happier, and her heart lighter than it had ever been before.

" Please accept my, thanks for bringing the box. It must have been a great trouble, — so large, and coming so far. From Albany, did you say? "

" Yes, to be sure; but indade you owe me no thanks. I am paid for it; and if you have iver any errands or missages to sind, you have only joost to let me know."

" Thank you. I will remember your kindness."

" Och! I had like to forgot one thing. Here is a letter

for ye's, that will tell you what's inside the box, and who it's from.   God bless you! for you are a good child."

The man was gone; and there stood Nettie, bewildered, not knowing exactly what to do next.   She brushed away the tears she was unconsciously shedding, when her little sister exclaimed, —

" See, they are dropping on the letter ! "

" Let the box contain what it may," she whispered, half audibly, " this is from *her*.   I had rather lose all the box contains than *this!*"   She clasped it closely to her heart, and rained kisses upon it; while her father was summoned from the field to break the seal : she had not the courage to take such a responsibility upon herself.

I laughed heartily in concert with " aunt Bessie," when she said this; and for the first time since the peremptory silence had been enjoined, I was permitted to ask questions and make comments.

" What was in the box, auntie? "

" All in good time, my dear."

" I would not have been five minutes in opening the box. The letter I could read afterwards."

" Yes; but you forget that it was Nettie's *first letter*, and that is quite a pleasant thing to remember by those whose lives have been far more eventful than was this little country maiden's.   To her a simple event — like the receiving of a letter — was a matter of some importance."

" The box! the box!" exclaimed I.   " Leave Nettie and her father to spell out the contents of the letter, and tell me all the contents of that mysterious parcel.   Gay dresses and beautiful presents, bought in the city for Nettie and the children!   I have thought, many a time, how delighted *I* should be, could I be the recipient of such treasures.   To sit on the carpet, unfolding parcel after parcel, and be surprised with things new, and beautiful, and strange, such as

I never saw before! I almost envy Nettie the pleasure of opening the box; but then she had so few pleasures, poor thing!"

"Gay dresses and beautiful things would hardly be in keeping with a humble home like hers; and her friend would have displayed little taste, and less judgment, had she sent such. There were only useful articles; but we ought always to combine the beautiful and the useful: besides, I would rather be the giver than the receiver. Which, think you, was the happier, Grace or Nettie?"

"It is hard to decide."

"Have a little patience, my dear: we will do as Nettie did, — read Grace's letter first."

CHAPTER XXI.

LETTERS AND PRESENTS.

" Slowly folding, how she lingered
　　O'er the words his hand had traced,
　　Though the plashing drops had fallen,
　　And the faint lines half effaced!"

　　　　　　　　　　　　Mrs. Neal.

Y dear Friend Nettie: I have made myself quite busy for a day or two packing the things you will find in the box. I only hope the unpacking will afford you as much pleasure. But I doubt if you will be happier in their possession than I have been in the purchasing and making up. The books are selected from my own library, with the exception of the ' set' of school Readers, Dictionary, and Copy-books. These I purchased expressly for you ; the Readers will be useful to the children after you have done with them. The stationery, and all that is in the writing-case, — the writing-case itself, — are presents from Mark ; and the little bundle tied with a pink cord you will please deliver to his mother. All the others are marked with the addresses of their respective owners. I hope the mantel-vases will not get broken, for they are really pretty ; and when you place fresh flowers in them you must think of the giver, who is always thinking of you, and who loves you dearly. I have guessed at the size of the little girls' frocks and pinafores and the boys' jackets. I hope none of them will be too small ; if too large, you will have to alter and make them fit. The little work-basket, with the thimble, needle-case, scissors, and bundles of patchwork, is for sister Susan, who must be quite a large girl — and a *good girl*, too. I wonder if she remembers me. Ask her if she remembers my rocking her to sleep in my arms the night that — the night I staid at your house. I presume the little thing has forgotten; but, Nettie dear, I can never grow so old as to forget.

" The larger basket, with the full set of sewing materials, combs, and brushes, is for you; the slippers and cravat are for your father. I hope the dresses will suit you. The dark one, if you do not need it sooner, will make you a nice winter dress. I would have made this, too, but Mrs. Miller writes that you have grown so tall we should not know you. I have put in a pattern to cut it by, and also a new-fashioned sleeve-pattern, which I think quite pretty.

" And now, dear Nettie, I come to the smaller box of bulbs and seeds for your garden. A little bird has told me how neatly it is laid out, and how nicely it is looking. These will be just in time for the spring's planting. Bulbous roots need a rich, soft loam, and plenty of sunshine. I would make, for the tulips, two beds of an oval shape — one each side of the main walk. A good many of them are already sprouted, and will blossom this year. The narcissus and jonquilles make beautiful borders; but they are very choice: I can only send a few. The daisies you can divide, and subdivide, and make all the bordering you want. The gladiolus and dahlias plant in hills wherever you wish them to stand. After they have done blossoming, and before the ground freezes, all these bulbs must be taken up, and kept where they will not freeze, in a barrel of dry sand, placed in the cellar. This is the surest way of preserving them. I give you these minute particulars, because I have taken great pains to get these bulbs, and, until quite recently, few have known how to manage them.

" I have packed the potted plants so I think they will go

safely. I was obliged to cut the tops off; but they will soon bud out fresh and new, and grow to be large plants. There are seven kinds of geraniums, and some monthly roses. You have a splendid place for these in your two south windows. The little leafless shrub in the smallest vase is a ' forget-me-not.' Plant *this* where the light and sunshine rest warmest and brightest. There are fifty varieties of *seeds*, comprising the useful as well as the ornamental. Some of the annuals are beautiful — the pink, and white, and purple china-aster, the double and variegated lady's-slipper, four-o'clocks, marigolds, mignonette, pinks, and lavender. You may have some of these seeds already, and can make whatever selections your taste dictates; and, if you like, divide with your neighbours.

" You will find my letter a very practical one; but I hope to write you many more; and if, amid your thousand cares, you can find time to answer some of them, it would please me much. Looking forward to a happy meeting somewhere in the hereafter, — if not in this world, in the one to come, when all that has made our lives sorrowful shall have passed away and been forgotten, —

" I remain, ever your affectionate friend,

" GRACE PEARSON."

It was after nightfall ere the pleasant task of " unpacking" was accomplished. The children were nearly wild with excitement; but Nettie's was a less demonstrative joy, partaking more of a feeling of gratitude to be thus remembered by the two beings who were to her the day-stars of her darkened existence. The night-dew dropped upon her hand as she passed under the low arch of woodbine; but the dew that lay upon her heart was sweeter than all the distillations of flowers.

She crept to the great open attic where her bed was, before venturing to unlock the little writing-case. In it was a short note from Mark to herself, and a long letter to his mother. Besides these, there was pink, blue, and white writing-paper, — and a great quantity of it; for Mark said she must learn to write neatly, and that he considered it " one of the greatest of feminine accomplishments." Then there were pens and penknife, wafers, sealing-wax, and a beautiful little inkstand, with a silver stopper. Was ever anything half so pretty?

It was a long, long night to Nettie, — the longest she had ever known, except that terrible one when her mother died. Whether she sat by the window, looking out into the darkness, or knelt at the low bedside, the one night was somehow strangely blended with the other. *Then*, a feeling of awe and desolation crept over her, as she contemplated her future life of toil, — unloved, alone, without the mother's hand to guide or lips to counsel. She knelt then, as now, in the same cold attic; but the soothing tears refused to flow: she wondered why she could not weep. Her lips moved not: she marvelled at their silence. But their trembling revealed the anguish of a troubled spirit prostrate before its Maker. *Now*, the world was brighter — the darkness was not *felt*. Tears would come. A grateful joy was swelling in her bosom, and the words gushed warm and ardent from her parted lips, " Make me worthy of their love and friendship, O my Father ! " murmured she. " Grant me strength, patience, and intelligence, to become all they would have me, and all Thou wouldst have me. Be Thou my Pattern, my Guide, my Saviour, through life and in death ! "

The following week a letter was despatched by post, breathing words of unaffected gratitude, acknowledging the kindness of her friends, and asking further instructions relative to planting, pruning, watering, and harvesting the precious seeds and bulbs. It was written in a small, childish, cramped hand, and some of the words not correctly spelled. But Grace, in her answers, — which were alway‡ punctual, — delicately corrected these, and all other mistakes, and craved the pleasing office of mentor and instructress. From this time they became regular and frequent correspondents.

The books were her greatest treasures; and scarcely a day passed that she did not snatch some little moment from the increasing cares which every year added to her store, and devote it to study or reading. In many of them she found pencil-marks, and notes on the margin, in the handwriting of Grace, showing they had been carefully perused by her, calling her attention to this and that charming passage, or expressing admiration of some beautiful sentiment.

The seeds were sown, the bulbs planted, and the pots set in the warm sunshine in the south windows. In Nettie's heart was also set a germ which in time would bear fruit abundantly, though for a season it lay within its wintry tomb of gloom and darkness, though its fresh young shoots were often forced back upon themselves, and their growth retarded by the uncongenial soil from which they received their life principle. But the spirit, like the bulbs and seeds, was heroically struggling for the light, and gathering daily aliment from each and every energizing influence around it, expanding and growing heavenward day by day.

Two years later 'Nettie wrote, in a bold, beautiful, feminine hand, as follows: —

"My dear, kind Friend: Your letter of May first, together with the little box of presents, came yesterday. Both assure me of your continued friendship and sympathy. Thank you for them. I find it most difficult to talk or write when my heart is fullest; and I have vainly sought for an hour when the tide of joy or grief (I hardly know which to call it) that fills my heart would ebb away, and leave me

calm, and in a mood to reply to you as I ought. I long to
see you, to have you by my side, to hold your hand in mine,
to look into your eyes, and then perhaps I could *tell* you all
that is in my heart, — all its joys, its sorrows, its hopes, fears,
and aspirations. I feel that my words would not be poured
into a listless ear. I remember myself as you first saw me;
I remember my home as it was *then*, and wonder much what
you could find in either to occupy your further thoughts.
Probably you saw in both something on which you could
bestow your great benevolence — something which you could
improve. A thousand thanks, dear friend, for your flattering
encomiums on my own progress! ‘ Proud of my letters ’?
and ‘ showing them to your friends ’? when I cautioned you
to hide or burn them? They must be more studied in future.
Yet I will not scold my best friend ; for all I am I owe, with
God's grace assisting me, to you, my more than sister. Your
thoughtfulness and generosity have made of our cheerless
home the little paradise it now is. It has gone on steadily improving, from the day your first invoice of treasures
came. And always since then, in the sweet spring-time, our
little home has been in a tumult of joy : such planning and
advising about the beds in the garden, — such rearranging
in doors and out, that at last I am quite contented when all
is complete.

" Never did the earth, ‘ with the blue above, and the green
below,’ look so beautiful to me as it does this spring. It
seems as if it might indeed be the ‘ threshold of heaven.’
And never did our home look so pleasant as now. Every
shrub and plant looks so beautiful, and the weather is so
charming ! One can almost *see them grow.* Who would
have thought, two months ago, that all those little bare twigs
would now be full of fresh young sprouts, and tender leaves,
and lovely buds bursting into blossom ? or that within those
dry bulbs (which the boys call little onions) was concealed
such unrivalled beauty ? Is it so, then, dear Grace, that we

too must lie low in the dust, ere our souls can be clothed
with that glorious beauty and perfection which God designs
for us? It seems to me a great miracle. Yet God can work
a greater than this.

" You surmised correctly when you asked after my 'increasing cares' and my 'little spare time.' It is true.
Every year brings an accumulation of care ; for the poultry
increases, and the dairy is large, and there is more flax and
wool to spin ; but I am growing older and stronger, and it
lightens half the toil to see things going on so nicely. I
shall make a long piece of cloth this year, and do it all myself. I fetch my wheel, and spin on the portico overlooking
the garden; and the warm sunshine peeping through the
sweet vine-leaves, and the garden itself, make me very
happy. But it is altogether a home-happiness; and as my
heart is brim full just now, I care for no other, or the extra
work the seasons bring.

" The snow-balls and peonies are now in full bloom. I have
just filled your little vases with them, and some smaller ones
with locust-blossoms and lilacs, with a dear little crocus
peeping out in the centre. They are on the mantel-shelf in
the west room, where dear little Janie lay *that night*. I
have a bright, home-made carpet on the floor, and Mr.
Sloper has given me such a beautiful case for the books,
with glass doors, and a drawer at the bottom for my nice
things. The cheerful, kind-hearted old man comes up to
see us occasionally, praising me more than I deserve, and
advising me when I am in a strait. I delivered Mrs. Loveland's parcel to her mother, and the kind messages you sent.
She is always pleased to hear about you, and sends much
love in return. Susan is just now busy setting out our little
family of house-plants, to give them their daily shower-bath
of water and sunshine. Benny is helping to carry the smaller
ones, insisting that he '*never did break one*,' and is quite
sure he '*never will*.' These are our special 'pets.' Not

only are the two south windows filled to overflowing, but —
thanks to James's mechanical genius — the whole south end
of the porch is converted into a conservatory. Every fresh
rose-bud and sweet-scented geranium leaf remind us of the
dear friend to whom we are so largely indebted. We all
have our favourites among them, or *make ourselves believe*
we have, just for the pleasure of saying *my* and *mine.*
Emma likes the calla and the blue violets best. Heaven
grant her spirit may be as pure and beautiful as the one, as
meek and sweet as the other. Frank pays daily homage to
a heliotrope, which he affirms to be the finest plant in the
lot. If I have a preference, it is for the sweet-scented ver-
bena, or lemon-balm, as some call it. And Lydia's *decided
preference* for fuchsias may be learned when pleading for
'*just two,* to make ear-rings with.' Her little winning ways
.re always irresistible ; and we generally gratify her, for she
.ever presumes to pluck one of these house-flowers without
the consent of some one older. To keep temptation out of
her way, we have placed this flower on the top pedestal,
or step, of our pyramid-shaped plant-stand ; but she looks
with such a wistful eye, we often hold her up to it, just to
see how carefully she snips off the delicate stems. Then
sister must hang them on her yellow curls, ' to make ear-
rings ; ' and then there are two little diamonds in her eyes
the rest of the day. She is our little ' wee lammie,' you know,
given us when mother died, — the pet and petted of all, yet,
strange to say, not spoiled. God grant her life be not as
mine, — so full of care and toil, — a constant yearning for
something unattained.

" The boys are stout, healthy, robust fellows, and will be
able to cope with the toils, and, I hope, the ills of life, like
men ; and the sisters are strong and healthy, too ; but when
I look at them, wondering what their future may be, I pray
God it may be different from mine. I have kept them almost
constantly at school ; and it cost me a deal of labour to make

them always look clean and neat, before that great bundle
of frocks and pinafores came.   We owe you more than we
can ever pay, for the many ' little trifles ' which you seem
to regard as ' things not worth mentioning.'   Small as they
were to you, they were of inestimable value to us.   But,
thanks to our increasing prosperity, we are now enjoying
the fruits of our industry and patient toil, and the children
look as well as our neighbours'.   Sometimes it troubles me,
when I think, ' What will become of me, when they are all
married and in homes of their own ? '   But that is looking
far ahead ; and I take my Bible and read those sweet passages about the lilies and the sparrows, and am comforted.
Our future is hidden from us, just as the germ was hidden
within those dry husks.   They have burst their shells, and
are now springing into life and beauty, making *unto themselves* a world of loveliness, and for me a world of reflection.

> ' They breathe
> Their lives so unobtrusively, like hearts
> Whose beatings are too gentle for the world.'

And so I am content to abide in my little home-sphere, and
to have my body planted on the hill-side yonder, under the
grassy turf where the warm sunshine rests, or,

> ' Swathed in the snowy robe that winter throws
> So kindly over Nature.'

In that glorious morning when

> ' awakening Nature hears
> The new-creating word, and starts to life,'

I shall know my destiny, and what my all-wise Father designs to make me.   Yet of one thing I am quite sure — that
my steps will be directed of Him who orders everything by
the highest wisdom and love.   I have longed to do some
good in the world ; but the thought that God has given me

my vocation, consecrates my humblest duties, and makes me, O, so thankful that I am spared to my family, and hopeful that my simple avocations may even please Him. This thought brings sweetness to my heart, like the fragrance in the air from the falling apple-blossoms, and the showers of rain dripping from the heliotrope.

"Can we ever hope, dear Grace, — the best of us, — to find in this life that genuine Christian excellence to which our hearts aspire? that intelligence and perfection which they long for? It seems too sublime a thing for me — in this work-day world — to attain. It is only for those who have leisure to study and improve themselves — who are surrounded by pleasing scenes and refined associations. I have no envy in my heart for people who enjoy these privileges. I only wish I could enjoy them too, and climb to those heights where my knowledge and experience would gain me the companionship of the great and good, and my example be thought worthy of imitation. But my path must ever be a lowly one; my world a little matter-of-fact, every-day, common-place existence; my life such as are the lives of thousands who live, and die, and are forgotten.

"In a dreamy summer afternoon like this, when, for the moment, I forget stubborn facts, and sweet fancy becomes my interpreter, we — the winged wanderer and I — soar away through fields of thought, far from this little home-sphere of toil and self-denial, and we say to ourselves, that some time in the hereafter a little leisure may be ours, wherein we can put into execution the plans and desires formed in the days of our early companionship. Now and then something like a dream of this happy hour will visit my sleepless pillow; but it will never be, dear Grace: facts are too stern, and my life too real a thing, to admit of much fanciful dreaming.

"Do you still think that 'our meeting was accidental'? — that your 'short stay in the little rural village' was a thing

13

of chance merely? Dear friend, you were sent to me; *I needed you;* and your *steps were ordered* by our One 'All Father.' And now you are a part of myself. I could not do without you. Your coming and going seem like a pleasant dream! Yet it was no dream, for the blessed reality lingers still. Do not I see the happy results of that ' short stay' all around me? You are pleased to say the ' meeting' was for ' our mutual good;' that here you learned 'lessons of humility and self-forgetfulness.' We were, indeed, apt scholars, could a month's tuition always leave such a lasting, wide-spread influence — an influence for good only. And yet, did I not, during that ' short stay,' learn something which has actuated my whole after-life? Have I not since then striven to emulate the example of that one friend who taught me to ' breast the wind, and wrestle with the storm'? to love the beauties of nature, and to see, in the stern and rugged, attractions which might have passed forever unheeded? That great, verdureless mountain, once looked upon as a formidable enemy, has, since we stood upon the brow of our own little hill-side, and talked of its grandeur, become an object of greater interest to me than many another that excited my childish admiration. Since then, I have loved the bold and rugged, the stern and grand, better than the simply beautiful things of earth.

" The most beautiful are generally the most delicate; they need something to lean upon, — something to trust to, — just as those little, meek, blue-eyed violets need to grow in the shade of some shrub, whose protecting foliage nurtures and enhances their modest beauty; or that little heavenly forget-me-not requires some stout, tough stick to support its fragile stems.

" Much as I love these delicate, dependent little treasures, I would not be like them. Neither *could* I be, here at home, where it has become a necessity for me to be the one on which others lean. To my brothers and sisters I seem the 'supporting pillar,' and sometimes, to my father, I am not unlike 'Help' pulling poor 'Christian' out of the 'Slough of Despond.' I often think, What would become of us all, were I one of those dependent little creatures, who, like some frail vine, lives by clinging to and drawing its sustenance from some stronger and sterner nature? Can you imagine your little rustic friend occupying such an exalted position?

" This evening I was sitting under our little arbour of jessa-mine, watching the shadows of the great hills creep over the valleys beneath, and listening to the birds singing their 'even-ing song to the sunset.' They sang so long and loud, I won-dered how their breath could hold out! I sat until the shade grew dense. The breeze had rocked the birdies to sleep, the stars lit up their leafy homes, the fireflies vying with the starlight, and the starlight with the moonlight, until the whole shone with a supernal splendor. I thought of my dear friend, far away in the great city, with its hot pavements, dusty streets, and vast aggregation of brick and mortar, and wondered much if there the sunsets were so charming, or the starlight nights so heavenly; or if such numbers of gay butterflies and glossy humming-birds, 'like gems and blos-soms on pinions,' flit around your home; whether your ear ever catches the wild words of the whip-poor-will, or the saddened strain of the mournful dove, —

'Singing her sorrows through the night,
Till wide around the woods
Sigh to her song, and with her wail resound.'

" I am writing you a long, and, I fear you will think, a very prosy letter. My dear friend will excuse the rambling style, and lack of more interesting topics. I have written upon the inspiration of the hour, as the thoughts came to me, but at intervals such as I could command. If I have enlarged upon our little home-scenes, and talked exclusively of our small domestic world, it is because I know but little of any other. All I hear of the great world outside is what you write me, and sometimes Mrs. Miller reads to me portions of Mark's letters, which are always full of interest. Occasionally a stray newspaper finds its way to our place, from which I gather information.

"And now, dear friend, I must bring my letter to a close. Be sure you write me as long a one in return. One day I hope to welcome you to our home. When shall it be? I will promise to be very good, and not monopolize you altogether. You will find the place much improved. I think it a beautiful town; but having never seen any other, perhaps I am not a good judge. As regards myself and my surroundings, the little gypsy's prophecy is fulfilled — ' In due season ye shall reap, if ye faint not.'

"That you may be ever happy, is the prayer of your friend,

"NETTIE STRANGE."

CHAPTER XXII.

MR. NEWELL AND MARK GO TO NEW YORK.

"Thy voice is a complaint, O crowned city,
The blue sky covering thee, like God's great pity."

BARRETT.

R. NEWELL and Mark were on their way to the great metropolis, or rather on the road to Mallowfield, where they were to take the stage. One of the "hands" drove them out, returning the same day with the carriage.

The day was charming; the turnpike smooth and level; the carriage, with its silver trimmings and soft, luxurious cushions; the span of superb "bays" stepping over the ground so loftily, were enough to warm the soul of a Stoic. But Mark was no Stoic; and this was his first ride in any vehicle more elegant than Mr. Sloper's little spring-waggon, in which he had sometimes taken a grist to mill. He questioned in his mind whether or not that light, one-horse waggon — with its elastic springs, and shining coat of green paint, striped all around with yellow — might not with propriety claim some relationship with gentility, inasmuch as its owner was a good, and great, and rich man. He turned the momentous thought over and over in his mind, until he arrived at the conclusion that it might, and ought. He was not going to be bribed into forgetfulness of, or to look contemptuously upon, aught belonging to " Sorrel Hill."

Away they spun, over the smooth road, on that calm

summer morning. Its bracing and delicious atmosphere gave to Mark's eye and cheek an unwonted brightness. Besides, his *heart* was all a-glow with the prospect before him, and with the pleasing memories of the past month. Even the "leave-taking," which he had dreaded nearly as much as the parting from mother and home, was over ; and now, in the society of one whom he has learned to love and trust, with his purse a little replenished, he is once more on his journey.

Mallowfield was ten miles distant; and they entered the town just in time to catch the shrill notes of the stage horn, echoing long and loud among the distant hills, —

"Waking the woods to new music."

Mark's heart thrilled with rapture, and was drawn for the time away from the perplexing cares and wild visions which for many a month had engrossed it. The stopping of the carriage, and the arrival of the stage at the same moment, gave him no time for further reflections.

The panting steeds, weary with their spirited travel, covered with fleck, waited patiently for their cool retreat in the stable. They were soon removed, and fresh ones attached, whose proud step, handsome arched necks, and glossy hides, showed that there was mettle in them, and their restless pawing of the ground, that they were impatient to display it. Mark was eighteen, and had never before seen a stage coach. The little lumbering vehicle that came once a week to "the hill," to bring the mail, and occasionally a passenger, or little articles of trade for the farmers, was quite a different concern from the one in which our young traveller found himself so comfortably seated. The farther he proceeded on his journey, the more he saw and learned. During his three days' travel he had time to take up the thread of his disjointed reflections, — which his stop at Mallowfield had interrupted, — and weave it into a beautiful web. Upon

the shining fabric was wrought his own fair destiny — " clear
as mud," said he, awakening from a lengthy nap, in which
he had been dreaming, he was sorry he could not remember
what.

" Were I less merciful, we would follow along in his train
of thought, describing all the scenery between Mallowfield
and New York, the subjects of discourse among the passen-
gers, and every minutia of incident."

" Spare me, dear, good aunt Bessie ! I do detest long
descriptions of scenery. I always skip that part of a story.
Please leave Mark to his sublime reveries, his naps and
dreams, and tell me what he thought of New York. I
know there's something rich coming."

" If by ' something rich ' you mean a laughable account
of a young country lad's shy, awkward demeanor, or amusing adventures, while being shown around the city, I fear
you will be disappointed. He was in company of a kind-
hearted gentleman, who, ' for value received,' to use his own
words, meant to pay off some of his indebtedness. To can-
cel the whole he felt would be impossible. One object Mr.
Newell had in bringing Mark to New York, was to show
him something of real life, — not as he had seen it in his
little native town, but as it really exists in all large cities,
especially in this great metropolis of the western world.
Here are always to be seen the high and the low, the rich
and the poor, the honoured and the degraded. Here are
assembled the great, the good, the refined, the intellectual.
The high-born and noble, of all lands, breathe the same
atmosphere, and live often in the same street, with persons
in the deepest poverty, and lowest in the scale of human
being."

Mark had never seen much of what is termed " high
life," nor had he an idea of the other great extreme, as it

existed here. He had heard of jails, almshouses, and peniten
tiaries ; of asylums for the homeless and the unfortunate of
all classes ; but a beggar he had never seen ; and if any one
had told him there were hundreds of homeless, destitute
children in New York, he would have set it down as an
idle tale. Dissipation, vice, and crime, he had little knowledge of; and when a daily paper reported the fact of there
being thousands of habitual drunkards, and thousands of
inmates of the city and county prisons, he thought there
must have been a mistake in the figures. Little could he
realize that here were young men of his own age, reared in
the lap of luxury, enjoying every advantage which wealth
and position give, — advantages and privileges which his
wildest dreams could scarcely picture, — devoting their
time, talents, and the best years of their lives, to idleness
and dissipation, — thrusting aside as worthless the very
object which he would give worlds to attain ; boys younger
than he, descending, step by step, from one fashionable vice
to another, soon to fill premature and dishonoured graves !

It was midday when they arrived and drew up in front
of the City Hotel, on Broadway. The Astor, St. Nicholas,
and Metropolitan were not built then ; but there were some
very fine hotels there forty years ago — quite palatial, so
people thought who came in from the country.

Not many hours elapsed ere Mark was made aware of
being the chosen companion of a man occupying no ordinary
position. On every hand was Mr. Newell greeted with a
deference and respect amounting to veneration. They were
shown to a room on the second floor, — or rather suite of
rooms, — Mark occupying a smaller one, opening into that
of Mr. Newell. To this arrangement Mark demurred ; but
Mr. Newell was peremptory.

" So far from your ' obtruding upon my privacy,' you
can, if you choose, make yourself useful to me. I shall have
some copying to do, and accounts to make out, and will test

your proficiency in these troublesome matters; but to-night we will rest, and during the few days that I am arranging some important business matters, you can look around at the sights."

Mark expressed his gratitude in a becoming manner, and his pleasure in being able to serve Mr. Newell. After the necessary preparations, they went to supper. He had brushed the dust from his thick boots and farmer's suit of homespun gray, and donned his new linen. But with his open, honest face, and hair combed back from his broad, handsome forehead, he looked every inch one of nature's noblemen. So Mr. Newell thought, as they walked arm in arm into the long dining-room. The splendid table-service, glittering chandeliers, the polite stewards, in their clean white livery, and the numerous well-dressed people of both sexes sitting directly opposite and all around him, were things well calculated to put his heart in such a state of nervous excitement as threatened to interfere with his appetite. Mr. Newell noticed his embarrassment, and while they were being served, engaged him in an easy, familiar conversation, that quite overcame his bashfulness, and renewed his desire for a good supper.

In the evening Mr. Newell received, in his own parlour, the few friends who chanced to know of his arrival. There were great shakings of hands, inquiries after his health and the health of his family. Had he come to stay? &c. And then Mark was introduced as " my young friend, Mr. Miller."

The next few days Mark was left to himself; and his experience in sight-seeing will be better expressed in a letter written to his mother, after he had been there a week.

" MY VERY DEAR MOTHER : I am one of the many thousands who comprise this great city. The broad fields, dense forests, purling brooks, hills, vales, and flowers, of my own loved home, are far away; and yet they are ever pres⁻

ent.   From my window I can see nothing but a mass of crowded houses, and the dense throng of living things that move to and fro before it; and my restless imagination has plenty of business on its hands.   So anxious was I to commence my career of sight-seeing, that notwithstanding the fatigue of our journey, I was awake ere the stars 'began to pale their ineffectual light,' and meek-eyed morn appeared in the east.   In half an hour every cupola and spire was bathed in a flood of liquid light, proclaiming the approach of the sun.   It was such a day as I should have selected from a thousand, — a season wherein if a man's heart fails to beat in harmony with all that is beautiful in nature, he must indeed be a victim of dulness, or, what is worse, a misanthrope.   The air is soft and cool, but I miss the delicious fragrance of the new-mown grass, and the familiar odour of the dainty flowers; but as it blows softly through the branches of the lindens and horse-chestnuts, stirring gently their summer suits of brilliant green, it appears quite like the fresh country air I breathed at home.   The mildness of these days gives me the pleasure of lengthy strolls through the beautiful Park and along the Battery, where the pure sea breeze comes up from the bay with soft and misty wings, scattering its little dews like a sweet, still, April shower. Here, while resting for a moment, I amuse myself in watching the hundreds of happy, rejoicing children, in their unrestrained sports.   I extend my rovings indefinitely, and take the liberty to gape and stare at everything that attracts my attention, and do not know but I am an object of curiosity; but ' I stare my fill with impunity, and take all stares myself in good part.'   I jostle my way through crowds of people, — young gentlemen, with dainty gloved hands, twirling attenuated little canes; ladies in pink, and blue, and pearl-green, and *couleur de rose*, gliding up and down with light steps and fresh complexions; beggars and blind men, black and white.

"On Broadway there is a double current, up and down, of beaver and broadcloth, exquisite and costly silks, velvets, furs, feathers, flounces, and flowers — a solid mass from St. Paul's to Bond Street. There is no crossing, for every vehicle in running order, I verily believe, is passing here. The *millionnaire*, with his magnificent 'turnout,' dashes past, while the sole occupant of a little fairy nut-shell, with two superb bays, comes up at a rapid pace, nearly running over a poor old man with a hand-cart. Ladies half buried in costly silks glide by like troops of fairies. I endeavour to get a second glimpse, but they are gone, and the phantom of the 'Flying Dutchman' looms up before the mind's eye. Little 'fast men,' with less discretion than mirthfulness beaming from their beardless physiognomies, urge on their foaming steeds, regardless of consequences, and despite the remonstrances of servants in livery, and a 'Hold on, there!' from a policeman. They *do* hold on to a tight rein, and are out of sight in less time than one can write it. Omnibuses, with four horses attached, seem as innumerable as the applicants for a ride. In one of these you can go from the Battery a mile up town for a sixpence. Opposite my hotel is the most magnificent panorama of confusion that could possibly present itself. There is a dray, heavily laden with long bars of iron, attempting to cross; the omnibus drivers break the third commandment because they have to 'hold up;' in their impatience to be the first to get by, one runs against the other, who threatens to annihilate the former on the spot. That great, huge coal-waggon runs leisurely alongside of a splendid carriage containing some of the aristocracy of this republican New York. On the other side is a little fancy, flashy affair, — I have no name for it, — in which sit two young men, dressed in the extreme of fashion, with jaunty little hats, and beards *à la bison*, driving a span of fast horses in tandem style. Here is a huge concern on wheels, taking up half the street, containing a band of music, and covered with placards announcing that this is ' positively the last week of Hamlet.' A candy express-man, pedlers of pills, porter, and other bad stuffs, close in with a train of carts laden with all manner of wares and merchandise. The driver of that omnibus has crowded those horses, belonging to some rich nabob, up on to the sidewalk, while the consequential son of Ham, with a gold band on his hat, and six capes to his overcoat, is pronoun-cing awful anathemas on all of plebeian and canine origin or occupation. Here comes a funeral train, with hearse and ' nodding plumes,' getting all mixed up with the carts and carriages, entirely separate from each other, until the hearse stops some three or four blocks ahead, and waits for the mourners to come up. Here, too, is a yoke of oxen drawing a sled; and driving them *quietly* does not seem to be among the Hibernian's accomplishments, for the way he talks to his cattle is very amusing. Such an entanglement of vehi-cles, horses, and human kind, needs a pen better adapted to ' descriptive pieces' than mine, to do it justice. Fancy must plume her wings from this point.

" These are only a few of the street scenes that constantly pass before me in my daily rambles. I have visited a few of the public buildings, the navy yard, and the receiving ship, where seamen are enlisted for the navy, the hospitals for the sick, the asylums for the poor, aged, the deaf and dumb, and blind, the gallery of painting and sculpture, the public libraries, the city prison, and a printing office, — all of which are of the deepest interest to me, adding much to my knowledge of the world, and the ways thereof. I have also visited a few of the churches. St. Paul's and Trinity are both superb structures — not much like our little meet-ing-house at Sorrel Hill. They both front on Broadway, and are in the busiest and most crowded portion of the city. Around both of these are the graveyards belonging to the societies. In Trinity churchyard are the graves of many of the heroes of the revolution. There is a splendid monument in process of erection commemorative of those martyrs who suffered and died in the New York revolutionary prisons. It stands upon the very spot where many of them were buried; and in excavating for the structure, a skull pierced by a bullet, and other revolutionary relics, were found.

" When night comes I am pretty well satisfied with my day's rambling and sight-seeing. If I could only get out of these *resounding* streets, it would be a richer treat than I have yet enjoyed. My poor head aches until I reach my room and take a good rest. Besides, I am made painfully sensible that my new boots are not just the things for comfort, or long tramps on hot pavements. We learn wisdom by the things we suffer; and to-morrow I shall fall back on the old ones, which after all will pass in a crowd. Some one has said, ' Were I called upon to put forward the most unique impersonation of comfort, I should give a plumper in favor of an old coat. The very mention of this luxury conjures up a thousand images of enjoyment.' Now, I can say the same of an old or half-worn shoe. It gives one such an unembarrassed, independent gait! But with feet imprisoned in a detestable pair of new ones, one can neither enjoy the blue sky nor a philosophic reverie. I found my clothes rather heavy and uncomfortable this warm weather, and bought a suit of light material, — quite a ' becoming fit,' — and not very expensive. I miss the dear mother, to tell me ' how well I look' in them. Had I been told that of my own free will I should be one day separated from that mother's side, I should have scouted the idea as a thing too absurd to think of; but now it is so, my only comfort is in thinking that it is right; and it is a pleasure for us to do many unpleasant things, if we know what we are doing is right and for the best.

" I shall write you again before I leave the city. We

shall go in about another week.　Mr. Newell is more like a father than a friend of a few weeks' acquaintance.　When he has time we go out together ; and, with his influence and assistance, I can hardly fail of getting something to do.

" Be cheerful, dear mother, and believe me to be
　　　　　　" Your affectionate son,
　　　　　　　　　　　　　　　" MARK."

CHAPTER XXIII.

BUSINESS LIFE IN ALBANY.

" Shortly his fortune shall be lifted higher;
True industry doth kindle honour's fire."

SHAKSPEARE.

AYS passed. At length Mark began to count the time by weeks; and then long months glided away without his seeing any one from home.

Through the influence of Mr. Newell, he was at length well established in a large wholesale mercantile house in Albany. Mr. Newell had written to this firm — who were old acquaintances — before leaving home, and had received a satisfactory reply. Before placing Mark in business, he wished to show him something of the world, and invited him to New York, where he remained as his guest. It would be better, he said, than a whole year's schooling.

The department to which he was at first assigned consisted principally of out-door work — the loading and unloading of stores, which came in and went out by the cargo. This was hard work; but Mark was used to that, and whatever he did was done cheerfully and faithfully, and with a will, that showed he was not ashamed of any honest employment. Were I to say that thenceforward his life was without cares and crosses, that no temptations, difficulties, or depression of spirits tried him, that no obstacles were surmounted, I should do injustice to the brave heart that met all these, but only to scatter and conquer them. So strong was his inherent sense of truth and justice, that never for a moment did pride interfere with principle. Pride always yielded, though his cheek were made to burn for the sacrifice. He had already the foundation of a good education, was quick at figures, and could generally make out a bill _mentally_, while the book-keeper was *ornamenting* his invoices and bills of lading with extra and superfluous flourishes. This mental and natural *activity*, together with his untiring industry, his regular and correct habits, his earnest, consistent, virtuous life, soon won for him the admiration of his associates and the implicit confidence of his employers.

Yet there are always some evil-disposed persons, whose delight is in annoying those whose consistent, upright characters contrast strongly with their own. Such a companion had Mark. He was a young man of showy exterior, who wore fine clothes, and prided himself upon his good looks and his gallantry. Mark was his especial aversion, and he never let slip an opportunity to tease and annoy him, often making him the butt of ridicule and a subject for practical jokes. Mark bore his raillery in silence, listened quietly to his coarse innuendoes, and sometimes joined in an innocent laugh against himself, retorting in a pleasant humour, and often hurling back upon the archer the shaft intended for himself. He could not compromise his manhood by tamely submitting to insults.

The two occupied a corner in the great loft, partitioned off by piles of empty boxes, carpetless and curtainless, and altogether a dreary-looking abode for one of Mr. Clinton's refined tastes and habits.

Mark had gone up one night to close and fasten the fireproof shutters. On descending the stairs he found himself locked in — a prisoner, literally, for the night. He made no outward sign of impatience, thinking his jailer within hearing distance, supposing — very properly, too — that when the

" freak " was over, he would come to his release. But he waited in vain. Hours passed; and he was still a prisoner, under as strong and secure a guard as though he were in the " Tombs." It grew quite dark. He was faint and hungry. There were no lights, save the soft starlight above and the sweeter love-light beaming in his soul. He had stood by the window two hours, though it seemed not as many minutes. An ever-changing panorama glides before him. All are hurrying homeward, and from those homes are streaming bright lights, and within are happy voices and smiling faces, and tender love-tones mingled with warm kisses, to welcome the tired footstep and gladden the weary of heart.

As he stands thus, motionless and sorrowful, another panorama, exhibiting the past, the present, the future, glides before his mental vision. The shifting, varying scenes grow dark or bright, as " fancy's wild imaginings " roll slowly by. He feels that he has indeed entered upon the world, — that world so replete with strange occurrences and parti-colored incident. Darkness overspreads the city. Dark and dreary seems the world below and around him. Above are the shining stars, and they alone of all the created universe seem without a cloud over their bright faces. Slowly glide the shifting scenes. He has passed the threshold of a new existence, and life in its sober reality is opening upon him. A murmur of indistinct, yet painfully audible sounds, reaches his ear from the busy world below; but no familiar voice, no tone of endearment, is here, no home-hearth nor home-comforts to cast a cheerful glow over the heart that is to be henceforth barred from social intercourse.

The bright stars seemed a great way off, and over the moon's disk a cloud had slowly gathered. A darker cloud gathered around his heart, until it seemed that no light was strong enough to penetrate its gloom! He opened the blind and leaned his forehead against the cool pane, and gazed out into the darkness, as if in that protracted, agonized stare, he

14

would pierce the veil of futurity, and learn, in a moment's time, the events of his future life. If such had been his thought, he thrust it back as impious. "O God, in Thee will I trust. Thou only knowest or canst know my future. Thy will be done." That perfect trust and holy faith, learned at his mother's knee and beside his father's death-bed, came like a beautiful beacon-light to a foundering bark. In this, the saddest hour his heart had ever known, he would not yield up the sweet hope that slept within the darkened chambers of his soul. It had kept watch with him through the mental storm, and now was growing brighter and more gayly-coloured as it neared the goal of his ambition. Years hence he might look back upon this hour with a smile.

Mr. Clinton did not return that night; but that did not prevent Mark's enjoying a good sound sleep, though he went to bed supperless, and with his head aching sadly. He was awakened the next morning by the approaching footsteps of his room-mate. He started to his feet, dressed himself hastily, then boldly confronting the gentleman, asked to know what was meant by this fresh insult. Mr. Clinton, nearly convulsed with laughter, attempted to pass it off as a good joke, when Mark interrupted his insolent harangue by saying, —

"Sir, I wish you to understand, from this time forth, you will not make me the subject of your insolence. *I will bear no more.* Your 'jokes' are getting to be serious affairs, and happen most too often.".

Clinton was a coward, and quailed beneath the fiery eye and towering form that confronted him. Mark could have crushed him, and he knew it. Never before had Mr. Clinton seen that bold, brave spirit aroused; but he saw it now, and trembled.

He attempted some further apology, but it was useless. Mark continued to lay his commands upon him until he was sufficiently humbled.

"Now you must go with me to Mr. Gedney, and we will talk this matter over. I am no pugilist, or I could redress my wrongs in a way less pleasant than for you to acknowledge them to our employer."

"O, Miller, you won't surely submit me to this humiliating ordeal! You may play me a dozen jokes, only don't take me before Gedney. I never could stand it; 'pon my honour, I couldn't."

"Your honour, I am sorry to say, is as little to be depended upon as your candour or truthfulness. I have little confidence in either. We will just go to the office and talk over this little affair, and let Mr. Gedney pass judgment. Perhaps he too will regard it as a 'good joke.' If so, I am willing to stand my chances against it, or any like it, happening again."

"Now, Miller, what's the use of pummelling a fellow when he's already down? Haven't I told you I was *sorry*, and begged your pardon?"

"No, you have not."

"Well, then, I *am;* 'pon my word I am; so let's shake hands, and say no more about it."

"Friends, or enemies?" asked Mark, as he took, rather reluctantly, the proffered hand.

"Friends — fast friends, for life, 'pon my honour."

And thus it proved. They never had any more difficulty.

Cheerless as was the great lumbering loft where he slept, Mark soon learned there were other homes, or houses, filled with elegant and costly things, more destitute of joy and the dear delights of social intercourse.

Mr. Gedney, the senior partner of the firm, was a gentleman of refinement and education, but somewhat after the pattern of Deacon Sloper in his notions about using all mankind as one common brotherhood, and all God's good gifts as though lent us to do good with. He had taken Mark to his house, "to keep him out of harm's way," he said, and,

after he knew him better, to keep one little ray of sunsline
beaming there.

It is said that " men like their opposites best." If this be
true in all cases, Mrs. Gedney must have shared largely in
her husband's affections. Two greater opposites never met.
Two greater contrasts of mind and disposition were never
wedded. He was all generosity and affection, — loved everybody, delighted to see everybody and everything, even the
lowest brute in creation, happy and cheerful. She — according to Mark's way of thinking — was a " frozen water spirit,"
— so pale, cold, and stately did she appear. The atmosphere of her house he likened to the damp fogs on the mill-
pond at Sorrel Hill after an autumn shower. An air of
deep gravity pervaded her manner; her speech was full of
big dictionary words, the meaning of which Mark could never
quite understand. The rooms, though furnished with taste
and elegance, partook of the same general discomfort and
chilliness, every article of furniture being arranged with a
stately and studied precision. Not a chair, not a book, was
ever out of place. No papers, no magazines, were lying
about, as if they had ever been read, or ever would be. No
children's toys, or little shoes, or bits of broken china, were
permitted to litter the carpets in that house. There were
birds in gilded cages, flowers in the conservatory, and children in the nursery. These latter were necessary evils, who
were pale and white like their mother, only making their
appearance at table, when they were very clean and very
dignified. If they were unusually good and still through
the day, they might dine with papa at five o'clock, or be
dressed nicely, and ride in the carriage with mamma. A
cat, or a dog, or a pet of any kind, never entered the sacred
precinct. A noble mastiff sometimes waited at the gate for
his master's coming, and, following him to the store, waited
there, with a loving fidelity, his return; but his home was his
kennel, — he never entered the house. A cat, also, " might

have been seen," shying around among the low shrubs in the garden, or leisurely sunning her shining sides, when there was no one around to stamp and cry, "*Scat!*" A beautiful tortoise-shell kitten it had once been; but long since it had been under the ban of the mistress's displeasure, for presum- ing to grow out of sweet, innocent kittenhood into a great, ugly, horrid creature! Was she so unfortunate as to cross the path of the said mistress, away, with tail erect, would poor puss scamper! slinking from God's sweet sunshine, as if there were not enough for all, and all had not the same right to life, and love, and happiness.

When immersed in the duties and excitement of business, Mr. Gedney appeared in the eyes of the world a man to be envied. He was rich, courteous, and charitable, and kept up a fine establishment. His wife, rather exclusive and dis- tant, — so the world thought, — gave elegant entertainments to the " dear five hundred friends," who knew little of their domestic arrangements. The world looked not into their inner life — they saw only the surface of their domestic ex- istence. Perhaps a few noticed the apparent dissonance, the want of kindred sympathy, a dissimilarity of taste and feel- ing; but then that, they said, " often happens among married couples : people — men especially — always prefer their op- posites." Society cast its homage at the feet of this cold, pas- sionless being; for society she reserved what little there was in her nature to love or admire. Mark was her aversion. She was too high-toned to tolerate any creature of low pro- pensities; and dogs, cats, rabbits, and children were his special admiration! Horse-flesh he idolized!

This cold, stately house was Mark's only home. Is it to be wondered at that his warm, impulsive heart yearned for the humble home and the dear mother he had left?

Thus the summer passed away. It seemed a very short summer to Mark, who was constantly seeing strange faces, and new and strange scenes were of daily occurrence. **He** kept on in the even tenor of his way, at the store, among the bales and boxes all day, and studying in the great attic all the evening. He had not seen Miss Pearson: she was spending the summer out of town. The warm summer months were gliding rapidly away. The approach of autumn was seen rather than felt, for the days were still pleasant; but the brown and yellow leaves were supplanting the bright green ones, and the delicate flowers one after another were skrinking into their beds of dusky shadow, just as man is hidden away in the tomb, awaiting the dawn of the resurrection morn to bring him forth to a new and more refined existence. At length Grace came home. As she sat looking over a numerous array of notes and cards, left during her absence, she found this note, written upon a small scrap of paper, lying at the bottom of her card-basket: —

" I have fulfilled my promise in that I called immediately on my arrival in the city. All well at home. These little faded violets were plucked fresh for you by Nettie, the morning I left; but that was two months ago.

"MARK."

The note was without date, and three months had elapsed since it was written. How provoking! If she only knew where to find him, she would set out immediately. She *must* find him. If he was still in the city, she *must* know where he was and what he was doing. Then a thousand ugly images arrayed themselves before her. He might be in want, seeking in vain for employment, looking in vain for a familiar face or friendly word. As these thoughts rushed through her mind, she became nervously excited — inquired of the servants; but he had never called again. She hastily wrote a few lines, and took them to the post-office herself. On her way thither, she unconsciously peered into the face of every passer-by who bore the slightest resemblance to Mark. Once she thought she had found him.

Her heart gave a sudden bound when, on turning a corner, she came up behind a man in a suit of gray homespun, with brass buttons. A nearer approach almost confirmed her suspicions. She thought she recognized the old — the peen-liar kind of hat he wore. Now she is close beside him, and looks smilingly into his face. O, horror of horrors! it is not Mark! No, those " weamy," leering eyes and carroty hair belong to no friend of hers. She felt somehow that she had insulted the brave, good-looking boy by supposing this dissipated vagabond could be at all like him. Having deposited the note in the post-office, she resolved on holding an indignation meeting, all by herself, which should last the whole evening.

She had not long to remain in suspense, for the next day Mark came. Her note had been very peremptory, demanding, in a girlish, playful tone, his immediate presence. With a light and bounding heart he sprang up the marble steps of the great brown mansion in —————— Street — Grace's home. Here were no icy barriers, though the lofty granite front and rosewood portal proclaimed the wealth and aristocracy of the owner. One there was within " waiting impatiently," " nearly dying to see him! " — so the little note read.

He was shown into a richly-furnished library, lighted by two large bay-windows of stained glass, that diffused a softened, mellow light throughout the room. Treasures of literature, art, and science were everywhere to be seen; paintings and maps adorned the walls; statues fitted nicely into the niches for which they were made; chairs of antique patterns, lounges made for comfort, —

> " 'Twas heaven to lounge upon a couch, said Gray,
>   And read new novels on a rainy day;"

tête-à-têtes, and steps, carpeted with velvet, to climb to the highest shelves; writing-tables, ready for use; and vases filled with fresh flowers.

The icebergs which had hemmed him around for the last three months, melted away before the genial, sunny smile of the fine, noble-looking man, who advanced to meet him. Though Mr. Guild — Grace's uncle — could count his possessions by thousands, was the owner of one of the finest estates in the country, stood high in the political and social world, was looked up to and quoted as a man of large influence and unbounded generosity, he never forgot that he was once a poor man, — that it was owing to his own earnest efforts and a combined train of circumstances, and that fortune favoured him in order that *he* might favour others.

The calm, easy, unstudied grace; the frank, generous, open countenance; the warm, genuine shake of the hand, disarmed the fears of the young country boy, putting him at once upon his easy, affable behaviour.

Ere the self-introductions and mutual congratulations are over, approaching footsteps and the sound of merry voices are heard. A moment more, and Grace comes forward, her eyes filling with a lustrous, familiar sweetness, and clasps his hand with the cordiality of an old, long-absent friend.

No, he was not forgotten! This noble, highly-gifted young lady, born in affluence, the petted child of fortune, the favourite of a brilliant circle of friends, the admired of all, the beloved of many, was still the friend of the shy, awkward country lad, who had been to her the hero of many a fancy-coloured day-dream, and who was to be " motive of more fancy."

From the library — where they spent an agreeable half hour — Mark was shown into a cosy family sitting-room. Here were children, and children's toys, and " heaps o' playthings " scattered over the soft carpet; and Grace had even to move a little bedstead from one end of the sofa before her guest could be seated. A home-like aspect pervaded the large and handsomely-furnished apartment. A matronly-looking lady, — Grace's aunt, — full of grace and innate sweetness herself, was seated at an open window, shaded by some rare creeping vine, whose profuse luxuriance added an azure softness to the festooned curtains of rich lace, falling in graceful folds at her feet. She rose hastily, gave Mark's hand a kind, motherly clasp, saying, " she had been almost as anxious to see him as had Grace; and now they had met, she hoped they would see him often. Could he not sometimes spend his evenings with them, after business hours? Had he a pleasant boarding-place? Would he not occupy a seat in their pew on the Sabbath? He must certainly accompany Grace to their Wednesday evening ' social circle,' held in the vestry, for the mutual improvement and better acquaintance of the younger members of the society."

To all these motherly interrogations Mark responded with a newly-awakened interest. New life, new hopes, higher aspirations, were swelling his great heart. He must indeed be aspiring, ambitious, zealous, far-reaching, to meet the expectations of these friends, who, he feared, over-estimated his abilities. But he would work with new energy, take another hour from sleep, and study with increased vigour.

Here, he felt, must be his *home*. Here were genial minds and sympathetic hearts.

> "The mind within him panted after mind;
> The spirit sighed to meet a kindred spirit."

And here, in this great palatial residence of one of the country's great and noble sons, he found it; and more, he found

> "Wisdom enshrined in beauty. O, how high
> The order of that loveliness!"

Grace bore a strong resemblance to her aunt, — she being her mother's only sister. Both were lovely, and seemingly one nature inhabited the two beautiful forms. Mark's heart was evidently " under the wand of the enchanter." He scarcely knew which he loved the more. "What a contrast to the cold, pale, marble-like beauty of Mrs. Gedney! What a striking contrast in the homes of the two!" were some of Mark's thoughts, when a frank, merry boy, full of mischief and animation, crossed the hall with a jump and a slide, and came bounding in at the half-open door, being unaware of the presence of a stranger. His little sister, a rosy-checked, healthy, happy-looking child, followed, bearing a whole apron full of kittens, which she fearlessly deposited upon the carpet. There were no little pale lilies in that household. Fresh air and plenty of healthful exercise kept their complexions ruddy and their eyes brilliant. There were no cold, stately rooms, "kept for company," into which the children might not enter, or where a ray of sunshine dare not intrude.

Mark was well pleased with his first visit, and was invited to come whenever he could spare the time. He was always made to feel at home when in company with this pleasant family. Two or three evenings in a week were generally spent here. Grace had become his instructress. To her he recited when his tasks were learned; and her kind, encouraging words often sent him cheered and strengthened to his daily toil, or to a night of sweet repose. He had access to the great library, and to the piano, both of which proved of inestimable value. The one satisfied his thirst for knowledge, the other charmed his senses, until "the listening heart forgot all duties and all cares." Together they read history, studied mathematics, conned the pages of ancient lore, or practised some charming duet, or tried the last new song. But for these few evenings of social intercourse with these much-valued friends, he sometimes felt he could not live in the cold, stately house where his home was.

Thus a whole year passed away. Mark entered upon his commercial life as junior clerk. He was honest, industrious, trustworthy, and made his patron's interest his own. Few young men of his age possessed better business qualifications. These brought him at once into favour. At the end of the year he was tendered the senior clerkship, with an advanced salary. He relaxes none of the interest he at first took, when he knew he must work or starve; sunrise and sunset find him at his post. He is happy comparatively, though a shade of sadness often steals over his brow when he thinks of "dear mother in her lonely home." But, then, letters from the dear old home come laden with sweet, comforting words, and his mother writes about everything of interest, always sends Mr. and Mrs. Sloper's regards, and dear Nettie's love, and says, "You don't know what a great girl Nettie has grown to be; and so good, too, that the old place does not look like the same." Winking away the tears that will sometimes blind him, he reads over again those sweet little passages referring to the poor girl who gave him, as a parting token, the Testament which is never forgotten or neglected.

This ever-dutiful son, during his junior clerkship, when his salary was scarcely more than was actually requisite to meet his own wants, was enabled, by practising the strictest economy, and by denying himself everything in the shape of luxury, to supply his darling mother with many of the little comforts her loneliness and increasing age demanded. Scarcely a month passed that a small parcel did not go out by the old lumbering stage which carried Nettie's box. It might be a pound of tea, a small box of sugar, a sample of nice West India fruit, a dress, or pair of shoes, or a cap-ribbon, selected with care and taste, to show that he was ever mindful of the mother he idolized.

So the months passed on. Mark's spirits were light, his step buoyant, while his heart clung fondly to the friends whom he met with in his desolation.

CHAPTER XXIV.

THE GOVERNOR'S RECEPTION.

"She may help you to many fair preferments,
And then deny her aiding hand therein,
And lay these honours on your high desert."

SHAKSPEARE.

HE second year of Mark's absence is drawing to a close. The winter is a delightful one: all is gayety and festivity in the capital of the Empire State. The legislature is still in session; and Mark, through the kindness of his ever-indulgent patron, passes an hour, almost daily, either in the Senate or Assembly chamber, listening to the speeches of the members, and learning much of parliamentary usage. These are hours well spent. He treasures up what he sees and hears. Sometimes Grace accompanies him; and it is during one of these brief visits that she introduces him to the governor. He repeated the name inquiringly. "Mark Miller? Are you not from Sorrel Hill?"

"Yes, sir; that is my native town."

"Why, my old friend, Enoch Sloper, wrote me about you over a year ago. I expected you to call on me ere this with your 'credentials.' And late as it is, I am happy to meet you."

"Fortunately, sir, my 'credentials' were not necessary; but I have the good deacon's *letter* stowed away safely, and if I am ever so unlucky as to be *out of place*, it may yet serve me for a '*character.*'"

"No danger of that, young man, if half what the deacon says of you is true."

"I can vouch for the truth of it *all*. The deacon is very moderate in his praises. When you want justice done him, come to me," said Grace, unblushingly.

"I see you are already *biassed*. You would not make an impartial report," rejoined the governor, good-humouredly. "You have a charming advocate in Miss Pearson," continned he, addressing Mark. "Her eloquence vanquishes all opponents; her judgment is infallible when character and principle are things to be passed upon, as many have found to their cost."

A half hour's pleasant conversation passed, when the governor took his leave, bidding them good morning, and saying, he hoped to meet them both in the evening at his "reception." It would be the last of the season, and Miss Pearson must use her powers of eloquence, and prevail on the "obdurate young man" to accompany her.

The executive mansion is blazing with bright lights, and the starry eyes of lovely women lend their added lustre to the brilliant scene. The beauty and fashion of the capital are there. *Mr. Miller* is there too; and leaning on his arm, as if proud of her companion, is one of the very *élite* of society; a fair girl in blue satin and pearls, the reigning belle — had she chosen to be a belle — of the old aristocratic society of Albany. Though several years his senior, she seems very proud of her young companion, scarcely permitting herself to be separated from him during the evening.

And the mistress of all this splendour, — the governor's estimable lady, — to whom he has been presented, invites him to a seat by her side, with the same courtesy and cordiality as are extended to her most honoured guests. This was Mark's first entrance into society; and the heart which he carried away from that scene of festivity was different somewhat from the one he took with him. Yet his lot in

life was the same; nothing was changed; only his own feelings and views of life were changed.

Here, too, he met Mr. and Mrs. Loveland. They have
been to him the kindest of friends. They look up and smile
when they meet him, with Grace leaning on his arm. They
have always so many questions to ask about Sorrel Hill!
and if they receive a letter it is always taken to Mark, as to
one of the family.

A few, whose fastidious tastes would never permit them
to move out of their own particular circle, or treat with
common politeness any one who did not belong to "*our*
set," were astonished to see "plebeians," and "people of *no*
note, putting on such airs." Mrs. Gedney was shocked.
Wondered if Mrs. Loveland, and that Miss Pearson, of
whom half the young gentlemen in the city were desperately
enamoured, knew they were promenading with one of *her
husband's clerks;* making fools of themselves and him too;
or did they do it to show their independence and indifference
to the speeches of people? Wondered if they were aware
of his low propensities and nameless pedigree?—that he
took his meals at the second table, along with the coachman
and gardener? She would be delighted when an opportunity
was given to enlighten them; but not to-night. No, she
took a secret satisfaction in seeing the thing go on, in order
that their humiliation and her own triumph might be the
more complete.

It was a grand affair, this levee of the governor—"the
last of the season." From early evening until the "wee sma'
hours of the morning," the great mansion, from the pave-
ment to the grand dome, is flooded with light and warmth.
Carriages are flying hither and thither in all directions;
load after load is whirled up the spacious carriage-drive,
depositing its lovely freight of gayly-dressed ladies. But not
a few of the honest plebeian population *walk to the* "*Govern-
or's Levee!*" Had Ben Franklin been there, and the weather

permitted, I presume he would have preferred to walk, or at least he would have shown his regard for those present by treating all with the same urbanity and Christian benevolence, and his disregard of those few purse-proud individuals, whose greatest aspirations seem to be to ape somebody more foolish than themselves. Franklin used to appear at court in a republican dress, set off by fine old republican manners; and that was honour enough for him: but people nowadays think too much of rank and station, caste, and the conditions of men, and are growing uproarious over the " importance of sustaining the dignity of office."

Such a man was not Governor Worth. He belonged to the old school of politicians, who have been out of date these many years. He was democratic in taste and feeling — loving all mankind, as brothers of the same great Father should love one another. He said he owed his political success and his present exalted position to the suffrage of the poor man, as well as the rich. He took special pleasure in patronizing the honest poor man, in preference to the rich, and would often stop to grasp the rough palm of the labourer, esteeming him one of the sovereigns of this great democratic republic. He would never think of questioning him as to whether his father was a Whig or a Tory; his grandfather a Puritan or an Infidel, or whether he himself was born north or south of " Mason and Dixon's line ;" with a silver or a pewter spoon in his mouth. It was enough for his excellency to know that he was an American citizen, — true blue, — " ennobled by himself," " whose country's welfare is his first concern," though

> " Of manners rude and insolent of speech,
>   If, when the public safety is in question,
>   His zeal flowed warm and eager from his tongue."

This great and good man was ever, we say, the friend of the poor. His grand levees, held once a month during the legislative session, were in keeping with all his other — and some may think strange — ideas of equality. They were free to all — high and low, rich and poor. *Here* at least, once a month, they were wont to meet, equal in all respects, so far as the general hospitalities were concerned, and treated with the same general regard by their honoured executive and his estimable lady. Some of their friends remonstrated when this arrangement was first announced. Not a few preferred staying at home to coming in contact with a rabble. Great was their surprise when they learned how splendidly everything passed off. *The scheme worked admirably.* There was no sign of a rabble; but a great throng of well-dressed and well-behaved people, passed in at the wide front entrance, paid their respects to their chief magistrate and his lady, chatted and looked around them for a few moments, passed on to the refreshment-rooms, where was an ample supply of plain as well as rich and delicate viands, and then, in the same quiet, deferential manner, left the house.

The governor and Mrs. Worth resolved that this first reception should be the standard for all the others; let all come who wished to; let those stay away whose prejudices would not permit them to mingle with trades-people and mechanics. " When we give a· private party," said they, " we are privileged to invite, few or many, our particular friends only; but our *public levees are for the public;* justice to ourselves and courtesy to them demand that we should entertain all by whose suffrage the governor holds his office."

" Your friend seems to be a very superior young man," said Governor Worth, addressing Miss Pearson.

" Yes; he is a noble fellow! high-minded, persevering, self-denying, aiming at something higher than contentment in obscurity: his energy is surprising. I wish my brother Frank had his talents and energy, and would make him his model."

" Frank is born to a fortune, and may, most likely, have an ambition above invoices and price-currents."

" He does not seem to have an ambition for anything use-ful. I wish he had. Instead of studying a profession, he wants to go out as supercargo on the ship Chesapeake, which sails next month. It goes on a three years' voyage to the East Indies."

" There is not much use in tying a boy down to a profes-sion, if his tastes lead him in an opposite direction. A three years' cruise round half the globe may satisfy his desire for travel ; and then he will not be too old to study for a profes-sion and settle down. He graduated well. Let him see something of the world, and then, depend upon it, he will resume his studies with increased zeal."

" You, sir, are older and wiser than I am ; but I feel as-sured, if he breaks in upon his studies now, and takes that voyage to China, he will never be a lawyer. He has little taste for study, and dislikes confinement above all things. Only for pa's promising him a one third interest in the ship Chesapeake, I fear he would have left college and run away to sea ! "

" Then let him go, by all means. If he does not make a lawyer, he may make something quite as useful ; and with his early correct training, and the influence of a pious father and a loving, praying sister, he will scarcely go astray."

" O, I wish he were like Mark Miller ! " sighed Grace. "*He* is toiling night and day to reach just what brother Frank has already within his grasp."

" That often happens. It were a queer world did all pos-sess the same tastes. If all our aspirations ran in the same channel, where were our statesmen, our noble mechanics, our authors and aitists, our great generals and naval com-manders, our painters, poets, printers, and professors, our worthy divines and self-sacrificing missionaries? Men of science, men who have become eminent in their professions,

15

have, as a general thing, pursued the bent of their own inclinations, not having had their young minds warped adversely to their own tastes and judgment."

Miss Pearson was but half convinced. She had ever opposed this wish of her only brother. It was quite natural that she should desire him to adopt a profession, or a business that would keep them together. Sometimes she felt that coercive measures were justifiable; but Frank had always been such a good brother to her, communicating his plans as soon as he formed them in his own thoughts, and with such an open, undisguised, confiding simplicity, that it seemed almost like betraying confidence to oppose him further.

As we shall not have occasion to speak of Frank Pearson again, — he having but little to do with the present history, — we will add, by way of parenthesis, that he sailed on the Chesapeake at the appointed time. That vessel was bound for the far eastern hemisphere, and back again, which "double voyage" then occupied about three years. His sister's prophecies were fulfilled. He never settled down to a profession, but became enamoured with the sea, often repeating, —

> "No scene half bright enough to win
> My young heart from the sea!"

For many years he was commander of a noble packet-ship, and noted for his uniform Christian life on sea and on land. Once or twice, Grace *and her family* sailed with him around half the globe, visiting many places of interest, and nearly all the principal cities in the old world.

Three full years had passed. They had not been altogether the happiest of Mark's life. A commercial life was not according to his taste. He had made it a very laborious one. At times it was irksome. He missed the free country air, the green and glossy fields, the bleating of the sheep on

the hills in this sweet pleasant spring weather, the com.
panionship of his mother, and the old familiar tinkle of the
brooklet that ran by her door.   He was getting just a little
bit homesick, if the truth were told.   But the cherished pur.
pose of his heart was every day drawing nearer its aecom.
plishment.   He was soon to enter college.

Deacon and Mrs. Sloper were on a visit to their daughter,
Mrs. Loveland.   They had seen Mark every day ; and it
would have done your heart good to see the kind, satisfied
smile of the old couple, when they found how well " their
dear boy " was getting on, and how his employers regarded
him.

" I have news for you, Mark," said the worthy deacon,
one day, entering the office in a glow of excitement.   " My
old friend Worth will doubtless be reëlected to a second
term of office, and you are to be appointed his private secretary.   Owing to the ill health of his present secretary,
you are to enter at once upon your duties. ·It is good for
another year, whether he is reëlected or not.   I trust you
will not decline this offer.   The situation will be more to
your taste than your present one, and you will have an opportunity of seeing something of political life.   You have
talents, energy, and ambition ; and, though no very great
thing in itself, you will be thrown among a different class of
men, and it may prove a stepping-stone to your farther advancement."

" It is very strange that Governor Worth should select me
for this position — a mere casual acquaintance of a few
months' standing."

" He has penetration, and he likes you ; and you have
abilities, and will apply yourself to whatever you undertake.
The road to honour and distinction is open before you, and
you justly deserve to win both."

" Many thanks for your unbounded generosity, my dear,
kind friend.   I feel that it is all owing to your love.   But if

I accept this situation, I must forego my long-cherished desire of entering upon a collegiate course of study.   This
may for the present appear the more advisable of the two.
It would certainly be more lucrative, and all I could desire.
I have hoarded my means with almost miserly care, and
have enough to take me through.   It would be a disappointment which I should scarcely outlive.   Besides, I shall have
my mother with me during the three years that I am in
college."

"I don't know but your plans are better than mine, Mark,
after all; and as you are so bent on it, the sooner you are
off to college the better.   But I never supposed you had half
enough money laid by to take you through college, seeing
you have always done so much for your mother.   There's
many a dollar that'll be wanting, I'm afeared.   And, Mark,
—now mind what I'm saying to you,—if you *should* ever want
money for your college expenses, or to start you in business
when you're through, remember uncle Enoch has a few
hundred at your disposal.   Yes, Mark, go to college, by all
means.   I sort o' opposed your pulling up stakes and leaving Sorreltown; but you was right about it.   Go ahead.   I
guess the govnor must find another secretary.   But what's
that you were saying about having your mother with you
while in college?   Do you suppose she is not well taken care
of?   I tell you, Mark, she is like one of the family,—we
should miss her sadly; though I know she pines about you,
and many a sigh escapes her when she is not aware of it."

"I am her only child, and our separation shall not be
protracted one hour longer than I can help it.   She must
be with me,—I cannot endure another three years' absence
from her."

"Yes, it has been a long, tedious absence to her; though
she is always cheerful and hopeful, because you write her
such loving letters, and she knows how well you are getting
along.   What mother's heart would not be happy to know

she had such a dutiful son? Mark, you are an honour to your birthplace. I hope to live to see you come back to us, to spend your days among those who will ever be proud of you."

"God bless and preserve you!" was Mark's tearful response. "When I send for my mother," he added, "you will please help her to dispose of her things, and see her comfortably started on her journey."

O, these partings and separations! How they wring the heart! Mark felt as if his father had left him. But the thought that in two months he should see his mother, and be living with her again under one roof, supported him under the trials of this and other partings that were soon to follow.

The "firm" had held out large inducements for him to remain with them. Mr. Loveland had said, "Miller, my dear fellow, here is the place of 'receiving teller' in the bank ready for your acceptance." Mr. Newell, who had returned with his family to New York, had written him that, did he feel disposed to relinquish his purpose of entering college, there was a fine opportunity for him to engage in a lucrative and permanent business.

But to all these generous offers he turned a deaf ear. His heart overflowed with gratitude to these friends for their continued kindness — gratitude which,

> "Like curls of holy incense, overtake
> Each other in his bosom, and enlarge
> With their embrace his sweet remembrance."

CHAPTER XXV.

COLLEGE LIFE.

"The youth
Proceeds the paths of science to explore;
And now, expanded to the beams of truth,
New energies and charms unknown before
His mind discloses."

BEATTIE.

E will avoid all the dry and uninteresting details of Mark's life while in college. The life of one student does not differ materially from that of another. One day is so very much like all the days of the year, that a student almost loses his count of time. Mark entered college with the same resolute will and steady perseverance that he entered upon his clerkship with Messrs. Gedney & Wright. As these qualities and principles of the heart and mind soon won for him the respect and confidence of his employers, so they afterwards won for him the esteem and admiration of his classmates and teachers. He had already the foundation of a good classical education. The text-books used in preparatory classes had all been gone through with under his gentle and efficient instructress Grace Pearson. His life had ever been, and would ever be, a laborious one; whatever he did was done with all the strength of his powerful will. Hard at work all day, studying hard far into night. In him his teachers discovered, if not an unusually brilliant, a *working*, *ambitious* scholar.

He soon became the star scholar of his class, and his classmates, to keep up with him, had to work with in-creased energy and take fewer hours for recreation.

Mark led no hermit's life. Neither did he isolate himself from his fellow-students during the hours of recreation, hut mingled freely in all their innocent and athletic sports, be-lieving that "nobody's healthful without exercise."

In the prosecution of the different sciences, and in the study of the languages, his great ability to acquire and re-tain knowledge was constantly displaying itself. The diffi-cult problems of the higher mathematics were mastered — not without effort and application — but they were *mastered;* and in them he found intense delight. His evenings were devoted to demonstrating them.

In the science of astronomy he took especial delight. He entered upon this with an alacrity and enthusiasm surprising even to himself. He loved to gaze upon the blue evening sky, when it was studded with bright stars, when the round full moon, midway in the firmament, —

"Hung like a gem on the brow of the night," —

while her serene, soft light fell like sheets of silver on all below. "Orion, with its circlet of hazy gold," Venus with her burning eye, the Polar Star, the Dipper, —

"Shining in order, like a living hymn
Written in light," —

had ever seemed like friends sympathizing in his utter lone-liness. His thoughts would turn aptly from contemplating "the pearly depths through which they spring" to a scene behind the veil of mortal ken.

From early childhood, when he was wont to give way to gloomy forebodings, did a weight of grief press upon his heart; did the world seem cold as the snow-clad hills with-out; did his hard fate seem by the "potent stars ordained;"

did a mist sometimes hang upon his brow and dissolve itself
into tears.   Those tearful orbs were raised heavenward,
where he learned the majesty and goodness of God, who
never errs in the disposition of the meanest creature of his
care.

Of rhetoric — a study that students generally consider remarkably dry and unprofitable — Mark was particularly fond.
While acquiring the elements of this all-important science,
he listened attentively to the declamations of the older students, thereby becoming master of much that he could never
have learned from books.

His first attempt at declamation (the first since he left
the old school-house at Sorrel Hill, where he was always
laughed at) was awkward in the extreme, provoking smiles
from the gravest faces.

He supposed, like many an older and more experienced
aspirant for oratorical fame, that great emphasis on certain
words, and much gesticulation, are calculated to impress upon
his auditors what, without these, they had not sense enough
to comprehend.

It did not occur during the regular daily session, when the
faculty and visitors were present, but on an evening set apart
for extemporaneous and oratorical exercises, when each and
all were granted the liberty of criticising their fellow-students' masterly efforts.   These evenings resulted in a little
benefit to each, and much merriment to all.

Mark stumbled through his " set speech," and descended
from the rostrum, amidst the wildest shouts of well-feigned
applause.   This being quite in order, he joined in the laugh
against himself, good naturedly, but paused, ere he took his
seat, to say, —

"Laugh on now, sirs! but you shall one day be made to
cry — when the charming strains of my classic eloquence
shall fill the world with dumb wonder, when the deep dia-
pason of my voice shall roll out like 'young earthquakes at

their birth.' Though the Fates have bequeathed to me no rich legacy of wit and humour, and though my commanding form and brilliant genius fail to win the hearts of my audi-tory (especially the feminine portion of it), yet I shall pro-ceed to demolish the beautifully-wrought theory of my an-tagonists, whoever they may be, in an eloquent strain, 'short particular metre.' The loud huzzas that ever follow sound logic and terse reasoning will drown the feeble acclaims which the eloquence of my opponent, with his fine poetical phrases and 'foppery of tongue' might call forth. I tell you, fellow-citizens, your necks will ache, gazing at me from my proud eminence. I shall never pause till a great height is won, and shall really pity the Liliputian efforts of any one who dares hazard life and limb in his attempts to outstrip me."

Mark took his seat amidst a burst of applause that made the house shake. There was something so thrillingly ludi-crous in his gesticulations and personations, that it was long ere order and quiet were restored.

This short impromptu speech inspired others to try their wits at extemporizing, which generally consisted in lively sallies of wit, and humorous repartee, in neither of which was Mark behind his fellows. He soon became a great fa-vourite in these debates, his presence calling forth the keenest witticisms, his absence deplored as a something missed which nothing else could supply.

These hours did not interfere with his studies, else his seat in the debating club had always been vacant. So great was his desire to graduate in a given time, that no more hours were given to recreation and pastime than health demanded. "His thirst for knowledge was insatiable, and such was the pleasure he derived from the pursuit of his different studies, that he seemed insensible to fatigue, and averse to trespassing in any wise upon hours allotted to study." One great thing in Mark's favour was his strong, healthy, robust constitution. He had seldom seen a sick day. It would not in all cases be wise for boys to take him for an example, and push themselves beyond what their strength can bear.

The superiority of his intellect was not more clearly defined than in other young men of his own age ; neither was he remarkable for the keenness of his perceptive faculties ; in his retentive memory, and his earnest, untiring industry, was the secret of his great proficiency.

In one of his letters Mark describes a secret society called the Mohegans. " They meet," writes he, " in the rooms of the members, and spend the evening in smoking tobacco and contriving some mischief. One of their favourite amusements is to adjourn to the room of some freshman, and under pretence of making him a friendly call, invite themselves to a smoke around his table, until the fumes are often so sickening as to drive him from the room. Meanwhile they secretly amuse themselves with his attempts to be civil and hospitable in spite of the blinding and strangling puffs they incessantly roll into his face. If any poor freshman resents this, or for any cause is suspected by them of being a spy, they visit his room, and having locked the door, and so made him prisoner, they place the hollow hemisphere of a large pumpkin on the table, fill it with tobacco, and then place the bowls of their long lighted pipes within this mass of the weed, and blow until the room is filled with smoke. When the tobacco is reduced to ashes, they seat the freshman before the pumpkin, and demand of him a chemical analysis of its contents. While he is looking into the ashes, one of the Mohegans suddenly claps the pumpkin on the head of the chemist, expressing the hope that the ideas contained in his new study-cap will strike through his skull, and so help him very materially in his scientific investigations. Two weeks ago last night the freshmen found a good opportunity to retaliate on the Mohegans. Early in the day some one of the former learned that the latter were going that night to make a bonfire of Professor Wells's old covered gig, a vehicle that, having been placed on the retired list, had long stood under an open woodshed. And so the freshmen contrived, in the dusk of the evening, to conceal a small keg of gunpowder under the seat of the gig, and at a late hour to hide themselves, armed with tin horns, cow-bells, and old muskets, in the trees that bordered one side of the field in which they observed the Mohegans were stealthily building a huge pile, made of rails, brush, straw, and such other combustibles as they could steal from haystacks, barns, and woodsheds. Accordingly, about midnight the flames were seen to burst suddenly from the martyr pyre, revealing the outline of the old gig, which had been placed astride the fuel. Not long after, the Mohegans appeared, disguised in a variety of Indian costumes and mounted upon horses, which they had either stolen or hired from the neighbouring farmers. They rode these horses without saddle or bridle, and some of them without even a halter. This savage procession galloped, yelling and whooping, round the bonfire in a circle, but at such a distance that they were but dimly visible, except when the flames flared with unusual splendor. When the powwow was at its height, the seat of the old gig *caved*, occasioning an alarming explosion, which scattered the bonfire in all directions, tossed the two flaming wheels across the field, right and left, and flung the old leathern gig-top high into the air. The horses were so frightened by this combustion, that they either threw their riders, or ran away with them into the distant darkness. The explosion was to have been the signal for the treed freshmen to blow their horns, ring their bells, and discharge their muskets. But the dispersion of the Mohegans was so sudden and complete that their adversaries could do nothing but laugh. And it was some time before any one could muster sufficient gravity to blow a horn or pull a trigger."

The weeks and months sped away. Mark was happier

than he had ever been before.   The one great desire of his
life had a fair beginning, and seemed most likely to have a
prosperous ending.   His little life-boat, now fairly afloat on
the sea of adventure, had thus far drifted smoothly with the
tide.   The " breakers " were far away in the distance, and
might never oppose so good a pilot as he.

The greatest source of his earthly happiness was his dear
mother's presence.   They were once more together.   Their
" ane ingle blinkin' bonnilie " warmed and cheered these
two devoted beings, who were never more in this life to be
separated.   They were enabled to rent a small house upon
the outskirts of the city, which was both neat and comforta-
ble, and furnished with everything necessary for their con-
venience and happiness.

A young student occupied a room with Mark ; and for the
three years that they were in college they were as brothers
of one family, — the good mother dispensing her love and
kindness to both, as though both were her sons.   They were
always seen together.   The boys used to say they lived in
each other's shadow.   Together they walked the three quarters of a mile between the college and home ; together they
conned their tasks by the bright lamp-light or the warm winter's fire.   Over this young student — his junior by three years
— Mark had an unbounded influence, as he seemed to have
over others who knew him well.   And so deep and true was
the affection of both mother and son for their young guest,
so devoted was he in his attachment to them, that in after
years — in their earlier and later manhood — they ever re-
verted to that humble home, and the time passed under that
lowly roof, as by far the happiest of their whole lives.

He was very unlike Mark in one respect — he seemed
wholly dependent on the circumstances that surrounded him.
On a calm, sunny day, or in the society of gay companions,
he would indulge in a flow of animal spirits that by some
was deemed excessive ; but in dull, rainy weather, — espe-

cially if left to himself, — he was gloomy and taciturn, in_
dulging in long, silent reveries, which were calculated to
leave unhappy impressions on his character. He was one
whom others would never think of looking up to or leaning
upon for support: he was ever the one to look up to and lean
upon others. Yet there was nothing weak or effeminate in
his character; he was true, and pure in heart and principle,
frank and generous, only he had never been taught the im_
portance of self-reliance. It was not strange that he should
cast himself upon and cling to a companion like Mark,
with his strong opinions, brave heart, and unconquerable
will.

During the three years that he was an inmate of the little
family, — whom he ever after regarded as allied to him by
the ties of a deep and lasting affection, — he learned that our
happiness, though it may be somewhat affected by, is not
wholly dependent on, externals, — that there is within our
souls a well-spring of happiness, fathomless and never-fail-
ing, which at times will overflow in little rills of joy and
love, bearing away upon its eddying bosom all the dark,
inhuman passions of our natures, and in its circling course,
returning with rich argosies freighted with the kindliest
feelings, the happiest thoughts, the noblest aspirations of
which we are capable, bringing forth to a new life, from
under the loam of selfishness and carnal enjoyments, ardent
longings for the good, the true, the beautiful, the heavenly.

Many other things he learned from these true friends. He
learned something of that home-happiness of which till now
he had little knowledge. He was taught, by the daily consistent Christian lives of mother and son, that "godliness,
with contentment, is great gain."

He used to say, " The great wide world must ever be my
home, and no more of love than what is shared by the common brotherhood of mankind." Experience had taught him
that the world was chary of its favours, — that Fortune gen-

erally caresses those who can brave her "threatening eye" with still more defiant looks!

He never would have had a heart to battle with either, but for the practical examples and lessons learned here.

Nothing unites people like a common interest, or a common object to work for, — unless it be a common sorrow: even then, —

> "Storms divided
> Abate their force, and with less rage are guided."

These two young men were striving for one and the same object, with the same goal in view. Born neither to affluence nor influence, they had both to carve out their destinies single-handed.

Prosperity was to crown the efforts of the one, though his classmates persisted in saying that oratory was not his forte; and it *was* not. An ever-active mind, and a strong, resolute purpose, enabled him to master this art.

The other, though a fine, generous, open-hearted fellow, always sanguine and hopeful, and quite sure that his plans will somehow succeed, and fully conscious of his abilities to do all that is required of him, lacks the great energizing powers of mind so absolutely necessary to the accomplishment of his purposes.

The world is full of just such men. For instance, — two are seeking the same office. The one is modest and retiring, though in every way qualified to perform the duties of said office acceptably and honourably, as his friends well know. But he is wanting in mental force, or is too diffident to push himself forward, and go to work to obtain it. And while he is waiting, and hoping to have his friends petition for his acceptance, or to have it thrust upon him, some other man — his inferior in every respect save that of energy, but one who can shrewdly pettifog his own case — will always slip in ahead of him, and bear away the honours.

There is an old adage — "Show me the father, and I will

show you the daughter; show me the mother, and I will show you the son." This may be true in most cases — the history of our two principal characters certainly leans that way; but what of the child who is left to himself? Thrown upon the world with no natural guardians, no one to love or take any particular interest in him, dependent on his own inherent principles and judgment, — with no other guide than these, he is apt to run into extremes. He forms a character to himself. He is either broken in spirit, has no heart to buffet with opposing elements, or brave those whose only wish is to make him a dependent. He will either become very brave and stout-hearted, or very timid and obedient. How sad is the destiny of such a child!

Days, weeks, and months passed away. They glided so imperceptibly one into the other, there was scarcely beginning or ending of the seasons, or the years. Their young *protégé* became every day more endeared to Mrs. Miller and her son, and they, in every way, necessary to his happiness. He was timid and dependent by nature; and Mark was often called upon to shield him from the mischievous persecutions of the younger students, whose delight it seemed to be to tease and annoy those of more quiet and docile temperaments. A feeling of loneliness, and often wretchedness, for his orphaned and unconnected situation, makes him at times a girl at heart — he sometimes wishes he was; for then some one would take' him kindly by the hand, and love him for sweet charity's sake. His young life had been a lonely one. Now he is with just such friends as a nature like his requires. Thanks to a kind, protecting Providence for directing him hither! Thanks to these friends for preserving him from that cold, unfeeling cynicism which unloved childhood is apt to acquire.

If a cup of water given to a wayfarer will receive its reward, many blessings shall be on the heads of those who administer " hearts-ease " to friendless, orphaned childhood.

Their healing leaves and heavenly balm shall sustain their own spirits when they faint under the burdens of life. The blessed memory of one such benevolent deed shall cheer the heart until it ceases to beat.

They are a very happy household. One is daily learning lessons of self-reliance, and independence of thought and action, which will in after years be a better capital than gold and silver to start him in business.

Another is already reaping the reward of these virtues. The precious seed sown in his young heart is bringing forth fruit a hundred fold: he is not only self-reliant, — he thinks for himself and others; and these virtues and graces of his character "spring from the best of all roots — a truthful, pious heart."

The mother moves cheerfully about her household matters, as in the old days, or sits quietly sewing or knitting all the evening, while the boys study, — her eyes glistening with silent joy, and her heart too full, and too near the one other throbbing in unison with her own, to need the "intervention of many words."

She looks just as she did that night when Mark and Nettie and she sat together in the glowing firelight at the old home.

CHAPTER XXVI.

NETTIE STRANGE AND HER MOTHERLESS CHARGE.

" Within her heart was his image,
  Clothed in the beauty of love and youth
  As last she beheld him,
  Only more beautiful made by his death-like
  Silence and absence."

LONGFELLOW.

IX years have passed away — years of indispensable, patient toil to Nettie Strange, who is now a blooming maiden of eighteen.

Six years had a graceful willow drooped over the little green hillock where lay her mother in that dreamless sleep that knows no waking until the resurrection. Long years had it cast its mournful shadow, or shed its soft dews upon a spot that had no monument to tell who slumbered beneath. It was known to few. But there was one loving heart that ever turned to it when oppressed with thoughts too holy and sacred for the world to know. All around were the stern emblems of death. Over the whole field brooded the spirit of desolation. There were a few plain white slabs, with the names and ages of the deceased engraved on them ; but the most were rough, flat rocks, with a single initial, or perhaps two, with the date rudely carved, and some with stakes at the head and foot, others with not even these. How lonesome and desolate it looked ! Save the willow that Nettie's hand had planted, no graceful trees, no sweet flowers, were there ; but everything spoke of

16

death and decay; nothing to remind one of the glorious reunion beyond.

From her mother's grave the child had come back a woman. She did not weep much; the tears had settled around her heart; for there was a heavy pain there. The little wailing infant, which her dying mother confided to her care, had always nestled to her heart, as if she was indeed its mother. The thought of self was gone, if it ever had a place in her nature. She had no separate life from the one which found its all of happiness in living for the welfare and happiness of others. Her father looks up to her as to a superior being; her brothers and sisters love and respect her, while they try to imitate her blessed example. They think sometimes, what if she too were to be taken from them! Their obedience and kindness to one another great- ly diminish the numberless household tasks of their sister. More like an angel than like a mortal she seemed when directing their young lips to form themselves in prayer, or their sweet voices in singing their evening hymn.

Benny, who seemed more self-willed and stubborn than the others, declined to say his prayers, unless he could pray for mother and Janie just the same as if they were living. Nettie had said to the children — as they were in the habit of asking God's blessing for " father and *mother*, brothers and sisters, and *Janie too* " — it was not necessary to in- clude mother and little sister Janie, as they were both in heaven, where they would never need our prayers more. The children were surprised at this doctrine. Benny re- mained incorrigible, and their sister could not easily explain it to them, or understand the *why* herself. Although she had appealed to her father, and he had told them that the prayers of the living availed nothing for the dead, yet it seemed such an act of filial love and reverence on Benny's part, Nettie had not the heart to remonstrate. Besides, she always said that it was so natural for *her* to include *all* her loved ones in her petitions to the throne of grace, she hoped it was no sin to pray for her beloved dead.

" They are ever in my thoughts," she said; " and when I ask for God's pitying, sustaining grace, to rest upon my father, his love, and watchcare, and guiding hand to keep the rest of us in the little path wherein we are to walk, I feel as if something were left unsaid, some great blessing yet unasked for. It seemed so singular that, though I had prayed for my mother ever since my infant lips could lisp her name, yet the night after she died I was to omit that name, now dearer than ever, and I must never again mingle it with ours, but my lips must henceforth be as silent as hers. I felt that I had slighted her love, that I had not paid the respect to her memory that it deserved. And though my lips were sealed, my heart was ever saying, ' Bless those whom Thou hast taken from us; our dear ones whom Thou hast with Thee in eternity. Let them, O my Father, dwell very near to Thee, and approach nearer and nearer the great white throne, until they are as the angels, who are forever singing praises to Thy great and holy name. May the sweet bond of affection ever remain unbroken, through time and in eternity.'" Nettie felt comforted, and better satisfied with herself, when her voiceless orisons were framed into words. She no longer was shocked at the idea of Benny's prayers for " dear mother and Janie too;" neither was her conscience disturbed when words bearing the same import, inspired by the same love, gushed warm and ardent from her own lips.

As the children grew older, they could understand the folly and the danger of praying for the dead. Their father taught them that they might nevertheless *remember* the dead in other ways and for other purposes; and that it was both safe and profitable to pray as follows: " Our heavenly Father, we thank Thee for the good examples we inherit from all our kindred who have finished their course in faith, and we beg of Thee grace to follow their virtuous and godly living, that we may finally share their glory and felicity."

In many another way Ben's obstinacy, or rather his independent and original way of thinking and acting, manifested itself. He was very fond of making a bargain, and would oftentimes surprise his father by the shrewdness and cleverness with which he effected a trade. He would say to his father and his brother James, his elder by four years, " Let us do this or that; let us summer-fallow this field, or put in such a crop, instead of the one you are intending to. We will make such and such improvements. That old unsightly hayrick *has got to come down*, for there is just where we want our new granary to stand. Let us not spend half our time in patching up that old stake-and-rider fence. Just demolish it at once, and build one that's decent and substantial."

His father's replies were generally to the effect that they had no time *now*. They would take the first rainy day, or some time when they were not so hurried, to do thus and so. Ben's obstinacy was made apparent by his not always waiting for the " rainy day," and by taking time into his own hands.

On looking out one spring morning, while the dew was yet heavy on the grass, the family were surprised to find the old *cave*, which had served for a milk-house, utterly demolished, not one old rotten log remaining upon another, and Ben busily engaged laying a good and solid foundation of stone and mortar for a new one in another place.

" What is *that boy* up to now? "

" Going to have a new milk-house, nice and clean from top to bottom."

" This is no time — the busiest in the whole year — to commence such a job as that. Why didn't you ask *me* about it? "

" Why, father, we have been two or three years waiting

for the right time to come. This old roof was just ready to tumble down, any way. My pulling it down may save some of us a broken head."

" But the *time!* the *time!* We are very busy now; and besides that, you can never do it *alone.* I was calculating, when we got round to it, to hire a mason and a carpenter, and have a good milk-house, built as it *ought* to be built."

Ben might have replied, had he been a disrespectful son, that he was quite sure the right time *had* come; that if they depended on a mason and a carpenter to do the work, and their father to superintend it, many a year would elapse before its completion.

He merely said, good naturedly, knowing his father's weak point about being consulted in all matters in doors and out, and making it appear as if really *he* could not expect to accomplish a task of such magnitude without his advice and assistance, —

" I can lay up the walls as good as a mason. They will be rough, but I am going to plaster it outside and in. When I come to the carpenter work, why, you must instruct me; and take a little time to help me on with the roof, and to put in the shelves. Which way would *you* have the roof slant? Better have the window on the north side, and the door south — hadn't *we?* "

" Well, y-e-s, I guess so; that's as good a way as any. And now you have commenced it, we may as well all turn to and get the pesky thing done at once. That old one *was* of very little account in its best days, and we shall have the milk of ten cows this summer. I really don't know how we could have got along with the old one."

" Two or three days' work *with your assistance, father,* will accomplish the whole thing. You can, if you please, wheel the rock from the old stone fence yonder, and I will lay the wall. If James wishes to serve a short apprenticeship

at the business, he might *'tend mason*, and that will hurry
things along still faster."

"I don't know as anything is suffering to be done in the
fields. It is a'most too wet and cold to commence planting,
and I guess, come to think on it, that this is just the best time
we shall ever have to do such little odd jobs. But what were
you saying about wheeling the rock from the old stone fence?
You don't suppose I'm going to pull down that fence, do
you? — and turn the front yard, with all of Nettie's posies,
into the street!"

"Why, father, we have been talking about moving that
old stone pile these five years. It mortifies us every time we
look at it. It is hardly in keeping with the nice, clean walks,
and beds of gay flowers, and sweet-climbing vines, which the
girls take so much pains with. See how hard they work,
father, and how much pride and pleasure they take in making the place look like a home! We must do *our* part, and
that will lighten their toil. The work of the dairy will not
be one half what it has been when we get this all arranged."

"Well, what's the use of pulling down a part of the fence
until we *get ready* to move the whole away? There's rock
enough in that fence to build half a dozen such small
houses."

"Every rock has got to come down," replied Ben, with
more warmth than he had yet addressed to his father. "And
we have use for them all. After the milk-house, we will
have a smoke-house, and not be obliged to hang our hams
in the chimney-top. We *want full half a dozen* nice out-
buildings, all standing in a row, plastered and whitewashed;
and the large rocks will lay the foundation to the new barn."

"But you talk as if everything could be done in a minute!
You have got such a way of plunging into business, one
would think, to hear you talk, that all this must be done
now or *never!*"

"No, father, we will do one thing at a time; but we

shall never accomplish *anything*, if we never make a beginning."

Wisely said, and as wisely acted upon, as one after another all these and many more improvements rose to view in and around the old homestead.

Ben was generally the one to put into execution, but his was not the only head that planned these improvements. He and his older sister were often seen consulting together in low tones, the influence of both being a thing quite necessary to bring the father over to their way of thinking.

James was sometimes exceedingly refractory; but he inherited, or at all events he possessed, his father's weakness about his advice being asked, and his coöperative measures being carried into execution.

Ben had said to him one day, "Let us try and make a wheelbarrow of our own, and not run a mile and a half to borrow one every time we want one to use."

"Make a wheelbarrow! We might as well undertake to build a meeting-house."

"I see nothing so very difficult in its construction, if we only had the tools to work with. The iron-work is very simple, and will not cost much. Suppose we try. I think it's a pity that two great strapping fellows like us should have it to say that we will not *try* to make so simple a thing as this, because we can borrow from our neighbours."

James had been *consulted* on the start, and after a little advice from the village carpenter, the wheelbarrow was commenced, and in due time *finished*, to the great satisfaction of the two joint owners.

They were so well pleased with their first piece of mechanism, that they made another and another, until twenty-five were made, and sold at two dollars apiece. Their reputation as architects was now established. They were not sure but they ought to get out a "patent right," and set up an extensive manufactory.

When Mrs. Miller moved away, she agreed with the boys
that for a small annuity they should till her land and take
care of the place. It was only ten acres, but so well was it
managed that at the end of the year they found themselves
in possession of a handsome little income; and then it was
all theirs. They had earned it with their own hands, and
could do what they pleased with it. How to invest it seemed
to perplex them more than how to earn it.

Great and mutual interests were to arise from these small
beginnings. For a certain per cent. the village blacksmith
agreed to iron all the wheelbarrows they would make; and
as they found a ready sale, and very fair profits, they set
themselves to work in good earnest. For several years they
carried on this business; and when the Erie Canal was finished, they had realized a small fortune from the sale of their
scrapers and wheelbarrows.

Very few of the villagers ever came to admire Nettie's
home, or cheer the patient, hard-working inmates. Few cared
whether it were prosperous and happy, or otherwise. Fewer
still were intimate friends of its lowly mistress, or they might
have discovered the changes a few years had wrought in her.
A serene spiritual beauty irradiated her not unlovely features,
giving to them a softer, sweeter, heavenlier expression, and
to her graceful form, as it moulded into womanhood, a lady-
like dignified bearing.

Within *her* heart was the same well-spring of cheerful
content that ever diffuses its genial influence on all around;
and yet there was so little, so very little, in her outer life to
soften its asperities, or cheer its monotonous round!

It was not until months after her departure that Nettie
could summon fortitude to visit the old home of Mrs. Miller.
At length her birthday, the ninth of November, came round.
The children had gone on a nutting excursion, and she resolved on making it a little holiday for herself. The days

were getting shorter and more chilly, and she could defer it no longer. She never visited places "sacred to memory dear" in company with others — the graveyard, and the old haunt under the great hickory, where the stile helped her over into the fields beyond. Others were permitted to go whenever they listed, but under one pretence or another, she always remained behind. These places — and now Mrs. Miller's cottage — were hallowed by remembrances too sacred to permit of her going accompanied by others; remembrances of the sweetest associations, the happiest, the holiest, the saddest she had ever known, and of the one short hour, the story of which she had shared with no other heart.

She followed the path that led close along by the old zig-zag rail fence, and jumped across the brooklet, babbling gayly as ever, idly telling its secrets to whatever ear was disposed to listen.

Nettie seated herself upon its green bank, while its garrulous little tongue rippled on in a low, murmuring tone, bewailing the untimely visits of King Frost away up in the mountains where it came from, and how, like a cold-hearted old tyrant as he was, he was usurping the reign of the beautiful Summer Queen, that gemmed its banks with green foliage and bright flowers; how day by day she was laying aside her gay robes for those of sober maturity, meekly resigning her royal sceptre to her stern successor. It told Nettie — for she sat listening a long time to its mournful story — how sorry they would be when the ruthless old monarch should take up his final abode with them, for then it seemed to say, as in so many words, " A seal will be set upon my lips, he will bind with icy chains my musical tongue, and we shall be strangers ! "

Not more than a hundred yards from where Nettie was sitting, by the silver brooklet, were the two green mounds where reposed the precious clay of her mother and sister.

There was another little spot, scarcely less sacred than these two, where the rank grass was not permitted to grow, because the same loving hands kept the sod green and fresh.

She sat down by her mother's grave, and thought of the last time she saw her, and of her dying commands, and, bowing her face down on the green earth, tearfully renewed the promise to be as a mother to those motherless ones, and resolved to bear her daily cross with more cheerfulness.

She emptied her lap of all the wild flowers she could find in her walk thither, and weaving them into wreaths, one smaller than the other, as though intended for the brows of the sleepers, laid them on the two graves.

There were some faded leaves twined among the flowers, and the autumn winds had rifled some of them of their fresh, delicate sweetness, but Nettie thought them all the more appropriate, for they told her heart at least of a home rifled of its sweetest song bird, when Janie was gathered to the heavenly home, and of faded hopes and withered affections when her mother died.

They were to her emblems of time and eternity. The fading flowers, fleeting as the breath of summer, reminded her of the fleeting years as they sped away on the wings of time. The sweet and holy affection that placed them there, would grow stronger and purer as the ages of eternity rolled away.

Nettie pressed her lips to the green sod, and hastened on her way to the cottage of Mrs. Miller. She recrossed the beautiful brooklet in order to follow the path, and paused only a moment to wish that when she too slept the long sleep, she might be laid where its sweet purling voice could forever murmur a requiem over her grave.

She followed a little by-path, at the extremity of which was the lane leading to the house; looking meanwhile this way and that, and listening for any voice that might be heard. All was still and quiet on that balmy autumn after-

noon. Save the splashing of the distant mill-wheel, coming
up through the still, pure air, softened to a low musical
sound, and the dripping of the water from the cattle-trough,
there was nothing to tell of the busy, bustling world beyond.

She entered the gate, and strolled through the little garden, overgrown with herbs and weeds, through which some
, hardy flowers were struggling for existence, living and growing, blossoming, and bringing forth the full ripe seed, in spite
of all the neglect and the coarser and harsher natures surrounding them.

How lonely and desolate it looked!

Poor girl! how lonely and desolate her life had been but
for those inherent graces of the spirit which sustained and
strengthened it, beyond the power of influences which might
have discouraged and crushed her!

She laid her hand on the head of the old dog coming
slowly up to meet her, wagging his shaggy tail, and licking
her hand with a low, pitiful whine. She almost fancied
Mrs. Miller's gentle footstep coming out and saying some
pleasant words, as in days past. She looked around
towards the window, over which the industrious spiders
had woven a gossamer curtain, and fancied that she could
almost see dear faces peering through the panes, the bright
glistening eyes bidding her welcome as she approached.
And these were like a spiritual presence, whose silent voices,
echoing softly the thoughts of her own heart, seemed to stir
in it the sweet instead of the bitter fountains of her being,
bathing it afresh in its strengthening, healing waters.

She went back to the house with her heart filled with awe
and dread. It was so silent and lonely, and when she opened
the door noiselessly and crept in, it seemed like rolling the
stone from a sepulchre.

There were a few articles of the old furniture ranged with
a rigid formality against the walls. There was the ample
fireplace, whose genial warmth and brightness had made

her heart glow as none other had. She looked at the vacant chairs of the twain, while her thoughts went back, " way back," to the time when the shadow of the death-angel first brooded over the hearth-stone. But she could not remember when she first thought of Mrs. Miller and her son, with that tender solicitude which true affection inspires. She had *always* loved them.

The tears could no longer be restrained. She leaned her head upon the low window-ledge, and wept silently.

She might never see them again; she hardly dared to hope as much, yet something whispered, and its sweet voice long afterwards echoed back the words, " There will come a day when they will return to the old home; perhaps not to live, but still they *will come.*"

. Silently the tear-drops fall, silently and swiftly her thoughts fly backward and onward.

She thinks of the times when Mark drew her on his little sled across the pond when it was frozen over, or rowed her in his skiff when its surface was smooth and glassy as a mirror. But then she was a child, and no doubt he had forgotten her, or thought of her only as a child.

" And what am I," she said with a sorrowful dignity, " that I should expect to be remembered? We are no longer children, but it is sweet for me to remember the past. I wonder if he ever thinks of the olden time — of our childhood days; the sleigh-ride, when we both — and we only — staid at home; and the party at Deacon Sloper's, where we both went. Pshaw! he does remember; he could *never* forget *that* if he would. And yet he must be so .changed, he doubtless wishes to forget, and, by me at least, to be forgotten."

Her heart glowed with the remembrance of a thousand little acts of kindness, while those few parting words, " whom, next to my mother, I love best on earth," held it in thrall. Mingled with this, there stole to her cheek a burning flush of shame, to think *she only* remembered; she *only* through all these years had not forgotten!

Pressing her hand on her throbbing and aching heart, so intense were her feelings that she crept away as noiselessly as she came. The poor girl, with her load of grief, had not the *one* little happy hope of her childhood left.

CHAPTER XXVII.

MARK MILLER IS ELECTED SENATOR.

" Still on it creeps,
Each little moment at another's heels,
Till hours, days, years, and ages are made up
Of such small parts as these, and men look back,
Worn and bewildered, wondering how it is."

JOANNA BAILLIE.

T is not necessary to relate how, step by step, the march of time had made great changes in the persons and things connected with our story. We will only allude to the most prominent events of these twelve long years.

The young collegian has graduated with high honours, entered at once upon the study of the law, and two years later found him a junior partner in the office of his preceptor. Never had a student graduated with greater honours to himself and the college. Never did a young man enter the arena of professional or political life under more flattering auspices. Success has crowned his efforts; it seemed as though a blessing attended everything he put his hand to. He is now a noble-looking young man, tall and finely formed, with that gentle, yet brave, determined look, which shows a spirit of self-reliance that can not easily yield to trifling obstacles. The pure principles that reigned in the heart of the boy guide the man, and will guide him through all time, come weal or woe. His praises are on every tongue. His splendid talents, fearless resolution, and fine personal endowments, are the all-absorbing topics of the day. He is advancing steadily in the road to prosperity and preferment. He is happy because he is good, prosperous because he is provident.

Miss Pearson has become a sober, staid matron of thirty-two; but time has dealt gently with her good looks. She often says, " The freshness and fulness of my husband's love keep my heart green." Of her little son, Mark, she is very proud. He is a beautiful child; but she hopes the beauty of his character may fully equal that of the noble man after whom he was named. From the exalted position where Mark and Nettie first placed her, Grace never fell. She was to them a true friend: her sweet influence and almost sisterly regard inspired them with greater confidence in their own powers, enabling them to place a juster estimate upon their own abilities. Though a hundred miles away from the place where once, as if by accident, her feet had strayed, and years had elapsed, her influence remained still. Her little benefits and her letters came regularly. But after Mark went away to college, she never wrote concerning him.

About that time two neat cards were sent, tied around with white ribbon, announcing her marriage. But her love, though shared with another, ever remained the same for her young friends.

Under her silent and unobtrusive tuition, and not altogether unknown to himself, Mark felt his nature expanding into broader sympathies with mankind. His own experience enlarged, and he advanced to a point where a doubt of his success did not venture to intrude.

The old " homestead on the hill" is now a most beautiful place. The house is no longer brown and bare; indeed, it is almost a new house, very little of the original structure remaining. Additions have been made, giving to it a more graceful style of architecture. Tall pillars support the long galleries, and handsome dormer windows in the great steep

roof, and many other conveniences, ornamental and substantial, have made it altogether such a home as people of
taste and refinement would choose for a country residence.
It is newly painted, inside and out, and finished and furnished
becomingly. Good fences, good barns, and other improvements, have added largely to the comfort and respectability
of its inmates. Large trees, shrubs, flowers, and creeping
vines are all around, almost hiding it from sight.

One had gone forth, a young and beautiful bride, to gladden the heart and home of him who sought and won her
love. Their home was in the far west, but Nettie was rec-
onciled to part with her young sister; for she had chosen,
wisely, a man every-way worthy of her. As Nettie gave
her into the hands of her husband, arrayed in a dress of soft,
white, fleecy muslin, with a wreath of pure bridal roses —
" sparkling in their own dew" — encircling her fair girlish
brow, she said, tearfully, " Take her, my brother, as a gift
from the Lord; though it cost me a pang, I resign her to
your keeping, cheerfully, willingly. Our homes will be far
apart, and she will often wish to see the old place and the
roof that sheltered her young head, and sigh for her girlish
days spent here. I have tried to make them happy, tried to
do my duty well, and if she be not all your fond fancy paints
her, remember that her instructress was but little older than
herself — that we were all alike motherless." A neater,
prettier little bride was never seen; a better, truer wife was
never won — just such a one as the young and enterprising
pioneer needed in his new home on the banks of the Ohio.

Nettie's face is not so young and fair as it was twelve
years ago, but the look of womanhood is far less grave than
that of girlhood. A sweeter expression is on it, mellowed
and ripened by the memories of these years. It wears so
bright a smile, one would never mistrust the care and anxiety at work in her heart.

Years passed; Mark never came; but at long intervals

there went out some little ripple from the great wave of life that reached the sluggish little town where her home was. They heard that he had graduated with high honours, that he had been admitted to the bar, that he was fast rising, and, as more years went by, that he had risen to honour and distinction. It was seldom that Nettie heard his name mentioned, yet always with a sweeter, sadder feeling than when other names were spoken ; and every time she heard it, he seemed farther removed from her. At length she schooled her heart to think it impossible they should ever meet in the same old way, and tried to reason herself into the belief that he had forgotten her. She thinks of the long years she has watched and prayed, waited and hoped. In a moment her heart travels over again the weary pathway her feet have come. It seems impossible that she could ever be so strong again ; and now she was to learn submission to a new sorrow. Rumour, with her viper tongue, whispers that the young and rising star on the political horizon is to lead to the altar a young and beautiful bride, daughter of the wealthy and honourable Mr. Newell, of New York.

"What if it be so?" she would say to herself. "What is it to me, a poor, hard-working country girl? If the report were not true, he would never think of me; so I wish them joy — O, so much joy! She is lovely, and an heiress. He is noble, and will win fame. They will be happy. I will at least be content."

The sweet little love-dream of her childhood had departed with that bright one dreamed at the stile long ago, the beauty of which had made her heart strong under many and sore trials. She shrank from coming in contact with those who would converse on the subject, thankful that this one secret was forever locked in her own breast. The world knew it not.

How God was trying her! And yet He has said, "As thy day so shall thy strength be." "O," said she, "that I could accept these promises without murmuring, and wear them as a shield over my heart!"

Other rumours ran rife, one of which proved to be not as unfounded as the other. It was to the effect that Mark was soon to have a great honour conferred upon him, one of the highest within the gift of the people. He was soon to take his seat in the United States Senate. That there could be no mistake in this was quite evident, from the fact that the public journals throughout the state were heralding it as a question already settled by the people. These reports were not long in finding their way into the little town, now grown quite proud in that it could claim the honour of being the birthplace and early home of this favourite son of the Empire State. One day Nettie's eye chanced to fall upon the following paragraph in one of the leading daily papers : —

" The legislature of New York will elect, at its next session, a successor to Judge Williams for the unexpired term, and also for the succeeding regular term. Public sentiment points to a most worthy and gifted son of —— County ; the selection of whom would benefit the country and meet universal approval. Mark Miller, Esq., is the person thus designated."

This news created no little sensation. The satisfaction was almost universal. Only a few partisans grumbled over this piece of intelligence.

There was one, an old and tried friend, to whom this last and crowning success was a joyful event. He had prophesied as much long ago. It fulfilled his early auguries.

Mark had written at long intervals. But latterly, through a press of business, his letters were hurried, and fewer than before.

There was one, lying upon the writing-desk of Deacon

Sloper, just received, over which the old couple were shedding tears of joy.

Could it be possible? Yes, it was really true that Mark and his mother were coming home! That long-promised visit to the home of his youth would be made ere he took up his residence in the nation's capital — this very spring, this month ; but another letter would determine the day when he might be expected. The letter came only on the eve of his own arrival, but his approach was heralded by the public prints. The name and fame of the young senator were now public property.

CHAPTER XXVIII.

HIS TRIUMPHAL RETURN TO HIS NATIVE VILLAGE.

> " We leave
> Our home in youth, — no matter to what end, —
> Study, or strife, or pleasure, or what not;
> And, coming back in few short years, we find
> All as we left it outside; the old elms,
> The house, the grass, gates, and latchet's self-same click;
> But lift that latchet, — all is changed as doom."
>
> BAILEY'S FESTUS.

HAT was a glorious day at Sorrel Hill!" continued aunt Bessie, tearfully, and with more emotion
than she could well suppress. " Will the few of
us who remain — like sere and yellow leaves upon
an aged tree — ever forget that day? It was like the dawning of a new advent to some of us, — the brightness and
beauty of a new creation!"

The sky was without a cloud, calm and serene, with a
soft breeze rippling through the old elms that skirted the
road-side, and scattering the apple-blossoms broadcast over
the greensward.

Well-tilled fields, thrifty orchards in full bloom, with neat
farm-houses nestling cosily amidst the flossy spring verdure,
and cattle grazing on the hill-sides or in the sweet, cool
valley pastures, are subjects of remark and observation.
The traveller's eye noted all these objects, as one after
another rose to view, and were passed in quick succession.
They are nearing the cross-roads, where Mark always felt

at home after the line was passed.   Two miles farther, and
the hill-top will be gained, where he can look down on the
dear valley home slumbering quietly in its rural beauty.

But what is this?   What startling event is to break in upon
his silent joy?   A great concourse of people are assembled
at the " Corners ; " the streets are thronged with carriages,
while over the road leading to the village are beautiful arches
of evergreens and flowers, streaming banners, and bands of
music enlivening the scene.   Some great gala day, no doubt,
though that were a strange sight indeed, and something altogether *new*, for the staid, sober citizens of a quiet little town
like this!   The booming of a cannon, and the wild enthusiastic huzza that followed, startled the horses into a quick
gallop.   They seemed to have caught the inspiration that
was swaying the hearts of the people.

As the plain, unostentatious travelling equipage neared
the scene of festivity, twelve horsemen advanced, with caps
raised, and circling around the travellers, drew up in true
military style, six on either side.

Two grooms advance to hold the restive horses, the
throng close around the carriage, loud and prolonged shouts
rise high on the air — a welcome cheering to one who has
long been an exile from home.

" Welcome!   Welcome home ! "

" Welcome to our hearts and homes ! "

Long and loud huzzas follow in quick succession.   The
cannon pours forth its wild peal, which is answered by
another far down the valley, while the echoing hills send
back a multiplied acclaim.   An open carriage, drawn by
four horses, and garlanded with flowers, is waiting to receive the honoured guest.

His mother felt at that hour that she must surrender her
son to a nation's care and protection.   Her heart is overflowing with silent, almost speechless joy; but she gives
him up willingly, well knowing that henceforth he will seek

counsel and advice from others — hers he will need no more. The old residents who remembered Mark were the most enthusiastic. He looks into their good, honest faces, and recognizes them all, though time has bent the forms' and silvered the locks of many.

The majority of this vast multitude are fine-looking young men, who are to him as strangers, and some are strangers indeed; but all are interested in showing their guest that respect and honour which is his just reward.

The clear, unclouded sky of that glorious June day was spread like a beautiful canopy of blue over the little village that lay enshrouded in a soft, hazy atmosphere; the hill-tops and tree-tops glowed like " golden arrows tipped with diamonds; " the sun's glad beams rested like a blessing on the noble brow, as he bared it to the multitude to thank them for this display of their regard.

A Sabbath-like stillness now prevailed, save the booming of the cannon, proclaiming from its bellowing throat that something unusual was about to happen. The old mill-wheel had ceased its industrious round, the hammer of the smith was silent, shops were closed or being bedecked in the national colours, interspersed with sprigs of evergreen and wreaths of flowers. A great flag floated from the tall liberty-pole on the Common, while, at intervals of a few rods, the road through the village was spanned by arches of evergreen and flowers, — twelve in number, — one for every year that he had been away; his initials, or some loving words of welcome, being interwoven in green and scarlet, or blue and gold. Doors and windows were gayly decked with flowers. On the silvery bosom of the great mill-pond rocked numerous little pleasure-craft, gorgeously trimmed with fluttering ensigns, or some token of regard for their honoured guest. On the green and glossy Common, overshadowed by native trees of elm and maple, were spread long tables of delicate viands. Such baking and brewing, slaughtering, roasting, and ornamenting, were never before seen or heard of by the good citizens of Sorrel Hill.

At last the cavalcade arrives. The booming cannon thunders, Welcome! the responsive hills echo back, Welcome! The people hurrah; the boys throw their caps high in air; the ladies wave their handkerchiefs, and throw bouquets from the windows; while every one in the street nearly stumbles over the other, in his eagerness to congratulate and welcome the old friend who had so nobly earned honour for himself and his birthplace. The multitude, that opened a path before him, closed in behind him as he passed on. Few could get near enough to speak to him, or take him by the hand. The prolonged huzzas, the echoing shouts, proclaimed the warmth of the respect, the genuineness of the enthusiasm. No victorious hero of modern times has been more gracefully, more enthusiastically, received!

What think you were the emotions of that brave heart at that hour? Was it pride and arrogance? Was it a spirit of triumph over those who had spurned him in his early youth? No; it was one of profound and tearful humility, of unspeakable gratitude to God, of warm and fervent gratitude to these friends, of an attachment which would grow stronger than, and lasting as, life.

Never in his whole after life — when he had reached the zenith of his fame, when his name had become associated with, and as a thing inseparable from, the nation's greatness and the nation's glory — did he experience aught that surpassed the pure joys of that day!

All was gayety and festivity; the people could scarcely restrain their wild joy; and Mark was equally excited. He ascended the platform, from which they hoped he would address them. His eye roved around the assembled multitude, his lips essayed to move; but his heart was too full for utterance. At length, with quivering lips, amidst the almost breathless silence that followed, he said, —

"My heart is too full to make a long speech to-day. Accept my gratitude for this display of generous friendship. It is more than words can express, and will last while life lasts. At some future time, during my stay among you, I shall be most happy to address you upon those great topics of the day which relate to the present and the future of our national policy. But, let me assure you, I am on no electioneering tour. My visit to my dear old home is purely one of affection. I love everything that exists here, and everybody that ever breathed this pure air, and who is so happy as to have been born here. Although I may not spend the sunset of my life where its dawn began, I shall feel that I must sometimes come back to look upon my native hills, the scenes of my early struggles, my old home by the brookside, and my father's grave.

"The vicissitudes of the past — the thoughts, feelings, and experience of twelve years — are crowding in upon my memory at this hour. It seems like a long dream, from which I have just awaked. Troubled as that dream may have been, the awakening is blissful. Be my future what it may, — whether it be overcast by clouds of adversity and sorrow, or made pleasant by the smiles of fortune and the sweets of friendship, — I know no greater happiness than that which fills my heart this day will ever, *can* ever, be mine. Never again shall I experience an hour like this; never again *could* my heart beat with the same wild throb of joy, though a nation's praises and a nation's honours were showered upon me. Though the proudest triumphs were achieved, the greenest laurels that ambition craves were won and worn, never could they bring to me the pure joys, the tender emotions, the tearful tributes of gratitude which I now feel. The memory of this hour will be like an hour passed in some little green Eden, where all before was doubt and darkness, and will serve to stimulate me to greater efforts and renewed exertions. This hour has called into being new thoughts, feelings, and aspirations, which MUST impel me onward in the path of duty; and if that path be upward, — if it lead eventually to any great eminence, — if my name, and the one little talent which I may possess, be not lost in obscurity among the great and gifted ones with whom I am to come in contact, I shall feel that I owe it to your kindness and your encouragement, more than to the circumstances which have governed me.

"My spirit faints sometimes when I think what is before me, and what great things are expected of me. I have often thought that my one little talent would make a poor show at Washington; but this display of your friendship sinks into my heart like the first spring rain, warming into life new hopes and high aspirations. Until this day I had never thought to win fame. Fame alone can never satisfy my ambition. But, for the sake of these my too partial friends, and this my beloved birthplace, I would not have my name lost to the world. Not for myself alone, not for my own individual honour, not for any personal glory that I may achieve, would I make my influence known and felt; but that I may reflect honour upon those who have thus inspired me with a hope of success.

"If my eyes are true interpreters of oracles, I read in your faces an assurance of continued sympathy and faithful friendship. It shall be to me like the embrace of loving arms, to cheer and strengthen me. I shall prize not life so much as I shall the commendations, the approval, of my old friends.

'Old friends, like old swords, still are trusted best.'

"Accept again my thanks for your thoughtful, generous kindness. I feel my heart energized, my soul braced to encounter whatever lies before me. I covet no higher honour, no prouder fame, no greater reward, than to be able so to live, that when I die, you may say of me, 'Faithful and beloved.'"

CHAPTER XXIX.

OLD ACQUAINTANCE NOT FORGOTTEN.

"All true love is grounded on esteem;
Plainness and truth gain more a generous heart
Than all the crooked subtleties of art."

BUCKINGHAM.

HE fêtes and feastings lasted a week. Day and night were the young senator's rooms, in the old mansion of Mr. Sloper, thronged with the good people of Sorrel Hill. The entire population seemed beside themselves with gayety, and to have given up all thoughts of business for pleasure. Days and weeks glided by. Still Mark remained the guest of the people. As often as he spoke of returning, so often would they interpose their objections; and somehow his own inclinations were in favour of his remaining longer.

Every spot sacred to memory was visited and revisited. The old cottage home had been wonderfully preserved, and was often the scene of little merry-makings, where the younger portion of the community came to frolic on the greensward, or to spread their luncheon under the great maples by the gate. Mark could recognize every tree, and it seemed almost as though the recognition must be mutual.

The bleating of the sheep, the lowing of the kine, the tic-tac of the wheel at the mill, the old familiar hum of the dam, were as though he had never been away. Time passed swiftly and pleasantly. Each day seemed happier than the preceding.

It was a happy reunion, but there were none who shed more tears of joy than Nettie. While others were loud in their adulations and profuse in their attentions, her tears flowed silently, for she felt that thenceforth there was to be forever a barrier between herself and the noble, gifted friend of her early years. The one little sunbeam in her darkened existence had been the thought that he would never cease to esteem her, but would sometimes think of her in her lonely home, and respect her for the good she had wrought there.

Nettie had made herself very efficient while the preparations for the reception were going forward. Her confections graced the tables, her wreaths of evergreen were the most beautiful, her flowers were indispensable, her frosted cakes, wreathed with fresh rose-buds, were pronounced exquisite.

Never before had the good ladies paid so much deference to her opinion; never before had her taste and skill been so extolled. Nothing was done, or could be done, seemingly, until her judgment had passed upon it. At her suggestion the arbour was festooned with flowers. Under her supervision the tables looked more like a fairy's banquet than a place in which to feast a hundred hungry men.

During the speaking, Nettie stood where she could both see and hear. Her heart gave one great throb when she first beheld him whom this display was designed to honour. And when in low, tremulous tones he thanked them for all their kindness, his voice had a strange sound. Though rich and manly, and full of pathos and affection, it was not the old voice that said "Good by," at the stile. Her first thought was, "He will never think of me as the friend of old; he *cannot*." There was such an air of lofty, yet gentle courtesy, such intellectual power beaming from his face, his words, the tones of his voice, as to her sensitive ear expressed a consciousness of the wide difference in their social position. And so she went back to her home unnoticed and unseen by

him, and the little gleam of sunshine which for a few days
had brightened up the old homestead, and *one* heart within
it, was shrouded in a deeper gloom than before.

Mark's coming, which had been the dream of her life,
was likely to end in a painful reality. She remained in her
own room silent and thoughtful, as by the light of the shaded
lamp she rocked to and fro. But her heart beat on and
hoped on in spite of that ever present conviction, that it
was in vain.

The meeting between Mrs. Miller and Nettie was more
like that of mother and daughter. They conversed in per-
feet simplicity and frankness. But the son was not present,
and there were few interruptions to their long, pleasant interview. Mrs. Miller's face beamed with pride and pleasure
to see her " dear child," as she persisted in calling her, grown
so tall and so handsome; and Nettie forgot the restraint
with which she at first met her old friend, and went away
happier than she came. The mother, at least, was un-
changed.

Nearly a week passed before Mark could find time to call
upon his friends. So entirely was every hour occupied, he
could do little else than remain at home to entertain those
who called, or to pay visits in cases where he received special invitations.

It was thought by some, that Miss Helen Maynard would
ere long have the young senator entirely to herself. That
she was lionizing him, and endeavouring to monopolize him
thoroughly, there could be but little doubt. There were
grand evening entertainments, and little *recherché* dinners,
and once they took a long ride together on horseback.
What more than this was wanting to confirm the most
doubting mind?

At length, one calm, hazy afternoon, when an Eden-like
stillness and beauty seemed to rest upon the whole world,
Mark stole away, unobserved by any, and wended his way

to the summit of the "Hill," where the *old* house of Mr. Strange used to stand.

Instead of going "cross-lots," and leaping over the old rail fence, and coming in at the side door, as he used to do, he took the highway, and went in at the arched gate, and up the broad gravel walk leading to the house. He gazed in silence, with a feeling of awe and admiration, at the beauti‑ ful picture spread out before him. It seemed to him as though an enchanter's wand had been waved over the place, so delightfully like, and yet unlike, was it to its old self.

Beyond were climbing vines and tall flowering shrubs; the arched doorway, the great pillars supporting the gal‑ leries, were almost hidden from view by the fairy touch of the floral angel.

Mark scarcely recognized the tall, commanding woman of twenty-five, standing under the low arch of jessamine; but a nearer approach confirmed his suspicions that it might be *she* whom he came especially to see.

He left her a little maiden, in short frocks and pinafores, with light golden hair hanging loosely about her shoulders, "waving in the wild freedom of childhood," but now gath‑ ered into large bands, and darker by several shades, rippling softly over her broad white forehead, showing the graceful contour of her head. Never had Mark thought of Nettie as being beautiful. It had never once entered his mind that she would *ever* be one who could command admiration; but as she stood before him then, in the midst of all this beauty which she had made, she appeared a being of queenly aspect, born to command the respect, the admiration, of the world.

Both were speechless, with hands clasped, each gazing fondly, earnestly, into the eyes of the other, until the long wistful look deepened into one of unspeakable tenderness. Her cheek grew warm under that long, admiring gaze, — for so she must have interpreted it, — and Mark seemed to have forgotten to speak the words of joy trembling on his lips.

" Mr. Miller, welcome back to your native town! I wish
you joy — much joy!"

" As you are formal with me, and so changed, I suppose
I must be ceremonious too, and call you Miss Strange."

" Strange indeed it would seem to be thus addressed by
you! No; call me Nettie, as of old. Though I should live
to be a gray-haired old woman, I would always be Nettie to
you."

" Let us then ever be Mark and Nettie to each other."

" Am I so very much changed, Mark?"

" Changed? Yes; O, so much! You are the same gentle, spiritual Nettie of old, only more graceful, more womanly, just as I would have you in every way — changed in form
and features, yet the same loving, confiding soul is yours."

They entered the house together. Here Nettie threw off
the embarrassment that at first oppressed her, and both engaged in a long, pleasant, unreserved conversation.

Here again he found cause for much surprise. A magi-
cian's wand, or the lamp of Aladdin, could scarcely effect a
greater change. The walls — no longer brown and bare —
are covered with fresh, delicate paper; the roses running
over the pale ground, vying, in beauty and harmony of
colour, with those overshadowing the porch outside. The
old rough floors — as Mark remembered them — are hidden
under neat carpets. At the windows are soft white curtains,
looped back to admit the cool evening breeze, which swept
over a garden of sweets, reviving even to those accustomed
to it. Lounges, easy-chairs, and little *tête-à-têtes*, covered
with neat chintz, are here and there; and over all is spread
an air of domestic purity and home comfort such as Mark
had often said should one day be his.

The evening was spent in showing Mark over the place.
Wonderful were the improvements. Charming was the
prospect. Instead of the old uncouth fences and fields of
stubble were smiling hedgerows and lawns of green, with

graceful trees casting their cool shadows upon the well-tilled fields. The visitor's admiration was unbounded, as well it might be. He could scarcely find words to express the pleasure which this visit afforded him, and awarded to Nettie her just meed of praise. He felt that nothing short of the consecration of her whole being to the task could have accomplished so noble a work.

He thought of her with more than the old usual tenderness, as he walked slowly homeward that calm, starlit night. He thought of the hard crosses of her girlhood, and noble self-denial of the woman; thought of the love, the almost idolatrous worship, she bore his mother; thought, too, — ay, he must have known it, — of the love she bore himself. He felt it deeply; but this seemed to be one of those hinderances to his preferment of which fortune bade him beware.

He often sighed for the companionship of some loving, womanly being to share the fame he had won. His fancy would often picture a fair home, with a highly intellectual, cultivated, refined woman there as its mistress and presiding genius; and — as he often whispered to himself — " one just like *Grace.*" Then he would think of fair-haired Effie Newell; and a vision of gentleness and almost angelic sweetness came too near his heart for its own peace. Again, Nettie, with her sweet, pensive face, would stand before him, as a reproof to his wandering fancies.

He knew Miss Newell possessed all that he could desire in a wife, and felt that he was largely indebted to her father for valuable introductions and political influence, which had served to facilitate his progress. Socially, the civilities extended to him by persons of talent and worth were in part owing to Mr. Newell's friendship. He fully intended *some day* to offer his heart and hand to Effie Newell. But life had suddenly put on a new aspect.

CHAPTER XXX.

THE FIRST LOVE IS THE LAST LOVE.

"The love that is kept in the beauty of trust
  Cannot pass like the foam from the seas,
Or a mark that the finger hath traced in the dust
  Where 'tis swept by the breath of the breeze."
                                MRS. WELBY.

ARK MILLER'S visits to the house of Mr. Strange were now of daily occurrence, his coming and going looked for as a thing of course, and commented upon by the good people, until each had things fixed up to his or her own peculiar liking.

Day by day he detected a growing interest, a new pleasure, in the society of Nettie; and at length she held a permanent place in his thoughts. To his surprise he found nothing vulgar or unbecoming in the manners or mind of his old friend; but every day brought with it new discoveries of the charming graces of both. He indulged without reserve in the pleasure which her presence afforded him, and soon found his growing admiration fast ripening into a warmer sentiment. Her manner was frank and natural, her judgment mature; and he marvelled much at the fitness of her language, and the pure, refined ideas it clothed. As nothing more or better than these did his heart demand in a wife, he determined to win her love, and make her his own.

She felt in her heart that her affection for him was daily

strengthened, and that the cold indifference with which she at first imagined he treated her, had long since melted away, like the little snowy pinnacle, which, twelve years before, she saw, in the soft moonlight of that starry evening, dissolve itself into tiny fragments of shining crystal. Although she could not but be aware of Mark's growing interest in her, she determined that no act or word of hers should betray him into an expression of his attachment; that no arts of hers should be brought to bear upon, or influence in any way, his finer feelings, or bias his better judgment.

A startled look greeted Mark as he one day stood at the stile, and parted the green boughs of the old grape-vine, and seated himself beside Nettie, who looked up timidly through the gathering twilight shadows to greet her visitor.

"I have been at the house, waiting for you," said he, "but you did not come; and instinct, or some powerful charm, directed my footsteps hither. Did you wish to shun me? Was I to go away on the morrow without a kind farewell from *all* my friends, and from you especially, the dearest and best?"

There was something in the tone in which this was said so earnest, so pathetic, and withal so sweet and sad, it made Nettie's heart beat violently; and the embarrassment she now felt in his presence was manifesting itself in the drooping eyes and blushing cheek, while a rich glow crept slowly over his own.

Nettie looked at Mark with a strange sort of bewilderment, in which doubt and fear, pain and pleasure, struggled for the mastery, while he poured into her not unwilling ear the story of his love; and to the words, "I must be a lonely wanderer wherever I am, or whatever I may become, unless I have your counsels to guide me, your love to strengthen me, and your faithful heart to lean upon," she replied with her characteristic humility and self-depreciation.

18

"I know not whether the feeling I cherish towards you deserves the name of *love*. I have read of it in books, and have seen it exemplified in the holy bond that unites the living and the dead, but scarcely thought of it as connected with myself. I did not suppose there was a being in the world who could love *me*."

But as her blue eyes and the radiant smile on her pure lips uttered the responsive "yes," which was to seal their betrothment, and make their paths in life one, she appeared to him the pure ideal of all he ever dreamed of noble woman — one who could make her home a place of blissful repose, and her husband's heart a sacred shrine, where would be hoarded away the best and purest of her affections ; her own, sanctified by an unswerving trust, and hallowed by a perfect love and perfect faith — one who would add to the strength of his character by the strength and beauty of her own.

That night Nettie pressed a sleepless, dreamless pillow, except when she dreamed over again that one long blissful, day-dream, which was to be, thenceforth, no dream, but a reality.

No doubt of Mark's love or sincerity crossed her mind ; and if, in an unguarded moment, the spectre stood before her, it was only to make her doubt her own efficiency and power to keep bright the flame of love that must forever feed his life. Some there were who wondered how one they considered so far her superior, so noble in character, so refined and graceful in person, so beloved and honoured by all, whose praises were sung by the passing breeze, who knew of the old days of friendless poverty, could either admire or love her. Respect her he might and did, they were sure, for all respected her nowadays ; but would not the memory of those days dampen the joy of his young life, should he link that life with hers? They little knew that this was the magic power which had started into being the half-forgotten boy-dreams.' In the scenes gone by which haunted his lonely hours, in the busy multitude of the great city, or the more secluded years of college life, the home of Nettie Strange arose oftenest, and her name repeated itself more distinctly than any other. The far-off days of the past, with all their painful reminiscences, swept into the nearness of yesterday, when the one true friend of *his* friendless years stood before him in her patient dignity and womanly pride, *self-made* and *self-reliant*.

He reverenced the woman for *what she was*. He knew she had made herself, and his profound appreciation of those very elements in her character first led him to think of her as a wife. He permitted no shallow prejudice to govern him, and resolved that no fear of what the world might say should influence him in his choice.

The curiosity of the good people of Sorrel Hill still continned to be rife, and Mrs. Miller was appealed to for the confirmation of their worst fears; but all they could get from her was, that " she hoped it would be so." They saw that the mother knew all, and was evidently happy in the knowledge. They saw, too, that any further comment, or any interference, would be utteily useless; and ere the wedding day dawned, the shock which their sensitive nerves at first received gave place to a more just and reasonable feeling, and finally the match came to be, with few exceptions, regarded with favour.

Mark took his departure for Albany on the following morning, his mother remaining until after the wedding. In little less than a month they were married.

IIow noble and beautiful they looked as they stood before the man of God, who pronounced those few solemn woids that made them *one !*

Her face was full of sweet, serene gravity, and his shone with a kind of happiness that did not depend on what others might think of it.

The wedding was to be as private as possible. So they had arranged. But ho ; the good people would not have it thus. As Mr. Miller's coming had been an event much thought off, could his marriage be less so? All Sorrel Hill took a holiday. The majority with no affected pleasure, but with heartfelt rejoicing, came to offer their sincere congratulations, to honour this crowning event in the life of him they so truly loved, and who, they felt, would ever be an honour to them and to the country.

Again were banners streaming in the soft morning air ; again were arches of evergreen, with their significant mottoes, erected over the principal thoroughfares. Even Helen Maynard, who had recovered somewhat from the stupefaction into which this event had thrown her, concluded, at the last moment, to do as the others did ; and for appearance' sake she permitted her father to run up, over his store, a flag of truce, in shape of a little piece of bunting made that morning of red and white cotton. She had not time to sew on the stars, and the whole was basted together so shabbily, that long before night each red and white strip was flapping forth its joy on its own individual responsibility, greatly to the amusement of all beholders, and much to her disgust. What more could she do to let them know that her heart was not broken, and to show her respect to the bride and groom?

A winter at Washington loomed up in the distance. She would commence a correspondence as soon as they had settled, and they would show their characteristic meanness if they did not invite her to pay them a visit. After revolving in her mind various ways in which she could bestow a small bridal favour, she concluded to send a bouquet for the bride, and a rose for Mark's button-hole. Accordingly the little front yard was rifled of some of its choicest treasures. Buds half blown blushed their sweetest in the midst of sweet elysian, and rose geranium very beautiful and very appropriate for a centre-table, where it was placed as soon as it arrived. A half-blown cabbage rose was despatched at the same time, with a request that her "dear friend" should wear it, as directed; but when he appeared at the little church, leading his bride up the aisle to the altar, where their solemn vows were pledged, without it, she never remembered to have been so agitated or so confounded.

She put on her blandest smile, however, and was among the first to press forward, and offer her congratulations. She looked him full in the face, and, so far as he could see, there was no pang of regret, no trace of bitter disappointment. The expression of his lips softened to pity, when he replied to her meaningless salutation; and as she could think of nothing further to say, and others crowded around and jostled her quite out of the way, she soon took her leave. The wedding was an unusually large one. Indeed, all Sorrel Hill was present. A few, who had marriageable daughters, were still disposed to remain at the church, and gossip concerning this singular choice of his. "There must be some mystery connected with it; time would show," said they. "If it had been anybody but her;" "I never would have believed it, had I not seen it with my own eyes;" and much more to the same purport.

The unaccountable fact was undeniable; but to them there seemed to be some mystery surrounding it, yet to be dispelled.

The wedding guests returned to the house of Mr. Strange, where a large quantity of bride-cake was served, and where the newly-married pair received the heartfelt congratulations of their true friends.

"What a noble pair!" said one; "She's just the wife for him," responded another; and all concluded that the wedding was a grand affair. Certainly Sorrel Hill had never seen anything like it.

Apart from the company, Mr. Miller found an opportunity to utter a few words, such as young brides seldom, if ever, forget.

"My own darling Nettie, my beloved *wife*, I bless thee for the great happiness of this hour, the crowning glory of my life. Take my mother's and my sainted father's blessing also. May it rest upon you always."

His happy, excited manner gave an exalted tone to his voice, and the words stole like a benediction into her heart. The white dove of peace was forever to nestle in downy softness there.

In the evening the old mansion of Deacon Sloper is brilliantly illuminated. Its many windows send their festive radiance over nearly the whole town. Even the great maples on the Common blaze with lamps which add to the splendor of the scene.

When Nettie threw herself upon her father's neck, at parting, she could not say many words; tears and sobs choked them back. But her faith in her father was strong and firm: for ten years he had been the sober, industrious man he now was, and she was confident that he would prove himself worthy to be loved, to the end of his life. She wondered if, in all the years that they had lived there together, — isolated from the world, as it were, — a thought had ever crossed his mind that she had been otherwise than happy. She hoped not.

In a few days they were gone; but long after their departure, and when life at Sorrel Hill went on again as before, the events of the few past weeks seemed like some pleasant romance, but all were proud and happy that it was a living reality.

Helen Maynard waited for years, thinking to make a splendid match, and just escaped being an old maid by marrying her father's clerk, a very worthy man, who deserved a better fate. She looked charming in her splendid bridal attire, and presided over her small house with becoming graciousness, ever mindful of her dignity, and the importance of maintaining her superiority over those in humble life. From her *works* we may best understand the purposes of her own.

" Our story is drawing to a close," said good aunt Bessie, as we were seated for the last time at the little round table in the cheerful antique chamber which had for years been the retired home, and was to be ere long the dying-place of our beloved ancestress.

The moisture gathered in her eyes when she said, " The old graveyard at Sorrel Hill does not now wear so gloomy and desolate an aspect. It has a neat white paling, and very handsome arched gateway, thanks to Mr. Miller's generosity. Many of the little hillocks are clothed with verdure, bright flowers are bursting into blossom, and birds are singing in the drooping willows, and the ' trees of heaven ' that have been planted there. I would wish my body to rest there, when my spirit has no more to do with earth."

" It shall be even so, dear aunt Bessie."

Old Mrs. Miller lived with her son and daughter many years, blessed beyond measure in that she realized in Nettie all that her fondest wishes could desire.

Mrs. Miller, the younger, was ever an active woman in all deeds of piety and benevolence, presiding, with an easy grace and unaffected simplicity, at the elegant festivities which were given at their splendid mansion, supporting the dignity pertaining to office with becoming fortitude and resignation, never having been known to complain of the honours and the privileges which power confers, and the many blessings she ever after enjoyed. But she often sighed for the retirement of private life, and the genuine happiness a humbler sphere affords.

Her ideas of what is termed " high life " were very much in contrast with those of women enjoying " position " generally. Her well-regulated mind shrank from ostentatious display, and from devoting time to the claims of the gay world, which, she said, might be better employed. Both were alike distasteful to her, while the blessings which wealth confers were properly appreciated and employed. By her works and words she won many thoughtless souls to admire the " beauty of holiness."

In a letter written to her old friends, Deacon and Mrs. Sloper, a year after her marriage, she said, —

"In the happiness that I now enjoy, I would not be so thoughtless as to forget the sorrows of others, nor so selfish as to hope for no cloud to shadow my pathway. I would have grace given me to kiss the cross when sorrow comes ; to be careful and thoughtful for others' happiness more than my own ; to live in and use this beautiful world as though it were not given me for merely temporal objects and selfish gratifications, but because it is the threshold of another and higher existence. I bless God that He has given me strength to endure, and to be of use to those around me, while I pass through this life to the life immortal."

THE END.

SHELDON & COMPANY'S

Standard and Miscellaneous Books.

THE WORKS OF MARION HARLAND,
THE GREATEST AMERICAN NOVELIST.

Alone. By MARION HARLAND. One vol., 12mo., cloth. Price, $1.75.

The Hidden Path. By MARION HARLAND. One vol., 12mo., cloth. Price, $1.75.

Moss-Side. By MARION HARLAND. One vol., 12mo., cloth. Price, $1.75.

Nemesis. By MARION HARLAND. One vol., 12mo., cloth. Price, $1.75.

Miraim. By MARION HARLAND. One vol., 12mo., cloth. Price, $1.75.

Husks. By MARION HARLAND. One vol., 12mo., cloth. Price, $1.75.

Husbands and Homes. By MARION HARLAND. One vol., 12mo., cloth. Price, $1.75.

Sunny Bank. By MARION HARLAND. One vol., 12mo., cloth. Price, $1.75.

"There is an originality in her thinking which strikes one with peculiar force, and he finds himself unconsciously recurring to what has had such a powerful effect upon him."
Boston Evening Gazette.

Waiting for the Verdict. By Mrs. REBECCA HARDING DAVIS, author of "Margaret Howth," "Life Among the Iron Mills," &c., &c. One vol., octavo, illustrated, bound in cloth. Price, $2.00.

This is a story of unusual power and thrilling interest.

"It is not only the most elaborate work of its author, but it is one of the most powerful works of fiction by any American writer."—*New York Times.*

The Life and Letters of Rev. Geo. W. Bethune, D.D. By Rev. ABRAHAM R. VAN NEST, D.D. One vol., large 12mo., illustrated by an elegant steel-plate Likeness of Dr. Bethune. Price, $2.00.

This is one of the most charming biographies ever written. As a genial and jovial friend, as an enthusiastic sportsman, as a thorough theologian, as one of the most eloquent and gifted divines of his day, Dr. Bethune took a firm hold of the hearts of all with whom he came in contact.

Dr. Bethune's Theology, or EXPOSITORY LECTURES ON THE HEIDELBERG CATECHISM. By GEO. W. BETHUNE, D.D. Two vols., crown octavo (Riverside edition), on tinted paper. Price, cloth, $4.50; half calf, or morocco, extra, $8.50.

This was the great life work of the late Dr. Bethune, and will remain a monument of his thorough scholarship, the classical purity and beauty of his style, and above all, his deep and abiding piety.

"When the Rev. Dr. Bethune, whose memory is yet green and fragrant in the Church, was about to leave this country, he committed his manuscripts to a few friends, giving them discretionary power with regard to their publication. Among them was the great work of his life; in his opinion *the* work, and that from which he hoped the most usefulness while he lived, and after he was dead, if it should then be given to the press. This work was his course of lectures on the Catechism of the Church in which he was a burning and

Fourth Series. Revised by the Author, and published with his sanction. Containing twenty-six Sermons. pp. 450. Price, $1.50.

Fifth Series. Revised by the Author, and published with his sanction. Illustrated with a fine steel plate representing the Rev. C. H. Spurgeon preaching in Surrey Music Hall. One vol , 12mo. Price, $1.50.

Sixth Series. Revised by the Author, and published with his sanction. Illustrated with a fine steel plate of Mr. Spurgeon's new Tabernacle. One vol., 12mo. Price, $1.50.

Seventh Series. Containing some of Mr. Spurgeon's later and more brilliant Sermons. One vol., 12mo. Price, $1.50.

Eighth Series. Containing Spurgeon's celebrated Doctrinal Discourses, which made a most profound impression throughout England. One vol., 12mo., cloth   Price, $1 50.

Morning by Morning, or Daily Bible Readings. By Rev. C. H. SPURGEON. One vol., 12mo. Price, $1.75.

"Though no printed sermon can give a perfect representation of the same thing spoken by an eloquent and impassioned orator, yet the reader of these will not wonder at their author's popularity. Though he may not sympathize with Mr. Spurgeon's theological opinions, he can not fail to see that the preacher is really in earnest, that he heartily believes what he says, and knows how to say it in a way to arouse and keep alive the attention of his hearers."—*Boston Advertiser.*

The Saint and His Saviour. By the Rev. C. H. SPURGEON. One vol., 12mo. Price, $1.50.

This is the first extended religious work by this distinguished preacher, and one which in its fervid devotional spirit, the richness of its sentiments, and the beauty of its imagery, fully sustains his high reputation..

Spurgeon's Gems. Being Brilliant Passages from the Sermons of the Rev. C. H. SPURGEON, of London. One vol., 12mo. Price, $1.50.

"The Publishers present this book as a specimen of Mr. Spurgeon's happiest thoughts,—gems from his discourses,—which will glow in the mind of the reader, and quicken in him a desire to read and hear more of this remarkable youthful preacher.

Neander's Planting and Training of the Christian Church by the Apostles. Translated from the German by J. E. RYLAND. Translation revised and corrected according to the fourth German edition. By E. G. ROBINSON, D.D., Professor in the Rochester Theological Seminary. One vol., octavo, cloth. Price, $4.00.

"The patient scholarship, the critical sagacity, and the simple and unaffected piety of the author, are manifest throughout. Such a history should find a place in the library of every one who seeks a familiar knowledge of the early shaping of the Christian Churches. An excellent index adds to its value."—*Evangelist.*

Bible Illustrations. Being a Store-house of Similies, Allegories, and Anecdotes—with an introduction by RICHARD NEWTON, D.D. One vol., 12mo. Price, $1.50. Every Sabbath School teacher should have this book.

"It is impossible not to commend a book like this."—*Editor of Encyc. of Religious Knowledge.*

"We think that Sabbath School teachers especially would be profited by reading it; and many of the anecdotes will help to point the arrow of the preacher."—*Christian Herald.*

SPURGEON'S WORKS.

Sermons of the Rev. C. H. Spurgeon, of London, in uniform styles of binding.

First Series. With an Introduction and Sketch of his Life, by the Rev. E. L. MAGOON, D.D. With a fine steel-plate Portrait. One vol., 12mo., pp. 400. Price, $1.50.

Second Series. Revised by the Author, and published with his sanction. Containing a new steel-plate Portrait, engraved expressly for the volume. Price, $1.50.

Third Series. Revised by the Author, and published with his sanction. Containing a steel-plate view of Surrey .Music Hall London engraved ex ressl for the volume. Price, $1.50.

Biblical Commentary on the New Testament.
By Dr. HERMANN OLSHAUSEN. Continued after his
death by Ebrard and Wiesinger. Carefully revised,
after the last German Edition, by A. C. KENDRICK,
D.D., Greek Professor in the University of Rochester. Six vols., large octavo. Price, cloth, $18.00.

"I regard the Commentary as the most valuable of those
on the New Testament in the English language, happily
combining the religious spirit of the English expositors with
the critical learning of the German. The American editor
has evidently performed his task well, as might be expected
from his eminent qualifications."—*President Sears, of Brown
University.*

The Annotated Paragraph Bible. According
to the authorized version, arranged in Paragraphs
and Parallelisms, with Explanatory Notes, Prefaces
to the several Books, and an entirely new Selection
of References to Parallel and Illustrative Passages.
An issue of the London Religious Tract Society,—
republished. Complete in one royal octavo volume,
with Maps, &c. Price, library sheep, $8.00.

The Annotated Paragraph New Testament.
In one octavo volume, uniform style. Price, muslin, $2.50.

"I have carefully examined a considerable portion of the
work, and consider it eminently adapted to increase and dif-
fuse a knowledge of the Word of God. I heartily recommend
it to Christians of every denomination, and especially to
teachers of Bible Classes and Sabbath Schools, to whom it
will prove an invaluable aid."—*Rev. Dr. Wayland.*

Tholuck on the Gospel of John. Translated by
CHARLES J. KRAUTH, D.D. One vol., octavo. Price,
$3.00.

"We hail with much pleasure the appearance of Krauth's
translation of 'Tholuck on the Gospel of John.' We trust
the work, in this its English dress, will find a wide circula-
tion."—*Bibliotheca Sacra.*

Baird's Classical Manual. By James S. S. Baird, F.C.D. One vol., 16mo. Price, cloth, 90 cts.

It is an epitome of Ancient Geography, Greek and Roman Mythology, Antiquities, and Chronology.

Croquet as played by "The Newport Croquet Club." By One of the Members. 16mo. Price, paper, 25 cts.; cloth, 50 cts.

"This manual is the only one which really grapples with a difficult case, and deals with it as if heaven and earth depended on the adjudication."—*Atlantic Monthly.*

Helps to the Pulpit. Sketches and Skeletons of Sermons. One vol., large 12mo. Price, $2.00.

"Here is a work that may be a help by its proper use, or a hindrance by its abuse."—*Christian Messenger.*

Pulpit Themes and Preacher's Assistant. By the author of "Helps to the Pulpit." One vol., large 12mo. Price, $2.00.

"We have no doubt but that it will be a welcome book to every candidate for the ministry, and also to pastors in almost every congregation."—*Lutheran Herald.*

A Text-Book of the History of Christian Doctrines. By K. R. Hagenbach, Professor of Theology in the University of Basle. The Edinburgh translation of C. W. Buch, revised, with large Additions from the fourth German Edition, and other sources, by Henry B. Smith, D.D., Professor in the Union Theological Seminary of the City of New York. Two vols., octavo. Price, cloth, $6.00.

"It exceeds, in point of completeness, every other treatise, English as well as German, and we have, therefore, no hesitation in calling it the most perfect manual of the History of Christian Doctrines which Protestant literature has as yet produced."—*Methodist, N. Y.*

Lieutenant-General Winfield Scott's Autobiography. Two vols., 12mo., illustrated with two steel-plate Likenesses of the General. Price, per set, in cloth, $4.00; half calf, $8.00. An elegant "large paper" edition of this valuable book, on tinted paper, price $10.00; half calf, or morocco, $12.50.

Milman's Latin Christianity. History of Latin Christianity, including that of the Popes to the pontificate of Nicolas V. By HENRY HART MILMAN, D.D., Dean of St. Paul's. Eight vols., crown octavo. Price, extra cloth, $20.00.

"In beauty and brilliancy of style he excels Hallam, approaches Gibbon, and is only surpassed by the unrivaled Macaulay."—*Mercersburg Review.*

Fleming's Vocabulary of Philosophy. With Additions by CHARLES P. KRAUTH, D.D. Small 8vo. Price, $2.50.

"To students of mental science this book is invaluable Dr. K. has done good service by the additions to the work of Dr. Fleming, and the whole volume is one which will be eagerly sought and cordially appreciated."—*Evangelical Quarterly.*

Long's Classical Atlas. Constructed by WM. HUGHES and edited by GEORGE LONG, with a Sketch of Classical Geography. With fifty-two Maps, and an Index of Places.

This Atlas will be an invaluable aid to the student of Ancient History, as well as the Bible student. One vol., quarto. Price, $4.50.

"Now that we are so well supplied with classical dictionaries, it is highly desirable that we should have an atlas worthy to accompany them. In the volume before us is to be found all that can be desired."—*London Athenæun.*

Life of George Washington. By EDWARD EVERETT, LL.D. With a steel-plate Likeness of Mr. Everett, from the celebrated bust by Hiram Powers. One vol., 12mo., pp. 348. Price, cloth, $1.50.

"The biography is a model of condensation, and, by its rapid narrative and attractive style, must commend itself to the mass of readers as the standard popular Life of Washington."—*Correspondence of the Boston Post.*

The Science of Government, in connection with American Institutions. By JOSEPH ALDEN, D.D., LL.D., President of State Normal School, Albany. One vol., 12mo. Price, $1.50. Adapted to the wants of High Schools and Colleges.

Alden's Citizen's Manual. A Text-Book on Government in connection with American Institutions, adapted to the wants of Common Schools. It is in the form of questions and answers. By JOSEPH ALDEN, D.D., LL.D., President of State Normal School, Albany. In one vol., 16mo. Price, 50 cts.

"There is no more important secular study than the study of the institutions of our own country ; and there is no book on the subject so clear, comprehensive, and complete in itself as the volume before us."—*New York Independent.*

Macaulay's Essays. The Critical, Historical, and Miscellaneous Essays of the Right Hon. THOMAS BABINGTON MACAULAY, with an Introduction and Biographical Sketch of the Author, by E. P. WHIPPLE, and containing a new steel-plate Likeness of Macaulay, and a complete index. Six vols., crown octavo. Price, on tinted paper, extra cloth, $13.50; on tinted paper, half calf or morocco, $27.00.

Sherman's March through the South. With Sketches and Incidents of the Campaign. By Capt. DAVID P. CONYNGHAM. 12mo., cloth. Price, $1.75.

"It is the only one that is entitled to credit for real ability,

Lightning Source UK Ltd.
Milton Keynes UK
UKHW011641160119
335572UK00013B/1422/P